BONNER'S
STALLION

BONNER'S STALLION

T. V. Olsen

FAWCETT GOLD MEDAL • NEW YORK

BONNER'S STALLION

Published by Fawcett Gold Medal Books, a unit of CBS Publications, the Consumer Publishing Division of CBS Inc.

ISBN: 0-449-13925-5

Printed in the United States of America

10 9 8 7 6 5 4 3 2

To Diane and Charcoal

Chapter One

Is it him, Pa? Diablo Red?"

"Hold your horses, Rainey."

Jonas smiled, but his own voice was taut with anticipation. His hand shook as the field glasses caught the sunlit crag in focus, causing them to waver off-target. He swore mildly, then caught the image again and held it steady.

Lord yes. Sure as sin, it was him. Diablo Red.

No mistaking that powerful clean-lined shape whose distinctive points Jonas could dredge instantly out of memory. This he did with the quick summing-up intuition of lifetime experience, unthinkingly and unerringly. There was no other horse in the country like Diablo Red. Jonas had never been sure of the stallion's breeding, but guessed it was predominantly Quarter, with that

7

rump of his that was so heavily muscled some would call it disproportionate. The neck was heavy, too, but had a striking arch that was almost classic, some Morgan or Arab blood showing in the high set of head and the long, clean refinement of bone structure.

Diablo Red was a blood bay whose bright red coat was set off by a black mane and tail. That was an easy thing to spot; taking Jonas's eye even from a distance, it had aroused his quick excitement.

He and his son had been returning from Moratown to their small outfit in the Neversummer foothills when, as the crude road slanted up a long rise, they had seen the horse standing motionless on this tall ridge to the north. Jonas had been occupied with handling the team and loaded wagon on the rocky switchbacks, and it was Rainey who had spotted the animal. But it was narrowing the glasses onto details of the horse's superb form that now cinched his identity.

Him all right, the big son of a bitch, Jonas thought in a reverie of pure admiration. Standing big as life, in fact bigger than ever, on a high lift of crag with his hide shining red-gold in the sunlight. Like the king of the mountain. God, if the son of a bitch didn't look it, every inch!

What had he been when Jonas had seen him last? Four years old, just about. Still comparatively green, but already magnificent in his young strength. That would put him in his prime now, with all the latent promise come to full maturity, swelling in neck and chest and haunch.

"It is him, Pa?" Rainey's young voice boiled with impatience now.

Slowly Jonas Bonner lowered the glasses. "It's him," he said quietly. "See for yourself."

He barely extended the field glasses before the boy seized them and set them to his eyes. After a moment Rainey whispered, "Oh, gee."

Jonas laid a hand on his shoulder, feeling the tense quiver of thin muscles, and he smiled wryly.

More than just any ten-year-old's fervor for horseflesh. Rainey shared his own feeling. In the blood maybe. Or the boy had caught it from hours of listening to old Mateo tell in his husking voice of his own mustanging and horse-breaking days, and of later times, not so many years past, when Mateo Baca had broken a younger —and damned well wilder—Jonas Bonner into the same trade. Like enough it was some of both—the blooding and the breeding.

Rainey was tall for his age, with a suggestion of big-boned heft to come in his gangling frame. Growing too fast, Jonas thought, same as I did. Rainey had his father's bony, long-jawed face; probably he would develop the same large capable hands and deliberate never-hasty way of moving. But the coal-black hair and the pale green eyes with that quick, merciless way of sizing up—those were Welda's undeniable legacy. The faint shock that sometimes came of memory aroused now touched Jonas as Rainey abruptly lowered the glasses and swung those eyes on his father.

"He's gone, Pa. He . . . he looked straight my way, and then he turned and he dropped out of sight. Right while I was watching him! He was there, and just like that he was gone. You reckon he saw us?"

Jonas hadn't been noticing. He took the binoculars now and slowly glassed the ridge once more. He swept its skyline and moved down the seaming of eroded pockets along its flank. "I wouldn't be surprised if he saw us a long ways off, Rainey. It's just he took his own time about letting us know it. He'd be curious about us, too."

"Wow." Now hushed, Rainey's voice still throbbed with a suppressed excitement. Then with a boy's swift directness: "What we going to do now, Pa?"

"About what?"

"Diablo Red! Do we catch him or what? Gee, he's come back, hasn't he, maybe he's back to stay!"

"That could be." Jonas took the glasses from his eyes, scrubbed a hand over his jaw and studied the ridge a moment longer, then looked at the boy. "I don't know what's going to happen now, Rainey. We best be getting home."

The sober, almost grim note in his father's tone wasn't lost on Rainey. He was silent as they trudged down the long rise to the switchback road where their spring wagon stood braked on the incline.

Hell, Jonas thought bleakly. Why couldn't that damn horse stay back in his mountains? He should have had it all there, everything he wanted. A harem of stolen mares, meadows of wild hay, pocketed valleys and deep canyons to shelter his herd in the high-country winters. All of this ringed by the lofty Neversummer peaks, guarding it from man's incursions for at least another hundred years. Freedom—all the freedom any wild thing could wish. And him the undisputed lord of all he surveyed, to boot.

Horse heaven. Yet Diablo Red had quit it. He had returned to the haunts of man.

Rainey had to run a little to keep up with his father's

driving, long-legged stride. The rise of frustrated anger Jonas Bonner felt was also reflected in the tight jut of jaw against his close-cropped beard, the smoldering darkness of his eyes deep-set under a level ridge of brows. His russet hair, the color of leaves after late frost, was thick and shaggy, fantailing over his ears and collar; it poked through the holes in his bandless, battered hat. His face was browned to the color of older leaves, with a graining of weather tracks that squinted his eyes at the outer corners.

Four inches over six feet, he was loose-jointed but not light; there was a bearish weight to his chest and shoulders and arms. His lower body was catty and gaunt with a horseman's whittled hips and the strong, tireless leg movement of a mountaineer. His clothes, soft-worn calico shirt and chalky-worn Levi's, held like a glove to his hard frame. Jonas carried himself with the tough-bitten independence of a man who, at thirty-six, knew his own way and could damned well make it stick.

But he hardly ever made up his mind in a hurry.

Rainey scrambled up to the high seat like a squirrel. Jonas swung up beside him, returned the old Army binoculars to their scratched case, and tucked it under the seat between the sideboard and his Winchester rifle. He took up his reins, kicked off the brake, and put the team in motion. Laden with the supplies purchased in Moratown, the wagon groaned and jolted up the last switchback rise, then onto a gentle length of downslope that leveled off to a grassy flat.

No longer occupied with maneuvering the wagon on a rough grade, Jonas gave a scowling attention to what was already shaping in his mind as a bitter dilemma. He thought he'd put it behind him forever on that day four years ago when he had laid a dynamite charge at the rim of Hawk Pass and sent tons of rock cascading into its cleft, closing it off and sealing Diablo Red and his herd away from the lower ranges of the Neversummer country.

Rainey said suddenly, "Pa, how did he get back here?"

Knowing his father for a moody man, knowing Jonas's moods weren't to be tested lightly, he gave him a slanting look. But Jonas, on his part, knew the crowding eagerness of the young couldn't be long denied. Knew too that no good ever came of suppressing a boy's curiosity.

"I don't know, son. But there's more than one side to that mountain range."

"You mean he could get out another way? But he'd have to make it over a lot of country he don't know, wouldn't he?"

"For a fact. Nearest way he could get out would be going a long way around, a hundred miles and more. Through some of the roughest country on earth."

"But," Rainey persisted, "how did he know how to find his way here?"

Jonas shrugged. "Horse sense, maybe. Your guess is as good as mine. But that's one smart *caballo*, boy."

Too smart for his own good. Mateo Baca had sworn he'd never run up against a *ladino* with so many wily twists to him. It was Mateo who'd first called the young wildling the Red Devil, and the name had fit him when he was only half grown. Repeatedly, the horse had eluded attempts by several horse-raisers and free-lance mustangers to capture him. Then Diablo Red had taken to running off mares from the valley ranches, and word had gone out to shoot the stallion on sight. King Canibar of the Big Crown, biggest cattle outfit in the country, had put a price on his carcass. But Canibar had been less concerned about losing a few mares than the possibility of what he called Diablo Red's "crazy blood" getting into his stock.

Jonas couldn't deny there might be some meat to the idea. Even Mateo had admitted he'd never seen such ferocity, strength, and intelligence in one *caballo*. Traits that might occur to a high degree in different animals, they weren't likely to find such a superb blend in one horse except by pure chance. But Diablo Red's unbridled savagery had seemed to negate his good points. Combined with his sheer cunning, it had enabled him to elude at least six sallies by men who'd been confident they'd had him cornered. A half-dozen close calls that had failed. On a dozen or so other tries, the horse-hunters hadn't even gotten close to the young stallion. . . .

By now Rainey had worked slyly back to his first question. "Pa . . . you think he *can* be catched?"

Damn Mateo and his horse stories, Jonas thought. He had the boy primed so his head was full of 'em. But a faint amusement at Rainey's oblique attack on the matter blunted his irritation. "It's been tried. Plenty good men tried it. You know how they fared."

"Sure, but *you* never tried. I bet you could catch him . . . you and Mr. Baca. Or you and Barney. *Any* of you!"

"That ain't the point. You know why I never tried taking him. You been told enough times."

Rainey nodded reluctantly.

"Then say it."

"You couldn't abide to see him catched."

"Or killed," Jonas said grimly. "It's a feeling a man gets, Rainey. You understand that?"

"I guess so." After a moment's silence the boy said tentatively: "Only you can't do that again, can you?

What you done before. I mean, Hawk Pass was the only way back to that high country from this side, and you—"

"No. I can't."

Jonas said it with a flat and final edge. Rainey fell silent, just slightly pushing out his lower lip. The question was now disposed of for a good while. Jonas disliked putting the boy down smartly, but he'd never found the knack of doing it gently. Mostly a seldom-spoken man, he was by nature brusque and close-mouthed on things that cut close to the nerve. Not the best way to be, he glumly allowed, when you had a boy to raise and no woman to help.

A mother, sure. Rainey had one, all right. But what the hell good was a mother who could live a few short miles from her growing son and not even give a solitary damn?

Late spring had mantled the Wyoming high country like a rich green carpet; bluebells and larkspurs and delphinium spattered it with pink and blue and lavender. The sky arched like a cobalt bowl, and an occasional chicken hawk or bald eagle swam the high currents of wind. The long flat petered out as the road mounted eastward into a range of low hills. It was formed by the remnants of ancient crags that showed here and there in shelving ledges and flinty spires sculptured to weird shapes by time and weather. Thin groves of pine and juniper grew tough and twisted from the shallow soil, interspersed by humpy belts of meadow. The road turned to switchbacks again as the land climbed. Some of the rockier places were overgrown with tangles of brush that Jonas knew were full of rabbit runways.

Jonas halted the team and took his Winchester from

under the seat. "Cottontail fricassee would go good," he said. "What do you say?"

Rainey kept his eyes turned down. "I guess so."

Jonas passed him the rifle. "Keep your eyes open. If you see ary cottontail, sing out and I'll stop."

He drove on slowly. It was only midafternoon and they could take their time getting home. Bagging a jackrabbit or two might take Rainey's mind off that damn horse. Mine too, Jonas thought wryly.

"Pa—"

Jonas hauled up. They were at the flat crest of a hill and Rainey was pointing down right of them. Jonas looked, not quite believing what he saw. Then he broke out the field glasses and looked again.

The hill tapered off to a pine-dotted park, and he could see four men. Three on horseback and one afoot.

One of the mounted men, his arm flailing up and down, was pushing his horse furiously back and forth in gyrating circles. The man on foot was stumbling wildly under the blows of a whip. Falling and then floundering back to his feet. Trying to run one way and then another, only to be headed off by the rider cutting in front of him. The other two men sat their horses and watched.

Sweeping their faces with the glasses, Jonas could identify the three horsemen. He couldn't be sure about the man being whipped, but then his face was a mask of blood. Even as Jonas watched, the whipped man slumped forward on his face and didn't move again.

Jonas growled something inarticulate. It was one of the times he made up his mind quickly. He picked up the reins, then looked at Rainey. "Get down, boy."

"Huh?"

"Out of the wagon. Here, give me the Winchester. Snap to, now!"

Rainey dropped to the ground and Jonas grunted, "You wait here," and hoorawed the team with a yell. As they surged into the harness, he pulled the wagon in a hard curve to the left and guided it down the slope. The man with the whip had stepped from his saddle and was tramping over to his victim. Now he looked up as the wagon came boiling down the incline. Jonas checked his speed a little at the slope's base and continued across the bumpy meadow toward the knot of men.

They had plenty of time to size him up before he reached them. All three stayed as they were, the two horsebackers motionless and watching, the third slowly coiling the whip between his hands. Jonas guessed he'd intended to give the fallen man a few more cuts. Just a logical guess, if you knew Frank Dance.

Jonas sawed the team to a halt and held the reins loose, his elbows resting on the Winchester across his thighs.

"Ol' Bonnie," Phil Canibar said agreeably. "Well, by God, it's been a spell. What brings you this way?"

Jonas eyed them for a moment, then dropped off his seat, Winchester in hand. It was Frank Dance he watched as he said, "You're a little off your range, Phil. I wondered why."

Dance began to grin. He was a knotty-muscled man, built like a solid keg and hard as nails. His head, bunched between his shoulders in a way that always put Jonas in mind of a ringy bull, was entirely hairless. With his scarred lips twitching back from his big yellow teeth, he looked all of the pure brute he was.

"We were following track on a missing mare of ours," Phil Canibar said. "From the sign, she got driven off from our north pasture by a wild stallion, something that hasn't happened in years. Anyway we came on a Big Crown beef a while ago." He waved a hand vaguely toward the south in his languid way. "A yearling calf that this hungry-looking soul," he nodded toward the unconscious man, "apparently butchered sometime this morning to fill his belly. We found a dead fire nearby, still smoking. Track of one man and one horse. David followed the sign and we overtook him at the edge of this park."

Jonas's glance shuttled to David Crow, sitting his horse quietly. He was about twenty-five, slender and still-faced, the son of a white trapper and a Cheyenne woman. Jonas didn't know him well, but he had the feeling David Crow wanted no more part of this than was necessary.

Looking back at Dance now, Jonas said: "I see you did."

Dance rumbled in his chest, his version of a laugh. He nudged the fallen man with a boot. "Don't reckon this should faze you a whole lot. You allus fancied horses better'n folks, as I recall."

"Times like this, that ain't hard to do," Jonas said quietly. "You don't fancy much of anything, do you, Frank?"

Dance said, "Not any," and laughed again.

"Come on, Bonnie—" Phil Canibar curbed his fiddle-footing horse as he took a "long nine" from his coat pocket, his smile very white and genial. "What would you do if it'd been one of your beeves?"

Jonas had always regarded Phil as something less than

half the man his brother King was, and now, seeing him
for the first time in nearly two years, could find no
reason to revise the opinion upward. Phil Canibar was
a well-built man, ten years his brother's junior—which
would make him around thirty now—and about the same
height, but considerably lighter, lean and elegant. His
handsome face was marred by his pale eyes: hooded
by folds of flesh at the outer corners, they gave him
a sly and show-nothing expression even when he smiled
broadly. He wore his yellow, curling hair long and his
mouth was bracketed by a thin mustache whose ends
drooped past his chin. He affected whipcord breeches
and a tweedy, belted jacket; his saddle was heavy wiih
silver trim.

"Slap his fingers maybe?" Phil clipped the end off his
cigar, then tucked it in a corner of his smile. "Quote
gospel at him? Doesn't sound like you some ways, but
how about it? What would you do, Bonnie boy?"

"Not cut a man to raw meat. Be better to hang him
and be done with it."

"Hell," grinned Dance. "This wa'n't nothing. Didn't
even work me up a good sweat."

He relaxed his grip on the whip, shaking out its
coils so the lash flopped across the downed man's body.
The end glistened wet red, Jonas saw. It was the same
whip Dance had always carried, or one very much like
it. Designed by Dance himself, it was halfway in length
between a quirt and a bullsnake, with a jag of lead sewn
to the tip. Dance could pop a fly off a horse's rump with
it and never touch flesh, but he'd hardly ever used it,
that Jonas knew of, without touching flesh.

He saw the taunting in Dance's eyes. Would the bronc-peeler use this moment to crowd a fight? He was plainly toying with the notion.

It was Dance's free use of his whip that had set off the one fight they'd had, now seven years ago. Jonas had still been working for the Big Crown then, and he had caught Dance abusing a horse. The two of them had beaten each other bloody and were still rolling in the corral dust when King Canibar had come on the scene and broken up the fight. The day had been memorable in more ways than one, for in the hot exchange of words that followed, Jonas had quit Big Crown for good, taking his young wife and son with him.

Dance, he knew, hadn't forgotten that time any more than he had. Any encounter that was inconclusive would stick in Frank's craw like a fishbone—he was that kind. Their paths hadn't crossed head-on since, so the dispute had never been settled.

Idly grinning, Dance flipped the lash up.

"Go on, Frank," Jonas murmured.

"Go on what?"

"You want it so damn bad, go ahead."

"You mean if I just give this jigger another little tap, say—"

"That's it."

Phil gave a short laugh. "Quit it. Frank, put that damn thing up. Well, Bonnie, you haven't changed any. Quite as red-headed as you ever were."

"Not quite, Phil," Jonas said gently. "I'm just apt to get that way."

"All right, all right. Frank, I said put that whip up!"

That was Phil's way. Not scrupulous in any way Jonas knew of, he was always cautious. Prone to head off any trouble that might get out of hand and for which he'd have to answer to his big brother. Not hurrying about it, Dance recoiled the whip. He never took his eyes off Jonas.

Phil snapped a match alight on his thumbnail and touched it to his cigar. "Bonnie, this drifter butchered a cow on our top range. I don't call that a hanging offense, but he had to be shown the vote."

"You showed him, all right."

"I suppose you'll take him home and bind his wounds, eh?"

"Any objection?"

Phil shrugged. "We're on public domain here; do as you like. But let him get caught that way again, he'll fare worse. Just be sure he understands it." His eyes flicked upward. "That your son standing on the hill yonder? Well, well. Even from here I can tell he's grown some. Raising a fine lad for yourself, I'll wager."

"I reckon I am."

"Well, well. You ought to bring him to Big Crown sometime." A baiting note touched Phil's voice. "Let his ma have a look at him."

Jonas's jaw ridged against his beard. "Phil, I tell you what's a better idea. You whistle up your dogs and get the hell out of here."

Canibar let out a stream of smoke, his shoulders jerking with mirth. "Jesus, you're touchy. All right, boys, you heard the lord o' the loners. Let us away."

Chapter Two

SET not very far off-side of the Continental
Divide, the high country of the Neversummer foothills was
a mixture of plains and dunes and low hills, bright with
green grass in spring and early summer, fading to yellow
and fawn as the season wore on. A bent arm of the
Neversummers crooked out to enclose partly the rugged
pocket of land where Jonas Bonner's Cross-B Ranch
was. Other settlers of the district had preferred to put
down roots in the great Washoe Basin's lower ranges to
the south and east. But the comfortable monotony of
those rolling lowlands, the convenience of neighbors
wasn't for an off-ox like Jonas. The feel of semiisolation
offered by this rugged northeast corner of the Basin
suited him to a T.

Cross-B was the only outfit in this high, lonely pocket,

and as Jonas had weighed that into account when he'd taken up his government patent here seven years ago, it was likely to remain so. If a man never took the itch to expand into his bones, there was enough good grass to support one outfit of middling size. Given that much, this upper range had its choice features. The barriers nature had laid down provided driftlines; the rocky headlands, pine-bearded cliffs, and secluded dells sheltered his cattle through the worst of any winter. A man-size chore, of course, working them out of the breaks and draws come spring, but you took the bitter with the sweet.

Dashing out of the peaks to the north, the Washoe River made a deep, churning cut along the west boundary of Jonas's land, taking a last steep plunge before it hit the levels and undulations of the lower Basin. Then it looped and crawled southwest, fanning lazily into broad ponds here and there, at the same time picking up a dozen tributaries—lesser streams that kept the range of valley ranches green and lush up till the height of summer's browning heat.

It was nearly sunset when Jonas drove his wagon over the Washoe, crossing it on a crude but sturdy bridge that had taken Mateo Baca and Barney Blue and him most of a month to build. Felling large, straight trees in a pine stand a mile distant, they'd skidded the trimmed logs by team and go-devil to a narrows where the river boiled between rocky walls. They'd dropped the logs across the gap with a "shears" of crossed timbers that hoisted and swung them into place with the aid of teampower. That had been Barney's idea—an adaptation of a device he'd seen employed to "grasshopper" river steamers across sandbars during his boyhood on the Mississippi. Once the supporting timbers were down, it had been a simple matter to nail whipsawed planks crosswise the whole length of the bridge, stabilizing the timbers and forming a pretty even span from one bank to the other. Even so, the team always balked at crossing it. Now Jonas coaxed and cursed them across more gently than usual.

He'd driven slowly along the lumpy and faintly marked road in order to minimize discomfort to the injured youth in the wagon bed. By now the drifter was conscious, teeth locked with pain. He'd held that gritting silence for hours, never making a sound, giving no response at all to any question put to him. His face was flushed by fever, his eyes varnished with it.

"Just a little farther, Mister," Rainey told him. "Gosh! Pa, he must be hurting awful, all cut up like that. You reckon we will have to fetch Doc Bellew?"

Jonas shrugged. "We'll see. Could be Mateo can fix him up after a fashion. He is a pretty fair hand with doctoring cows and horses."

From the river crossing it was a short distance to Cross-B headquarters. Here, on Jonas's own land, the road had been smoothly graded by team-drawn scraper —another tough and lengthy chore—and inside twenty minutes they came in sight of the ranch buildings.

Seven years ago Jonas had planned the layout with care, hoping that a snug and sightly home would help allay the wifely discontents that were already plaguing his marriage. He had built solidly, built to last. Cutting massive logs, snaking them out of the surrounding timber, hewing them to shape to "roll up" his walls. Set between pine-crowned hills, the main house followed the downslope of one in a pleasant, rambling way, dropping a step from kitchen to dining room, from dining room to parlor.

A shallow gorge between the hills led to a wide, rolling pasture, at the head of which the outbuildings were clustered, bunkhouse and barn and tackshed, and a big stable with a horse corral set off behind it.

Minita's dog picked them up and barked a couple of times, then slunk away, growling, as Jonas pulled up in the hard-packed yard. Mateo Baca was seated on the stone step of the house, working a cud of tobacco in his cheek while he patched a piece of worn harness with gnarled, sensitive hands.

"Heh, you're late enough, you two." He spat across his left arm with an old man's care. "Minita, she's keep your supper warm. You better get to it. Then we unload wagon, eh?"

Jonas set the brake and stepped down. "Something else wants unloading first, *viejo*. Have a look."

"Eh?"

Mateo got up and hobbled over to the wagon, favoring the stiff leg that was a memento of his horse-breaking youth. Slight and wiry, he had a grooved and wattled face that had baked to brown leather and was divided by the handsome droop of a white mustache. His pale brown eyes were as quick and young as a boy's; age and a crippled leg and the rich aroma of sour wine that always engulfed him after a good meal didn't diminish by a jot his crotchety and unstooped dignity.

"Santa Maria, what's this?" He peered at the hurt man. "Looks like this *niño*, he get chewed up and spit out. You save what's left of him from a bear, maybe?"

"From a few curly wolves, say. Tell you about it later. Give me a hand fetching him inside." Jonas hesitated. "Where's Barney?"

"He ain' come in yet." Old Mateo bristled, his pride

touched. "Hell, I can carry any gringo in my myself."

"I'll lend a hand, you don't mind," Jonas said dryly. "Rainey, you run ahead and tell Minita to boil some water and set out some dressings."

"Her sewing stuff, too," grunted Mateo. "This one, he's tore to hell, I'm think. Anything busted?"

"I don't think so, but go light with him."

Between them, the two men eased the youth out of the wagon and carried him into the parlor. They were about to set him on the leather-covered couch when Minita came hurrying from the kitchen.

"Not, not there," she told them sharply. "It's too hard, that old couch, for a man who is hurt. . . ." She stopped, gazing in shock at the youth's face. "*Dios,* that's terrible! Who would do such a thing?"

Old Mateo gave her a testy glare, saying sarcastically in Spanish, "Where then, my small dove, would you suggest we place this disabled caballero? *¡Ándale!* My arms ache."

Minita tossed her head. Small and golden-skinned, she was just touching sixteen. She looked even younger, her figure slim and coltish in a shapeless calico dress. Her heart-shaped face was delicately modeled, framed by black hair that was crow's-wing shiny and pulled to a tight knot back of her small head. Her straight brows were pertly winged at the ends, setting off fine eyes as gentle as her voice; but she had a share of her grand-sire's spirit.

She said: "In my room, little Grandfather. Where else?"

"*¡Qué!*"

"He is hurt, he's bleeding. He needs good care. Don't argue, bring him."

The girl was already moving ahead of them into the sleeping area that adjoined the parlor. It was a large wing, for Jonas had planned it for the big family he'd never have: a master chamber and two other good-sized rooms where kids could double or triple up. He and Rainey now occupied the master bedroom, Mateo and Minita the other two.

The men clumped into her room, old Mateo glowering and muttering, and Minita threw back the covers of her bed. "Lay him down. Gently now . . . gently!"

Jonas said dryly, "You hear her, *viejo?* Gently. You're going to have you some messy sheets, Sis."

"So? Sheets can be washed. Pull off his boots, *Abuelito*. If you'll raise his shoulders, Jonas, I will undo his clothes. . . ."

Old Mateo's mustache quivered angrily. "You will *not!* We will do that. Go to the kitchen, 'Nita, and get the water."

Minita gave him a dark-eyed look of patience. "There is no water, *Abuelito*. I have sent Rainey to the well for some—"

"Then prepare bandages. Needle and thread to sew these wounds. *¡Andale!*"

They found the youth's clothes crusted fast to his skin with dried blood. He was feverish by now; spots of color came and went in his face. Jonas got a bottle of whiskey and filled a tin cup from it and told him, "You'd better take this if you can keep it down." The drifter said nothing, but he heaved himself painfully onto his elbows and gulped the liquor down as Jonas held the cup to his lips. When the water was heated, Jonas and Mateo soaked the clothes away while the youth jerked and shuddered uncontrollably.

Most of his body was covered with raw welts, the flesh bruised and purpled and broken in a score of places. He didn't let out a peep as Mateo washed the oozing wounds with whiskey and warm water, and closed them with small neat stitches, including several ugly gashes on his face. Then the old Mexican salved the hurts with a tarry-looking ointment and fixed bandages of torn-up calico in place.

"That is all I can do," he said. "I hope this wolfling is worth it."

The kid had something of a wolf's look at that, Jonas thought. Not over nineteen, he was medium-sized and wiry-muscled; under a shaggy tumble of chestnut hair, his face was gaunt and hungry and marked with older scars. His lips stayed clamped against speech as he studied each of his benefactors in turn, the woodsmoke eyes fierce with pain and suspicion.

"How deep he must hurt," Minita said softly. "Will he be well, little Grandfather?"

"How can I say? I think yes, if there is no infection. But he will not move about for a long time. I suppose you will take care of him, eh?"

"Who else? So I would do for a sick calf or a bird with a broken wing."

"Bah. This is neither. It is a wolfling. I think its teeth are sharp." Mateo glowered at her. "You will take care of yourself, too. You will sleep in the loft."

"But I should be close by if he needs—"

"*¡Por Dios!* In the loft, I say."

Minita knew when not to belabor an argument. "*Sí, Abuelito.* . . ."

Rainey came in from unhitching and turning in the team horses and the drifter's horse, which had been tied to the tailgate of the wagon. The two Bonners took their places at the puncheon table while Minita ladled out bowls of beef stew from an iron pot suspended on a trammel hook in the fieldstone fireplace. The kitchen was equipped with a big range, but often as not Minita preferred to cook as her mother had taught her, over open coals. Jonas and Rainey had grown a taste for her highly seasoned cookery. They dug in hungrily.

While they were eating, Barney Blue came in from the day's work.

" 'Evening, folks." He flipped his battered hat onto a wall peg. "Sorry I'm late for grub. Was setting out salt by the crick 'long Five-Mile Pasture and come on this yearling stuck in the mud. Had me a time roping him out."

"Sit and eat," Jonas said.

"Yassuh, massa, thankee. This ole colored boy sho' 'preciate how you do equalize things." Barney limped to the table, rubbing his big hands together. "Mm-mm! Them's some savory fixings I smell, Miss Minnie. I swear, you white folks know how to set one fancy-fine table."

Minita laughed, spooning stew into a bowl. "Always you joke, Barney. *Abuelito* and me, you know we are mostly *Indio*."

Barney dropped onto a rawhide-rigged stool between old Mateo and Rainey, ruffling the boy's hair. "Have a good day, young 'un? How you doing, Gran'pop?" He gaves Minita a sober wink. "Well now, I dunno 'bout that, Miss Minnie. This *viejo* here, he get a good skinful o' that berry sweat he is tucking away, he will swear seven ways to sundown he is of the pure blood of Castile. Ain't that right, Gran'pop?"

"That is right, Negro," old Mateo said tranquilly. His

usual irascibility mellowed by several more cups from the demijohn by his elbow, he wasn't to be baited. "The blood of *grandees*. And the *Indio*, this part is of the true line of Aztec kings. . . . *¡Alto!* Put that back."

As she set the bowl of stew in front of Barney, Minita whisked the demijohn away. She marched with it to a cupboard and placed it inside and firmly closed the door. "No. That is enough of an evening. Your spleen of the days would be less were your nights without it."

"You are a scold," Mateo Baca said in a mellow tone. "See, Negro? Day or night, it is no matter. I am beset by this termagant and her scolding."

Barney chuckled, saying around a mouthful of stew, "You are lucky to have such a termagant, old one. It lessens your senile folly, I think."

"Bah! Hear the son of servitude."

Sometime in his life, Barney Blue had learned to speak the old and pure Spanish as well as Mateo himself; Jonas could just manage to follow it. Barney was a lanky, rawboned man in his mid-forties, hawk-faced and balding. A mesh of kindly humor lines around his eyes and mouth softened the craggy angles of his face. Three-quarters Negro and one-quarter Cherokee, he was the son of slaves who'd fled to Mexico before the war, and he'd learned all he knew of cattle and horses—which was considerable—from Sonoran *vaqueros*.

Minita poured cups of steaming coffee for the men. Then she sat at the table and said with a note of eagerness: "Jonas, will you tell now how you found the young man?"

"What's 'at?" Barney asked.

Jonas, the edge off his appetite now, briefly told them

of the encounter with Phil Canibar, Dance, and David Crow.

"A cow thief then," muttered old Mateo. "He has brought a cow thief under his roof. Ai-yi! I am not surprised."

Barney grinned. "Yeah, he pick up all kinds o' strays, the boss does."

"You ought to know, Negro."

"You, too. That's what I mean."

Mateo yawned and nodded, rubbing a hand over his white head. "*Sí*, there's something to that, I suppose. Is a cross-log outfit you got here, Jonas. Ain't that what people call us?"

Jonas grinned. "I guess we're a pack of cross-dogs, *viejo*. Recall how you picked me up? I wasn't much older'n this drifter boy. Not in much better shape, either."

"Ah." Mateo chuckled, stroking his mustache. "I'm remember, yes. You were a wild one, Jonas. Ver' wild. Is why we took to you, I'm think."

Jonas had been twenty years old, fresh from helping trail a herd to Laramie. Had blown his pay on booze and then drunkenly had ridden his horse full tilt through town, shooting out windows. Had escaped in the night followed by a hail of gunfire from angry citizens, and one bullet had found its mark. Long miles later, still drunk and weak from loss of blood, he'd fallen from his saddle. That was how Mateo Baca and his people had found him next day. They'd taken him, a strange wounded gringo, to their camp and nursed him back to health.

At that time there had been four of them: Mateo, his younger brother, Mateo's son-in-law, and Mateo's daughter who was swollen with child. The Bacas were *mesteneros*—a family of mustangers who followed the wild herds and laid their traps. When they'd broken camp to resume their hunt, their number had grown to six, for Mateo's daughter had given birth to a girl, Minita —and with them went young Jonas Bonner. It was a free and wild life, one tailor-made to his nature, and he had ridden with them for three years, helping them snare the *mestenadas* and learning to rough-break and gentle them under Mateo's careful tutelage.

It had changed his life. An orphan himself, Jonas had taken a family feeling from those years with the Balas.

"That was a long time ago, *viejo*." Jonas's voice unconsciously roughened; to cover a faint embarrassment, he raised his coffee cup and drained it.

Rainey, unable to contain himself any longer, blurted out: "Mr. Baca, you know what we saw today? Diablo Red!"

Mateo's brows arched, then scowled. "How's this, *niño?* What strangeness do you say? *Diablo Rojo*—"

"It's true, sir! Tell 'em, Pa."

Jonas felt all their eyes on him. He fumbled out his pipe and bit on the stem. "It was him all right, Mateo. We seen him over by Castle Rock. He saw us too."

"Hah. So . . . he is come back. Yes, that horse, he could do this. You sure there's no mistake, amigo?"

"No mistake. It was him." Jonas explained how they had spotted the stallion.

"Now that's sure something." Barney shook his head. "Think o' that *caballo salvaje* finding his way clear back to his ole stamping grounds. Seeing's you dynamited Hawk Pass and they's no other near way back, he must-a come 'round the long way. He'd-a had to bypass glaciers, cliffs, canyons, a reg'lar maze. Less'n he sprouted wings, though, I reckon that's what he done. Sure is a curiosity *why*. Had him ever'thing back in them mountains a big ole *manadero* like him could want. And not a human soul to argufy him."

"It was a ver' hard winter, this last one," old Mateo observed. "Maybe he lose his *manada*."

"That could be it," Jonas said slowly.

"I bet, sure," Barney nodded. "Most time he could look after his mares 'n' colts just dandy. But them mountain blizzards hit like they done last year, they must-a raised hell with his herd. Way-down temperatures 'n' deep snow. Couldn't scratch 'em up no forage and couldn't keep on the move. No feed and stone-iron cold. Weak 'uns would-a starved and froze even if they wa'n't wolves and lions to pull 'em down. Them meat-eaters be half-starved 'emselves, they get plenty bold, you bet. Old Diablo, he'd-a toughed it out himself, and I lay odds he fought like all furies for his folks. But that there was a seven-month winter. Time she was finished, I reckon they wa'n't a one of them wildlings left, cep'n . . ."

Abruptly Jonas got up and walked to the fireplace. Squatting on his heels, he picked up the bubbling coffee-pot in a calloused hand that was impervious to its scalding heat, refilled his cup, and set the pot down. He stayed that way, hunkered down with his back to the room, staring into the fire.

"So," Mateo said softly. "This time, my friend, I think there's no way you keep that big *caballo* free."

Jonas nodded, not looking up. "Don't seem so, does it?"

"Not if he up to his ole tricks again," said Barney. "I reckon that's why he come back. To get him another *manada*."

"He's at it already," Jonas said tightly. "Phil Canibar said him and the others were out trailing a mare that got taken off."

"Then," Mateo murmured, "soon King Canibar will know that Diablo Rojo is back. Again he will put men on the hunt—with orders to kill."

"I reckon."

"Oh, it is too bad," said Minita in a pained voice. "I know how you feel, Jonas, about the horse."

"Eh, you know nothing," growled her grandfather. "It is a woman's softness you feel. Nobody feels for the wild ones like this Jonas Bonner who is half horse himself. *Amigo*, I don' think this time you save him, not if—"

"Let it go, all of you," Jonas said harshly. He stood now and swung around, giving them a frosty stare. "We got no damn time to fret over outlaw horses. This is a working outfit, remember? It's drawing dark. Let's get this wagon unloaded and turn in."

"Pa," Rainey began.

"No more talk, boy. Help Minita clean up. Then you both got an hour of study before you turn in. Get to it. Barney, give me a hand."

When they finished putting up the supplies, Jonas and Barney Blue sat on the front stoop and lighted their pipes.

It was part of a nightly pattern, a ritual of household habit. Usually, comfortable habit. After supper old Mateo would take his way carefully and unsteadily to bed, full of wine and weariness. Minita and Rainey would sit at the table with primers and copybooks spread in front of them and apply themselves to the study they were too far from any school to get otherwise. At first Jonas and Barney had taken turns teaching the kids, but both youngsters had quickly overtaken their elders' meager acquirements in the three R's; now they coached each other. Weather permitting, Jonas and Barney often sat outsde and whiled away evenings with talk or companionable silence till it was time to turn in.

Tonight the two of them sat and smoked and had little to say. Jonas felt withdrawn and a little touchy; Barney sensed his mood and respected it. Presently Barney would say good night and head for the bunkhouse where he had his solitary quarters; basically a loner, he liked it that way.

Reckon we're all pretty much loners, Jonas thought, even the young 'uns. For neither Rainey nor Minita appeared to miss the company of kids their age, yet neither was shy or lacking in confidence. Still—for both there remained a whale of a lot to be seen, to be learned, that couldn't be come by on a backwoods ranch. In Rainey's case it might not matter a great deal. He's be taking a restless itch in foot before too many years, but having grown up around three men, he'd probably make his way in a man's world one day with—so Jonas figured—no more'n the usual quota of lumps and bruises. For Minita, having no woman about to tell her what a girl ought to know, the road was likely to be a sight bumpier. Fortunately, she had a straight head on her shoulders and plenty of natural savvy. Not a bad thing, meantime, that this man's outfit had a touch of female to keep the place orderly and its menfolk more or less curried and mannered. . . .

Cricket song thickened the dusk; the day's heat was lifting. A cool wind coming off the high country carried the tang of pine pitch; it mingled with the pipesmoke, not unpleasantly. Jonas stirred restlessly, thinking of Diablo Red. Where was he tonight? Again on the prowl along valley ranges?

Damn that *caballo*, anyway! Jonas remembered the first time he'd seen the blood bay. It had been five years ago this spring—at a distance and unexpectedly, like today.

Hard to put into words how he felt about the horse, then and now. Damned near as hard to put into thoughts. Some of it, Jonas supposed, was tied up with the reason why, years ago, the trade of trapping wild horses had gone sour on him. He'd mustanged for three years with Mateo's family, then three years on his own. When he'd quit the business it wasn't because the rough freedom of the mustanger's life had palled on him. It was the catching and penning up of wild things that he could no longer abide.

That personal decision hadn't caused him to pass judgment on other horse-hunters. They were his kind of man, in love with a way of life. Sure-to-hell a life where you bitterly earned every dollar you turned. Not many in this part of the country plied the trade any longer. The numbers of the *mestenadas* had dwindled over the years, trapped out or driven to other ranges. Going after the few bands of scrubby broomtails that still frequented the remote places wasn't worth the time or trouble.

So it had been by the time the red colt called Diablo Red had made his appearance. And he'd been wholly a different proposition. Men coveting him had gone out in bunches; they had set elaborate traps. Twice they'd nearly succeeded in taking him, each time running him into a box canyon and fencing up its mouth. Diablo Red had escaped from the first trap by clearing the pole barrier with an incredible leap. The second time they'd built a higher fence, but not strongly enough; he'd smashed his way through it. By the time he was old enough to begin raiding for mares, the horse had learned all the tricks, literally outthinking his pursuers, eluding them with uncanny ease. When the order had gone out to shoot him, nobody had been able to get close to him.

But in the end, one way or the other, they would have gotten him. And Jonas Bonner hadn't wanted that to happen.

Seeing the stallion only a few times and always from a distance, Jonas had taken irresistible feeling for him. Not the desire for possession. In fact no feeling he could easily define. In some obscure way, Jonas supposed, Diablo Red represented a wild remnant of that life he had given up. Something he could keep alive in himself by knowing the big horse was out there somewhere— anywhere, just so he was running free.

With the skilled help of Mateo Baca and Barney Blue, Jonas had managed to accomplish what no others had: to maneuver Diablo Red and his band of stolen mares into a trap of sorts. With infinite patience and matchless teamwork, the three men had gradually hoorawed him toward Hawk Pass which formed the only break in a mountain cordon that cut off the high ranges of the Neversummers from the Washoe Basin's east flank. It had taken three days to work the band finally into the vast funnel-shaped mouth of the pass. Finding himself bottled, Diablo Red's only choice had been to take his *manada* through. Then the setting of dynamite charges . . .

Jonas's pipe had gone dead. Irritably, he gave it a couple hard whacks on the step to knock out ash, then jammed in another thumb of tobacco.

From inside the house came the soft drone of Minita's voice as she read with a halting care from *McGuffey's Third Eclectic Reader:* " 'If I wish to know whether it is George or his brother who is sick, I speak the words *George* and *brother* with more force than the other words. I say, is it *George* or his *brother* who is sick?' . . ."

Barney chuckled, his pipe coal drawing brightly. "Man, it sure shines how fast them young 'uns learn. Me, I learnt most o' my letters offen making powder cans and the like."

"Uh-huh. We had the same teacher."

The lanky Negro gave him an oblique glance. "If you got your grub settled and all, I would like to put a question."

Jonas grunted. "So long it don't mean an answer I already give, go ahead."

"No-o," Barney said judiciously. "I reckon not. You only *thought* you give it. You still got something mighty strong in your innards about that Diablo horse. You ain't about to let go of it neither."

"All right. Get it said."

"Man can maybe put a thing like that out o' his head, but not out o' his craw. Trouble with you, *caporal*, you get a burr under your saddle and you just gotta buck yourself to death. Sure makes living 'round you a caution."

"Is that a fact."

"Yeh. Turns you sore as a scalded dog. I know."

Jonas couldn't keep back a wry grin.

Likely Barney Blue knew him better than anyone ever had. Barney had been breaking and gentling horses for Canibar's Big Crown when Jonas had first hired on there for the same work. A quick bond had formed between them, the kind of understanding that only two lonely maverick men in the same trade could know.

Six years ago, when Barney had been badly busted-up after getting stomped by an outlaw bronc, he'd been left with the choice of quitting Big Crown or staying on as its all-around chore boy, a flunky job. Even in the rough democracy of a ranch crew, a colored man had few choices, and King Canibar didn't hold with the view that getting stove-up in an outfit's service earned a man his right to pride. A half-crippled man, as Canibar saw it, couldn't handle a full man's job. So Barney had come to Jonas and put it flat: crooked leg or no, he could still give a day's work for a man's pay and asked nothing but a chance to prove it. This was right after Jonas had fired the two shiftless hands he'd first taken on— the only kind he could get for the wages he could afford to pay—but he'd have counted himself lucky to take on Barney Blue under any circumstances.

Not long after that, Jonas had learned that another old friend, Mateo Baca, was in sorry straits. Mateo's brother and daughter and son-in-law had all been taken off by the same outbreak of typhus, leaving the old man with a young granddaughter to care for and his trade wiped out, no outfit willing to take on a man of his years and no family left to help. Unhesitatingly, Jonas had sought out Mateo and urged him to come to Cross-B. Accepting charity of any sort was beneath the old *mestenero's* fierce pride, but he'd understood Jonas's need to pay a debt. And Mateo had known, as Jonas had too, that his lifetime knowledge of range conditions would be invaluable to his gringo friend.

So it had proved to be. Easy to weigh a man's handicaps. But there was no measure or price you could put on the loyalty and experience of two men like Blue and Baca.

"All right," Jonas said resignedly. "I pay you for advice too, even if I don't pay much."

"Ain't that the truth." Barney's voice held a grin. "Well, *caporal*, you wanta keep that Diablo horse alive, you can't keep him free. You can't have it both ways. Reckon that there's my advice."

Jonas didn't reply immediately. "Catch him is what you mean."

"Uh-huh. And don't tell me it didn't cross your mind noways."

"Seeing you're so damn full of ideas, what the hell do I do with him if I get him?"

"Man, I never tried to tame a tornado. One thing at a time. It's catch him or you know what, is all I'm saying."

"Some good men have tried it."

Barney's teeth flashed. "Sure, but not you or me or the *viejo*. Put the three together and we can show that red devil some tall odds. We got the time to spare for it, seeing the spring gather is done with and the calf branding, too."

Jonas was silent again, turning the reluctant decision in his mind. *It's catch him or you know what*. Then he said abruptly, "Let's get some sleep. We'll be starting out first thing tomorrow."

Chapter Three

NEXT morning after breakfast, the men made ready for a back-country trip that might last several days. They chose three saddle mounts that would be long on speed and endurance. Along with axes, utensils, camp gear, slickers, and blanket rolls, they put up ample provisions and lashed the whole pack to a spare horse. If there was a long trail ahead and any hard chasing to do, they'd want their mounts to carry as little extra weight as possible. As they prepared their animals at the corral, Jonas studied the sky above the Buckhorn Hills to the north where they'd begin the hunt. Weather looked promising enough. It was a clear spring day, bright but crisp.

As he cinched on his saddle, old Mateo grumbled, "I don't know it's a good idea, all us *hombres* going. The *niño* and the *niña*, we leave them alone. All *solo!*"

Barney looked up from tightening a diamond hitch on the pack. "What you fretting 'bout, Gran'pop? Them young 'uns have held down the place by 'emselves before this."

"Not with a wolfling under the roof, Negro. This is a worry."

"Man, that boy ain't just bunged all to hell, you got him sewed all over like a Christmas turkey. He try to move, he be tearing stitches. He plain helpless as a baby."

"Heh, yes. Now he is helpless. *Now.*"

"Well, I dunno," Barney said innocently. "Seeing it's giving you such a burr under your blanket, maybe you best stay behind. Could be some mighty hard riding ahead o' us. Get them old bones o' yourn too stiffed up, they will just naturally spring at the seams."

Mateo shook a fist at him. "*¡Ay qué risa!* Don't laugh at me, you black goat, you son of servitude! This decrepit can yet run circles around your spindly shanks—"

Jonas shook his head, grinning, as he swung open the corral gate and led out his and Mateo's mounts. This was relatively mild grousing from Mateo, whose frame of mind was always testiest early in the day. Like any old warhorse rousing to the bugle, he was eager as a boy for this adventure. If he hadn't been invited to share in it, he'd have been fit to tie.

"It's like Barney says, *viejo*. That ridge-runner won't be off his bed for a week anyway. We'll be gone two, three days at the most. We ain't raised Diablo Red by then, we will quit. And the kids got Tigre about to mind 'em. They'll be fine."

"So," Mateo muttered, leading out the packhorse. "Have you thought about this wolfling, what he may be? What do we know of him? From his look, I'm think maybe he's a *ladrón.*"

"He looks like a spooky kid is all," Jonas grunted. "What he got fetched 'ud make anyone spooky."

"Heh. He is a thief, you know this."

"Man gets hungry enough, he'll steal. Damn near any man will."

Barney led out his mount and closed the gate, and the three of them mounted and rode through the shallow gorge to the house. Minita was in the yard setting out scraps for her dog. Tigre was a huge yellow cur of indeterminate breed, thickly built, with powerful jaws like a mastiff's. Snapping up his food in great gulps, he paused long enough to show his teeth at the men, then growled continuously as he finished eating. He had no use for anyone but Minita, who had fed him from the day he'd shown up at the place, a bad-tempered stray looking for a handout.

Quite a bodyguard, all right, if she had need of one.

Mateo gave his granddaughter a final stern warning to be wary of "the wolfling," and she nodded patiently. "All will be well with us, *Abuelito.* Do not worry."

Rainey wasn't around to see them off. Jonas felt a nudge of guilt as they rode away from Cross-B headquarters, thinking how he had lost his temper with the boy this morning. He had been out of patience with Rainey's persistent eager wheedling to go along on the horse hunt, that was true, but it was no good excuse. Rainey had moped about at his morning chores, then had disappeared.

Always alert to Jonas's broodings, Barney pulled up stirrup to stirrup with him, saying mildly, "Don't fret 'bout the young 'un. He didn't go far; I found him back of the tack shed a little while back. Sulking some, but he be all right."

"He say anything?"

"Not much. Tol' him it's needful one man stays here to look after Miss Minnie 'n' mind the place. Dunno he took it to heart right off, but he get thinking on it, it will sink in."

Jonas nodded bleakly. "I could of said that. I should of."

"Be better if it came from his pa, for a fact."

"Afraid I keep botching things with the boy, Barney."

Barney shook his head. "Man, you done the best you can. Hard for some men to talk to a kid. You ain't an open sort o' man, and you ain't no damn shucks at putting on, neither. Best that boy know his pa for what he is, not what he ain't."

"You think he does?"

"Yeh." Barney grinned a little. "I think he does. Most times you ain't done as bad as you think."

The Buckhorn Hills undulated away northward into a jumble of serrated badlands that bordered the higher ramparts of the Neversummers. After an hour's ride, the three men came up on a crest where they had a panoramic view of the bad country. It was miles of wild and broken terrain, which had been a refuge for roving bands of wild mustangs since the white man's encroachments had driven them from the valley ranges. Even when the close-pressed *mestenadas* had no longer found the area a refuge from the horse-hunters, Diablo Red had made a successful stand of his own there.

Just surveying as much as you could see of it from this height gave you a foretaste of the difficulties. Yet Jonas felt confident. He hadn't prepared for a drag-out chase; he was depending on his hard-won savvy and his companions' to make a swift capture of the red wildling. Not allowing himself to dwell on what might happen if they couldn't manage it. Well, both he and Barney had worked this district at one time or another during their mustanging days. They knew the trails, the waterholes, the whole lay of the country as well as any man alive. They'd used that common savvy to get the stallion pointed the way they wanted him, toward Hawk Pass, four years ago.

Not with the aim of catching him, though. This was opening a whole different can of beans.

What the hell. The procedure was basic. Find Diablo Red and trail him up till you had his pattern. Watch your chance and then close in. Head him into a tight place and hold him there. Simple enough. It was the details that would require patience and some wily thinking out. Man sense against horse cunning. Just don't get thinking too much about it now. You'd get tripping yourself up on some fancy fixed scheme. This was no ordinary *caballo* they were up against. They'd have to improvise like hell according to the set of the land and the unexpected turns that damn horse might try.

Finding him: that came first.

The three reviewed what they knew of the stallion's old habits.

The Washoe River cut along the west edge of the badlands, and there, as it did farther down, the stream offered few easy crossings. Jonas recalled that Diablo Red had first favored one crossing in particular, a place where the river surged tightly through a canyon or wide fissure whose rims tapered almost together at the top. A horse or man could practically step across it. The *caballo* had come and gone by that route in his mare-raiding forays. Later, as men had sized up his habits, the stallion had changed them. But that had been four years ago. For now, maybe, he might have reverted to his early patterns.

"He taken one Big Crown mare we know of," Barney said. "So if he looking to build him a new *manada* . . ."

Jonas nodded. "We'll have a look at that crossing first. Good a place as any to start."

"*Bueno*," grunted Mateo Baca.

For close to another hour they worked north through a maze of canyons, then swung west. Another mile brought them onto a wide bench covered with big pines, and they crossed it easily and came to the edge of timber. Almost from their horses' feet the land fell away in a dizzying sweep. Just right of them was the sparkling snake of the Washoe, pinched off from sight at that narrow point where the crossing lay. Ahead of them the land dipped widely and then abruptly rose in a rugged series of terraced benches. The valley below was miles across, a mixture of shouldering ridges and pine parks and belts of meadow.

With no exchange of words, the men reached with one accord for their field glasses. They took the time for a long scrutiny of the open places.

"Ah!" Mateo husked. "There—there, *hombres!*"

"Where?" Barney demanded.

"To the left of that needle rock, then down the slope . . . you see?"

Almost concealed by dense timber, a pocket of humpy meadow slanted off from the rock, and halfway across it four horses could be picked out. "Him, all right,"

Jonas muttered when he had the focus. "And three more. He'd been busy, right enough."

"Now—" Mateo's old voice cracked with excitement; he was actually smiling. "—we find how good you remember the game, Jonas."

Jonas scrubbed a hand over his jaw. "Them benches over north are pretty tall and rough. I hazard he won't make for 'em if he thinks he sees a better out. The river'll block him on the west—'cept for that crossing. Barney, you get over by it and wait. Mateo and me will lay a few 'spooks' along the west and north, see if we can crowd him against them ridges yonder. Might be we can fetch him up short there. Soon's you hear me fire a shot, you work straight east, get him moving our way. Stay behind him then, but take it slow and easy, all right?"

The three men put their horses down the steep, long incline with care, dirt and rock rattling away under their horses' descent. The animals were almost sliding on their haunches when the slope began to level off. At the bottom the men broke apart, Barney turning west toward the river, Jonas and Mateo swinging at a loose angle toward the needle rock. The meadow where Diablo Red and his fledgling *manada* grazed was hedged on the south by a dense forest that would cover their advance; the light wind was in their faces and wouldn't carry their scent to the stallion.

They rode into the pine woods, their passage almost noiseless on its needle-carpeted floor. Presently, through the tree trunks, the gray pinnacle came into sight. As Jonas had noted from above, it was part of a wedge-shaped mass of granite that jutted deep into the meadow at its east end. The trick now was to get Diablo Red headed past the north side of the formation and toward the ridges, rather than taking the easier route that lay open along its south flank.

Jonas and Mateo rode to the point of the wedge. Here, still well cut off from the stallion by a grassy swell, Jonas dismounted. He unbuckled his narrow Cheyenne-style chaps and draped them across a bush just south of the rock. As he stepped into the saddle again, old Mateo chuckled softly.

"Yes, *amigo*, that will turn most wild ones. But *Diablo Rojo?* He learned about such tricks ver' quick before. He *thinks*, that horse."

"He ain't come up against men in four years. I'm gambling he's forgot a few things."

"Eh, he will learn 'em again. *Pronto!*"

"But maybe not *pronto* enough. Let's find out."

They skirted wide around the formation and worked northeast toward the ridges, Jonas carefully sizing up the more open ground to which he was fairly sure Diablo Red would stick. Coming to a second place where the trail might easily split one way or the other, this time by a stand of aspen, he told Mateo to hang his chaps from a tree limb that projected across the south fork.

Mateo obeyed, but he grumbled: "If he's smart enough by now, maybe he go into the trees here."

"He might," Jonas conceded. "But being so all-fired smart, he might figure he'd be wiser yet to stay always in the open where he can keep a good watch on his front and sides. Herding stallion is like a good general, he don't let his vantage get cut off."

In the saddle again, they pressed on across boulder-strewn ground to the first massive fold of ridges. From the meadow to this point, Diablo Red's line of retreat should follow that rough alley that wended between rock formations and stands of timber, provided he shied off from the two "spooks" they'd laid. Once he got this far, the tricky part would begin. Jonas pointed to a wide gap that yawned between two towering ridges.

"Right through there, *viejo*. That's where we'll push him."

Mateo's old bones were plainly starting to ache; he shifted in his saddle to ease a hip cramp, saying grumpily, "So, and then?"

"Well, you can't tell it from right here, but that gap heads into a pass. Farther you follow it, the narrower it gets. And the steeper it gets on each side. Maybe a half mile from here it pinches off in a box canyon."

"Before you push him that far, I'm think he find some places he can climb out."

"If he takes it in his head to. But it'd be a hard climb, and he's got them mares to look after. We'll push him right along, Barney and me, but not so hard he'll spook. I hope. It's all by guess and by God, old-timer."

"Eh? You and the Negro? What am I doing then?"

"There's one place up ahead where the pass slants down so low on one side, he could take his *manada* right out of the trap easy as pie. About then he is going to be onto us, and I reckon he'll try it. Want you to get up forward at that place and turn him if he does. With Barney and me right behind him, only one place he can go then. Right into the box canyon."

The old man scowled. "A two years' child could do this work. Ha! I see. You are getting *el viejo* out of the way. The good work, you and the Negro will do it all."

Jonas clamped him on one bony shoulder. "Not all. Right after we get him that far, you'll be joining us. Ain't no place he can climb out after that. The three of us'll run him square into that box. All right?"

"You are the *caporal*," Mateo grumbled. "Where is this place I must wait?"

"Ride about a quarter mile straight in and you'll see a slide on your right. The wall is busted clean down, you can't miss it."

As Mateo jogged away into the broad cleft, Jonas lifted his Winchester from its boot and fired it off once. Afterward, he gave the whole area roundabout a sweeping study. It was too open here, that was the trouble. Plenty of room for Diablo Red to swing wide of the gap's mouth. He'd been caught in such places before, last at Hawk Pass. Memory might have dimmed, but not completely. In that case he'd almost certainly make for the sparse timber to the left.

Jonas rode across the open and into the timber a ways. Then he settled down to wait . . . .

At last he picked up the slow rattle of hoofs. Diablo Red had swallowed the two "spooks"; he was coming. So far, so good. A minute later he broke into view, pushing his three mares steadily, nipping flanks and keeping them bunched, yet never relaxed a taut vigilance. His head was up, all senses alert and conning the rocky scape. Sunfire hit on his burnished coat.

Jonas rose in his stirrups, pulse thickening. Lord God— to see that critter this close!

The stallion came uncertainly to a stop. He extended his head toward the gap; suspicion flattened his ears. He struck the ground with a forehoof, irritably. Then he wheeled with a snort and tailed up the mares, heading them straight toward the timber.

Come on, Barney, Jonas thought. Come on!

And Barney Blue came into sight then, out of the long

alley down which he'd pushed the herd. *Now.* Jonas rode slowly out of the timber. Diablo Red pulled up short of it, giving an angry nicker.

"Close up, Barney!" Jonas yelled. "Close it up now —and take it easy!"

The two men moved in gradually. Jonas's throat was tight with anticipation. Let the stallion feel too crowded, and that savage unpredictability of his could flare; he might bolt in any direction. But the easiest way that now remained open to him was the gap.

And he chose it, whirling around the mares and urging them sharp and fast into the broad cleft. Jonas and Barney converged behind him and met in the shroud of dust raised by the four horses. Barney scooped off his hat and sleeved his sweating face, shaking his head.

"Man, I don't believe it. This here's been too damn easy." But he was grinning. "You sure had him pegged all the way, *caporal.*"

"So far. Let's keep him on the move. Slow and easy like before."

"Sure. What's next?"

Jonas explained the rest of it as they rode into the gap, keeping the horses just in sight.

"You'll have him ketched in a dead end," Barney nodded. "But he been boxed before. Iffen he spooks, he could run right back through us."

"We won't push him hard at any point. That box can-yon is long and it's narrow. One of us'll cover the mouth while the other two fetch timbers and get a fence built across it. One he can't jump or bust down. After that we'll take our time figuring how to handle him."

"Whee-oo, that gonna take some figuring, sure enough.

So will fetching him home. I reckon our troubles is just starting."

Jonas reckoned the same.

Frank Dance and David Crow watched the whole thing.

The two of them were on a high, narrow ridge a little to the northwest. They had heard the shot and were curious enough to leave their horses and climb the promontory to its highest point. From here Dance glassed the area.

"I don't see a thing," he muttered. "But that shot was damn close."

"There, Frank." David Crow pointed.

A man had ridden into sight at a break in the gap, and now he turned and rode up a broad slide where the wall had collapsed. He dismounted and settled wearily on his haunches.

David Crow didn't need glasses to identify him. "That's old Baca."

"Sure enough. But what'n hell's he up to?"

"To your right, Frank. Look sharp."

They saw four horses trot into sight, and Dance said: "There's our mares, by God. And there's the big bastard who took 'em. Jesus! That's . . . naw, it can't be."

"Diablo Red," David Crow said softly. "It's him. No other like him."

"How'n hell could that be? Wait . . . there's someone tailing 'em up. That nigger of Bonner's for sure. And that's Bonner himself coming out of the timber."

For a minute they watched in silence as Jonas Bonner and Barney Blue headed off the stallion and Diablo Red swung away into the gap with his mares, the two men following him.

Dance lowered the glasses with a grunt. "Seems they're looking to catch that Diablo horse."

"Maybe they will. That gap goes back till it narrows for a long way and it boxes off."

"Yeah? Ain't nobody held that red bastard in no box before."

"Maybe these fellows will, Frank. They all got plenty savvy for it. Bonner, he knows what happens if anyone else gets to Diablo Red first. He won't want that."

"Uh-uh. He wouldn't."

Dance's scarred lips peeled back in a slow grin, and seeing it made David Crow uneasy.

There was no love lost between Dance and him, and mostly they didn't work together. Big Crown's horse operation was marginal; King Canibar had built his fortune on cattle. There was a small profit to be turned by breeding and raising horses for the Army, and King always retained a couple of men on his crew whose sole duty was handling that end of things. Both Jonas Bonner and Barney Blue had worked for Canibar in this capacity, and now Dance and David Crow were Big Crown's horse-handlers.

The young half-breed had an instinctive feel for horse-flesh; training animals with sensitivity and patience was close to being a creed with him. David Crow barely knew Jonas Bonner, for he had come to Big Crown just after Bonner had quit, but he knew Bonner had been the same with horses. And he could understand why Bonner had lit into Frank Dance. King Canibar believed in using an easy hand only so long as it got results. Canibar wasn't noted for patience with men or animals; if the velvet glove didn't work, there was always the iron fist. Men he handled himself; Frank Dance took care of the animals.

With horses Dance had a streak of pure-quill meanness that wouldn't have been tolerated by Big Crown's cowhands, who were no rougher than they had to be. Dance had no friends among them and couldn't have cared less; he had a shanty of his own back of the barns and was well paid. His only recreation aside from getting drunk was visiting a whorehouse in the Mex village near Moratown where he was a great favorite because his lavish spending more than made up for his occasional wildman sprees of breaking furniture and beating one or two girls. The outcome was always the same: Sanchez, the big proprietor, would lay a blackjack across Dance's hard skull, and Dance would be sober and peaceable when he came to.

Canibar kept a pretty fair cinch on Frank's worst excesses, and one of the periodic flings in Mextown always drained off his bottled-up spleen for a spell. All the same David Crow had seen enough of Dance's free use of whip and spur, taking the rough edges off broncs that couldn't otherwise be gentled fast enough to suit Canibar, to be glad their separate operations usually kept them away from each other.

But David Crow didn't hate Dance. It took all kinds, he phlegmatically supposed. The country was hard, the living was hard. That was just how it was.

From here the lower part of the gap was cut off enough from view so that they couldn't make out the horses or the men trailing them. Until Diablo Red and the mares came to that wide break by the slide. Here the stallion had the plain intention of driving his *manada* up the slanting rubble and out of the gap. But old Baca was on his feet now, yelling and waving a hunk of red cloth.

You couldn't tell about a *caballo* like that one. He might try to run past the old man. But he didn't. Diablo Red gave an angry high-pitched squeal and headed the mares straight on down the pass. Moments later Bonner and his two men were pushing behind them.

Smart, thought David Crow. They were giving the stallion no chance to think the situation out, hustling him right along, but not so tightly as to panic him into an unexpected countermove. Even if they had him boxed, holding into him would be no cinch.

Dance scratched his jaw. "Ain't that a thing, though." he murmured. "Too bad we can't make out no more right here. You reckon if we take a swing over east a ways, we could get a look down in that canyon?"

"From that big ridge over yonder, sure. You can sight straight into the canyon a good ways." David Crow pointed with his chin, then eyed his companion narrowly. "What you got in mind, Frank?"

Grinning a little, Dance wheeled and tramped back down to his horse, and David Crow followed him. They stepped into their saddles. "I tell you, Injun boy—" Still grinning, Dance reached under his knee, yanked his .45–.70 from its boot and checked the action. "I am on a long-time peck with that Bonner, I ever tell you that?"

"I think you mentioned it."

"Yeah. Kind of an old account to square." Dance stroked a thumb along the breech of his Winchester.

David Crow gave him a flat-eyed look. "Is that right."

Dance laughed. "Nothing like that. How dumb you think I am? But that big wild 'un, now. Bonner sets a heap o' store by him."

The half-breed shook his head, his mouth tight.

"Look," said Dance. "The King sent us after them mares got stole, didn't he? All right. He finds out Diablo Red's back, he'll want him fetched *dead*. You might say this comes under orders."

"You're kicking up a hornet's nest, Frank. I want no part of it."

"Up to you, shorthorn," Dance said amusedly. "You don't need to do nothing 'cept ride back to the Big Crown and tell the King he don't need to worry 'bout them mares. They'll be just fine. He won't have no more worry 'bout Diablo Red, neither. You tell him, all right?"

"Just like that."

"Injun boy, you do it, that's all."

There was a flat challenge in Dance's stare, and David Crow wasn't about to argue it. The man was as pure a brute in body as in brain. And he meant to have his way. No point getting your own brains beaten out when it wouldn't do a lick of good.

Without a word, David Crow turned his horse and headed away.

The gap had pinched down steadily till it tapered suddenly into this entrance of the long, chute-shaped box canyon. If Diablo Red tried to turn back, it would be now. Jonas and his companions gave him no chance. They rode three abreast those last few yards, yelling at the tops of their voices. The stallion and his three charges raced into the cramped passage and were lost in a choking blur of dust. The men's throats were raw, their eyes leaking, as they halted at the canyon mouth.

They pulled down the bandannas covering their mouths and noses. Jonas spat grit and looked at Barney and

Mateo. Both were grinning; it was like like old times, and Jonas, though he had little taste for this particular job, couldn't help sharing their exultance.

"We'll put up that fence here," he said. "I'll keep guard. You two cut some poles from that grove at the front of the pass and snake 'em back here."

"Okay, *caporal*," Barney grinned. "You watch yourself, hear? C'mon, Gran'pop. I'll do the cutting, you take the easy part. Can't put your ole ass in much of a sweat, just having your horse lug poles."

Mateo snapped, "I don't give *dos reales* for your kind thoughts, Negro," and the two continued to wrangle as they rode back down the pass.

Jonas rode back and forth in the settling dust, studying where the fence ends would abut against each wall and where a couple of posts could be sunk between to reinforce it. Building a strong high barrier would take a while, and he could only hope Diablo Red wouldn't attempt a break before it was finished . . . .

The rifle shot made a flat impact on the hot stillness. A whole string of shots followed, echoes crackling between the ridges like Chinese firecrackers. *What the hell!* Jonas reined his skittish pinto under control.

Son of a bitch with a repeating rifle. Sounded like he was up on one of those back ridges. What the hell was he trying to do?

A running clatter of hoofs sounded in the cul-de-sac, and Jonas braced for the expected. Moments later Diablo Red came pounding into sight. Not checking his momentum he whickered a wild challenge.

Spooked by the shooting, Jonas thought. Then he saw the horse's bright coat was streaked with darker red. Blood . . . .

No time even to think about attempting to cut off the stallion's flight. For Diablo Red was barreling straight at him, teeth bared. Jonas tried to swing away from that savage charge, in the same moment realizing it was too late. He jerked the pinto back around to avoid being hit flank-on. And only partly succeeded.

At the last instant before collision, he saw the stallion's upflung head, his rolling eyes, and heard the snap and gnash of his teeth. The pinto screamed.

Diablo Red swerved just as the smash of his shoulder drove the pinto off his feet, backward and sidelong. Jonas was already kicking free of the stirrups, flinging himself off-side, his body loosening in the horse-breaker's roll. He saw the stony ground rush up; he lit on his shoulder and hip and kept rolling. The pinto's fall shook the ground a couple of feet away.

Stunned, Jonas lay on his belly and watched Diablo Red cut away out of sight down the pass. He had no shred of hope that Barney or Mateo, even if they caught on in time to what had happened, would be able to halt him. He climbed to his feet, grabbing the pinto's rein as it floundered up; he spoke to the animal as it stood trembling. Jonas himself was shaking, bruised and hurting in a dozen places; blood ran into his beard from a nick on his cheek.

A scouring rage lifted in him and spread through his gut in hot waves. He tried to calm the boil of his thoughts, to think out what this meant and what it would mean.

Mateo and Barney came up the pass on the gallop, slowing their horses when they saw him. By the time they reached him, Jonas was able to talk in a controlled voice, telling what had happened.

"Ole Diablo come out straight past us," said Barney.

"Looked plumb crazy. Wa'n't no stopping him, *caporal*. Blood on his rump, but I reckon he wa'n't hit bad."

Mateo rode up by the pinto, peering at his withers. "*Dios* . . . this horse, a piece is tore from his neck. Just skin, I'm think, but he's bleeding bad."

"Diablo Red took a snap at me," said Jonas. "He didn't go after the pinto, he went after *me*. Then he settled for Woboy."

"Ah. I have said it. That is one *caballo salvaje*. But this Dance, it was his doing."

"Dance—" Jonas's head tipped up sharply. "Frank Dance?"

"*Sí*. Is his doing."

"How the hell do you know?"

"We seen him," said Barney. "When that shooting started up, I couldn't tell where it was at. But ole *viejo* here, he's got the ears. Put it on that big ridge off back o' the box canyon. Yes sir, he's got the ears. From where we was, using our glasses, we could just make sight on the top o' that ridge. Dance, he was riding down off it. Man up there could shoot straight into that box canyon."

"You sure of that? It was Frank Dance?"

"I see him, too, *por Dios*." Mateo spat, rubbing a sleeve across his mustache. "I know that foul *cabrón*. A spoiler of good horseflesh."

Jonas's hand knotted around his rein. "He was out looking for them mares, I reckon. He must of seen what we was up to."

"Sure," said Barney. "Done it out o' pure meanness. Well—" He let his shoulders lift and fall. "Ain't no law says a man can't take a potshot at a wild horse. Reckon we just got to start all over."

"Not yet," Jonas said softly. "Not just yet." He rubbed

the pinto's muzzle. "*Viejo*, you look to Woboy's hurt. Barney, I want the loan of your horse."

Both men looked at him. A slow worry crept into Barney's long face as he swung to the ground. "What you got in mind, *caporal?*"

"You two stay here. Them mares is still in the canyon. Get that fence across to hold 'em there."

"That ain't no answer." Barney shook his head. "That look o' yours says it. Man, you best cool down."

Old Mateo's chuckle was a cynical rasp. "It's no good to talk, Negro. You know this Jonas Bonner. He will have his way."

Jonas walked to Barney's grulla and took the reins, and stepped into the saddle. He looked at both men, his face bleak as iron. "Just so Frank Dance don't have his," he said. "I aim to make damn sure King Canibar gets the same message."

He turned the grulla with a touch of his heel and rode down the pass, heading south.

Chapter Four

JONAS didn't bother trying to pick up Dance's trail. It seemed certain Dance would make tracks to Big Crown now. Undoubtedly he'd had orders to find and bring back the stolen mares, but the temptation to take a shot at Diablo Red and frustrate Jonas's plans must have been too great to resist. Having muffed his chance, inflicting only a slight wound on the stallion, Dance would quickly retreat, not knowing he'd been spotted.

Maybe he hadn't shot to kill, but Jonas bleakly discounted the possibility. Four years ago King Canibar had put out orders to kill the horse; learning Diablo Red was back, hearing from Dance that it was he who'd run off those mares, Canibar would renew that order. In Frank's own mind, then, he'd been running no risk.

Damned shortly he was going to find out otherwise.

When his first rage had cooled, Jonas argued a little with himself about the wisdom of what he meant to do. He could be running a tall chance himself, bracing Dance on his own grounds. What good would it really do?

The hell with that. Since he and Dance had clashed seven years back, a strained truce had held between them any time they encountered one another. Dance's action today had tipped the balance, and Jonas fixed on this with a cold ferocity. Meeting Dance head-on and settling the old grudge—win or lose—was something he had to do, sensible or not.

It was nearly sunset when the buildings of Half Moon came in sight. The coal of Jonas's anger was still ripe and hot, and now he could give all his attention to satisfying it.

Big Crown headquarters was built in a shallow timbered valley where a lower bend of the Washoe River made a wide, rambling arc. The house itself was set in a park of rolling lawn dotted by big trees. The main part was two stories high, large and boxy; built of massve timbers, it was flanked by two one-story wings of stone construction. Stables and a carriage house separated the big house from the barrackslike cookshack-bunkhouse, and beyond these a vast tangle of barns, sheds and pole corrals stretched to the east.

The mottes of pine that studded the valley floor permitted Jonas to move up fairly close to the place without being seen. He went ahead carefully, keeping his eyes open. Once he spotted a pair of riders coming off-range and ducked into the timber till they were well past.

The headquarters area was so big that getting inside it without being seen shouldn't pose too much of a problem. Locating Dance would be the hard part. To deal with him without inviting interference from others would be tougher still.

The breaking corral might be the best place to start looking, but the whole working part of the ranch was too open to approach from the east. Better to work in toward it by way of the tree-flanked carriage house and stables, and Jonas, remembering the layout well though he hadn't set foot on it in years, had already picked out his point of approach. He left Barney's grulla in a grove west of the house, then circled it on foot, crossing behind belts of trees and shrubbery, making short runs across open places.

The sun was low, the shadows long and flat, when he reached the corner of the carriage house. The cook's triangle sounded high and tinny, as he peered across the grassless, hard-scuffed open area that lay beyond. Men were converging on the cookshack for supper. It was just close enough for him to make out faces, but few of them were familiar.

He picked out Dance's trim and thickset form, his muscular walk that was bouncy and slightly rolling, as soon as he came up from the corrals. He was the last man to wash up and enter the cookshack.

What now? Jonas fingered his rifle as he weighed the question. He could walk right in and put a gun on the room and order Dance outside. But then? He'd have no ally in this fight, not even the law in Moratown. As Barney had said, it was no crime to potshoot at a wild horse.

All right, just do it then. This wasn't supposed to be any damn picnic excursion, was it? Get him out of there. Then see what.

Jonas slid around the carriage house and moved swiftly

across to one of the stables, hugging its wall for partial cover while he worked up closer to the cookshack. Then he heard a quick step—someone coming along the gravel path that curved back of the stable. Coming from the direction of the house. He had just time enough to duck inside the open stable doors and flatten himself against the wall behind one of them.

A horse stamped restively in the gloom. This was the stable reserved for the "fast rackers" kept by the Canibars for their own use. Jonas silently cursed his luck—and waited.

A woman came through the doorway. She didn't immediately see him, and then she turned quickly. For a moment he didn't think he knew her, but recognition came fast enough.

"Step in here," he told her. "And keep your mouth shut."

She was tall and supple in a riding habit that matched her rain-gray eyes. Her face was handsome and sharply chiseled, framed by pale blond hair caught in a careless knot back of her head. She'd be in her early twenties now, and he remembered that bold and imperious look of hers before anything else; it went with being King Canibar's sister.

She ignored his order. "What are you doing here? Who the devil are you?"

"Jonas Bonner. I used to work here."

"Oh." She nodded slowly, a smile tipping her wide mouth. "Oh yes, the former husband. Well, well. It's been a while, hasn't it? You haven't changed a whole lot. I don't suppose you remember me."

"Margaret. They called you Meg. You never liked it." She made a face. "It always sounded wishy-washy, like

someone's maiden aunt. But I like Margaret a lot less."
She nodded at the rifle he held pointed off-side. "I guess
I needn't ask if this is a friendly call. And I assume
you're not skulking in our stable for the fun of it. But
just what do you want?"

"You don't know, eh?"

"What am I supposed to know?"

Jonas felt a thin irritation at this sparring.

He'd barely known Meg Canibar in her teens; most
of the time he'd spent at Big Crown, she's been away at
one fancy school or another in the East. But coming of
age hadn't changed her by a jot. She'd evinced only a
mild surprise at seeing him here, and not a trace of fear.
No dissembling or false bravado to the pose either: it
was merely the same brand of cocksure arrogance that
her older brother had, a trait that had always set a lot
of people's hackles bristling. I'm a Canibar, it seemed
to say, and you'd better damned well not forget it.

"I could just give a yell," she murmured. "and bring
a dozen men running, Mister. What'll you do then, shoot
'em all? Or maybe you'll start with me."

The faintest smile held on her mouth, full of amused
speculation, but he sensed she was curious too. Obviously
Dance hadn't told what had happened, or at least it
hadn't reached her ears.

"Talk up, Jonas, and I'll listen. For maybe one minute."

Resigned to it, he told in spare phrases about the
attempt to catch Diablo Red, aborted by Frank Dance.
Before he finished, her smile had faded and she broke
in: "These mares . . . was one a blaze-face sorrel?"

He nodded.

"That's Blazes, she's my horse. Is she all right?"

"Far as I could tell. My men are holding 'em in that

canyon. They'll be fetched back here."

"But first you have something to settle with Frank, is that it?"

"That's right."

"Well, boy howdy," she said amusedly. "Maybe, just maybe, I owe you something. How would you like to collect it?"

He eyed her warily, wondering if she'd learned her damned unseemly forwardness at an Eastern school. Not likely, though the militant suffragettes he'd read of in a tattered copy of *Harper's Monthly* were said to be popping up everywhere these days. No—just more of her natural sass busting out, like sap from a spring tree. And her brother had never put much of a curb on it.

" 'Pends what you mean."

She laughed. "I've heard folks describe you as a kind of wild man, Jonas. But a mighty cautious one, I'd say. Well, what I mean is, suppose I could fetch Frank Dance off some place where you could be alone, just the two of you. Would you shoot him?"

Jonas shook his head.

"Beat hell out of him, then?" She smiled at his twitch of distaste. "All right, whale the tar out of him? Or try?"

"I had it in mind." He watched her narrowly. "Why would you do that?"

"I told you, I'm owing you. How about it?"

A reckless glint touched her voice; it mocked him. So that was it. The perverse whim of a bored, spoiled woman who'd never had to work a day for anything she wanted. But if it could be bent to his use, why not? Besides, what other way was there?

"You think you can do that?"

"Oh, I can do it, don't you fret. Is it a go?"

"I reckon. And thanks."

"I'd hold off on any thanks. Nobody's ever put that fellow down and kept him there long. He could just mop up the ground with you, Mister. Odds are, he will."

The words suggested that she didn't find the idea uncongenial: it might go either way for all of her. But she surprised him then, saying abruptly: "I don't like the way Frank treats animals. I never have. If you can give him even a dose of how it feels, it'll be worth it."

He waited in an isolated grove of pine on the west side of the layout.

He wasn't sure how far to trust her; she might show up with her brother instead of Dance. But even if she had no reason to help Jonas Bonner, her dislike of Dance seemed genuine. He figured he could trust that much of it. Apparently, she had no fear of what her brother might do when he heard of this, and he soon would.

She would accost Dance when he left the cookshack, Meg had said, and persuade him to walk back here with her. She hadn't spelled out exactly how she'd manage it, but knowing Frank's hell-for-women reputation, he didn't bother to second-guess. She'd get Frank here, all right. Jonas had wondered if she'd be missed at the house. No worry on that score, Meg had said carelessly; the family always took supper later than the crew, and it was her custom to go for a ride around sunset.

Jonas loaded up his pipe and sat on his hunkers, watching the sun's last flare turn the pine needles to gold slivers. When he heard the tread of feet, a sound of voices approaching, he rose to his feet, rifle in hand.

Meg came strolling into the glade, smiling a little, talking in a quietly amused tone to the man tramping a

little behind her and to one side. All of Dance's attention
was on her; he looked pretty hungry for a fed man. The
two of them were well inside the glade before he noticed
Jonas standing at the clearing's edge.

Jonas half-lifted the Winchester. "You just stand,
Frank. Stand right there."

Dance stopped in his tracks. His jaw knotted; his fists
curled. Showing no other signs of surprise or anger, he
said mildly, "So you two cooked up something between
you. That's why you walked out with ol' Frank, eh,
Missy?"

"That seems to be the case," said Meg. "Think you
can whip him, Frank?"

"You don't need to worry about it," Jonas told her.
"You done your part. You best go for that ride now."

"Oh, I don't know, Jonas." Her smile held a small
malice. "It might be fun to watch."

"It ain't nothing for a woman's eyes," he said grimly.

"Goodness. Am I ordered to leave?"

"I'm telling you it's nothing to see."

"All right. You've told me."

Meg walked over to a large deadfall and seated herself
on it, arranging her skirts about her ankles. There was
a demure mockery to the pose. To hell with it, he thought;
no odds arguing with a spoiled chit like this one. He
looked at Dance who stood hands on his hips, his expression almost sleepily unconcerned.

"You got seen, Frank. You didn't know that."

"Yeah, well—" Dance rolled his shoulders in a shrug.
"That artillery you are toting, I reckon you can put my
saddle in a sack."

"Think that's why I'm here?"

"Uh-uh." Dance's lips peeled back in a scarred grin.

"Either way, you're one dumb son of a bitch, man. You always was."

"Let's see."

Jonas swung the rifle sideways, and let go, sailing it into the underbrush. Dance dropped his hands and gathered himself, a tightening of his hard body that was barely perceptible: the action-ready stance of a physical man who was totally sure of himself. Jonas was the bigger man, but he knew from that one matching of their strength that where he was loose-strung rawhide, Frank was more like bunched rawhide, tense as iron. But not slow at all, and he was long-armed, his reach equal to Jonas's.

The light was starting to fade, twilight shaping toward dusk. Dance moved in bouncily on the balls of his feet, his grin a grayish streak in his dark face. He looked ready to spar a little, but Jonas was impatient. Just to draw Dance out, he gave him a hard clout on the arm, then caught Frank's answering swing on his own raised arm.

For maybe ten seconds they met toe to toe and exchanged a flurry of body blows, then broke apart. Following up fast, Jonas rocked Dance's head with a stiff right; he felt the jolting ache of the blow clear to his shoulders. Dance growled and shook his head, then bored in like a ringy bull. Jonas caught him in the mouth with a left hook, at the same time grunting to the sledge of Dance's fist against his ribs.

Dance closed again, trying abruptly to knee him in the groin. Jonas managed to turn enough to take the knee on his thigh. It threw him a little off balance, and in that moment Dance tried for a crushing hold, snaking in his long powerful arms under Jonas's guard. Momentarily Jonas's arms were pinned to his sides, and he jerked one free before the hold took. They scuffled back and forth, Jonas punching with his free hand at Dance's head and neck. He felt his ribs creak under the balled power of Frank's applied strength, and then he drove a heel into the bronc-peeler's instep.

Dance gave a howl and twisted, flinging Jonas away. He hit the ground on his back as Frank took a long stride, then dived for him. Jonas straightened his leg in a savage kick that smacked Dance in the jaw. Dance fell to his hands and knees, shaking his head to clear it. Both men were on their feet at the same time. Dance was bleeding from the mouth, but a cold maniacal fury lit his eyes; he wasn't even dazed.

Jonas met his charge and hit him twice in the face, and Dance looped a high right against his ear. Jonas fell back, his head ringing; red lights popped in his eyes. His head quickly cleared, and now he realized that punishment was slowing Dance at last; he'd failed to follow up that instant's advantage. His face wore the bloody print of knuckles; it was streaming blood in several places.

Again they met with a rush of close-in blows; again they fell apart. Jonas's upper body felt pummeled to a raw pulse; a weary numbness ate at his muscles. No stand-up, bare-handed fight between two men could last for long even if they were equally matched, not when they went at each other like a pair of feral dogs. Most always they'd clip the edges off each other in short order; then it could go either way, riding on a hair balance where a chance blow might end the fight.

Jonas had only a blind sense that the battle had turned in his favor. It enable him to dredge up the blunted core of his rage and wade in again.

Dance tried belatedly to protect his face with one hand, pawing out the other in a couple of blows that had no force. Deliberately Jonas slugged him in the throat, and Frank stumbled back. Jonas crowded him hard now, feinting twice at his face and slamming him twice in the body, and with each blow Frank gave a step back. He'd won too many fights too easily; hurt now, he was quickly losing heart for it. Yet he wouldn't ask for quarter, and Jonas hammered him steadily backward.

Meg Canibar had stepped away from the fallen log as Dance's retreat carried them close to it. And now she was crying, "Stop it! Stop it!"

Feeling his own strength going, Jonas paused. Placed his weight and mustered his force for a blow that he brought up from his knees. His knuckles skidded off the red smear of Frank's face. Dance flipped over backward, the deadfall catching him in the small of the back. His body arched across it, he groaned and tried to lift himself and failed. Half falling across the log beside him, Jonas pushed himself to his knees and grabbed a handful of Dance's shirt and yanked his head up, hitting him again.

The gunshot rang like an angry slap through the glade. Jonas pulled back off Dance and tried to straighten up, but his knees folded and he slumped against the side of the mossy log, one arm flung across it. Blinking exhaustedly, he turned his head till he saw the blurred whiteness of Meg's face. She was holding his rifle pointed upward, and now she levered it and fired again.

The shots would fetch someone on the run. Well, that was all right, he reasoned dully, now that it was finished.

He fumbled for a thought and managed to form it into

words. "You . . . found out . . . didn't you?"

"Animals!" Her mouth and eyes were dark stains in the dusk; her voice shook with a wild disbelief. "My God . . . men? You are nothing but animals?"

The shots brought several of the Big Crown crew to the spot. Two of them carried Dance to his shanty. The others helped Jonas to the bunkhouse and eased him onto the washbench outside. Someone handed him a wet cloth, and he swabbed at his stinging eyes with it. Then it was taken from his hand, and Meg said flatly: "Hold your head up." She cleaned the blood from his face. There wasn't very much; his body had taken most of Dance's mule-kick punches. He felt like one vast, sore bruise, and thought if he tried to take a step by himself, he'd fall on his face.

One puncher had gone to tell King Canibar what had happened. And in a few minutes the King himself came striding toward the bunkhouse. In the last light of dusk Jonas could make out only his big swinging outline, but there was no mistaking it. Or that driving, impatient stride that had always mirrored the man's whole nature.

Canibar hauled up in front of Jonas, drew his cigar to a bright coal, and then flung it away in a flurry of sparks. "One of you men bring a lamp out here," he ordered.

The lamp was brought. Its glow picked out Meg's pale face, the men standing around, and Canibar's bulking form.

King Canibar dominated the scene without trying. Not an unusually tall man, he had the meaty musculature of a young bull; his expensive suits were tailored to minimize the massive chest and shoulders that would have split any clothes off the shelf. King's head was heavy and imperial with its saddle of golden curls starting to recede from his broad forehead. His bluntly handsome face was fleshier than Jonas remembered, and his Roman nose divided it like a thick blade. His hands, planted on his hips now, were like square hams.

He looked chill-eyed at his sister. "You had a piece of this, did you?" And raised a hand to cut off her reply. "Never mind. Get up to the house. I can damn well guess, but I'll hear it later."

"It was my fault, Lenny," she said quietly. "I'm sorry."

King studied her a moment. "Yeah," he said slowly. "I think for once you really are. Get up to the house now."

She walked swiftly away, passing Phil Canibar as he sauntered up, rolling a long nine between his teeth. "How you doing, Bonnie?" he asked cheerfully. "Better than Frank, I allow. I had a look at him like you said, Leonard."

Only members of his family called King Canibar by his given name, Jonas remembered.

King said, "How is he?"

"You know Frank. Too mean to die." At his brother's warning frown, Phil added quickly, "Banged up some, nothing broken that I could tell."

"A lucky thing for you, Bonner," King said heavily. "What kind of hell are you trying to play, barging onto my place and pulling a stunt like that?"

"Just Frank's style," Jonas said. "He's a real gut-buster, Frank is. Has a fine sense of fun."

"All right. I heard what he done today. David Crow told me, and I gave Frank hell. No call for what he did— not the way he done it. But you wanted satisfaction, you could of come to me."

"Sure it wouldn't cost you too much?"

A flick of contempt touched King Canibar's broad mouth. "You know something, Bonner? You ain't a whole lot different, you and Dance. You both think with your guts. You trimmed his wick, fine. I could just trim yours, couldn't I?"

"Right now, you likely could."

"Any time. You want it like that, you come to me any time you feel sandy again. I'll show you."

The taunts fanned the banked spark of Jonas's anger. He got to his feet now, legs apart, swaying a little. "That so? What're you thinking with these days, Leonard? Your ass? You taken enough lard on it since I last seen you."

He watched a cold temper flare and die in Canibar's face, and then King made a brusque gesture. "No need for this kind of talk. All right, Frank bought what he got, I'll not gainsay it. But he was acting in my interests, too. Diablo Red is back. He knew what that meant. So do you."

"I had him," Jonas said thinly. "I had Diablo Red cold. We could have taken him, my men and me. Till Dance threw a wrench in the works."

"Yeah, that's what David Crow thought." King took out another cigar and scowled at it. "Well, mostly you have always kept to your own business, Bonner, I'll give you that. Even when—" He checked himself, then said roughly, "I know how you feel about that damn horse, in a way. But—"

"Like hell you do."

"In a way, I said. I like to own a thing. You don't. That's the difference."

This flat declaration, coming almost like a bald admission, surprised Jonas a little. He said nothing, just gave a guarded nod.

"It ain't so much the mares he took," King said. "It's . . . by the way, what's happened to them mares?"

Jonas told him.

King nodded curtly. "I was about to say, that ain't what's rubbing in my craw. You know my stallion Alacrán? He's been turned onto the range this spring. I'm afraid that red devil keeps coming back, one time him and Alacrán will be bound to tangle. They fought four years ago when Diablo Red come lifting mares, and Alacrán got ripped up some. Well, that Diablo Red 'ud be in his prime now, and Alacrán ain't young no more."

Jonas was silent. Yes, King Canibar had his own feeling for a horse. Different in the way he said. But a deep feeling all the same.

"I mean to protect my own, Bonner. I got no hankering to have that *manadero* done away with. But Alacrán's a *manadero* himself, a herding stallion, and you damn well know what that could mean if they tangle again. A fight to the death." He paused, then said coldly: "I'll see that red horse strung out for buzzard bait before I let it happen."

"I'll have them mares of yours brought back here," Jonas said. "That worth anything to you?"

Canibar grunted. "Maybe. I suppose you want to try running down Diablo Red again. Your way."

"Just that."

"All right. Say I owe you that much. I'll give you a week, Bonner. I'll hold off that long. Then I'll do it *my* way." King's teeth snapped together with a click of finality. "You want to, you can lay over in the bunkhouse tonight. That's if taking Big Crown hospitality won't sour your belly."

He wasn't in any shape to do otherwise, Jonas decided. "I'm obliged."

Without another word, not even a nod, Canibar swung around and tramped away toward the house. Phil grinned and shrugged, then followed him.

Jonas went back to the grove where he'd left Barney's horse. Feeling too sore to mount, he led the animal back across the layout toward the corrals. It took him past the broad front veranda of the big house whose windows glowed with lamplight. A man sitting in the shadows got up and moved unsteadily to the veranda's edge. He walked with a slap-slap sound made by the carpet slippers he wore, and this gave away his identity even before he stepped into a square of windowlight.

"Well, the Lord love Jesus if it ain't Jonas Bonner."

Jonas halted, giving the old man a civil nod. "How are you, Sam?"

"Piddlin', Bonnie, just piddlin'. 'Bout the same as ever."

Sam gave a short laugh that ended in a wracking cough. Runty and white-haired, he was about the opposite of anything you might expect King Canibar's father to be. A failure in everything he'd ever tried, Sam Canibar was content to live in his son's shadow and on his son's largess. Or at least he kept any lurking sense of humiliation well salved with booze. Jonas had rarely seen him in any condition other than mildly drunk. He must be close to seventy now, and it was a pure wonder the tanglefoot hadn't carried him off long ago.

"How long's it been, Bonnie? Six years?"

"Closer to seven."

"That long, hey?" Old Sam teetered on his heels,

somehow managing not to tip over. "Well, you're looking fit for a man's just trimmed Frank Dance's whiskers—just heerd about that. You still got your guts, boy." He chuckled thinly. "That's a compliment."

"Thanks."

The front door opened and a woman stood outlined against the light. Jonas felt a hard jar of his pulse as she spoke. "Come in, Sam. We're about to have din—"

She broke off and stepped onto the veranda, her crisp taffeta frock rustling. "Jonas . . . hello."

"Hello, Welda."

He replied woodenly; he didn't touch his hat. Just watched her.

Five years. Not long enough for her to have changed much. If anything, she looked somehow younger: more regally beautiful, even, than treacherous memory had ever shaped her. But then these last years would have been satisfying ones, full of the fine living she had once coveted so desperately. Under middle height, slight and dainty, she looked born to be the mistress of a manor, made for the wearing of costly gowns. Soft light glinted on the rich blue-black of her piled hair and on her smoothly olive skin.

But for Jonas Bonner the picture was mixed with too many memories. Maybe only memory was left, but it had a quality that was gritty and tearing. The last time he'd seen her they had been shouting at one another, and now there was nothing to say.

Nothing at all.

"Well, I'll be getting inside," old Canibar said with a sly lopsided grin. "You two must have plenty sweet nothings to pour out." He guffawed, hiccoughed, and slap-slapped his way into the house.

"How is . . . . " Welda moistened her lips. "How is Rainey?"

Bare courtesy demanded that he answer—briefly and affirmatively—and then he turned and started away.

"Jonas!"

Her voice arrested him sharply; he noticed it had taken on that imperious Canibar ring. He came to a stop and looked back, and she said quickly: "I . . . I would like to see the boy sometime. Is that too much to ask?"

"Too much and too damn late," he said harshly. And walked away into the gathering dark, putting his back to the woman he had once given his name. Who now wore the name of Mrs. King Canibar.

Chapter Five

NEXT morning Jonas was almost too sore and stiff to walk, but he had no intention of accepting Canibar hospitality one hour longer than he had to. After breakfast at the cookshack, he went to the corral and got Barney's horse and headed for home. He rode slowly, stopping often to rest. It was early afternoon when he finally dismounted at Cross-B headquarters, almost falling out of the saddle. Stretched out on the porch, Tigre raised his head and growled.

"Shut up, you son of a miswhelped bitch," Jonas growled back.

Rainey came running out of the house. He pulled up short, staring at Jonas's battered face. "Pa! What happened to you?"

"Tell you later." Jonas handed him the reins. "Take

Sandy to the corral and turn him in, son." His glance dropped to a tangle of string dangling from Rainey's hand. "What's that?"

"This? It's a cat's cradle. You ever make one, Pa? Grif showed me how." Rainey dropped the reins, eager to demonstrate. "See you slip it over your fingers of both hands like this and if you do it right you can give a jerk and comes out straight, no knots at all. There!"

"Yeah, I see." Jonas blinked wearily, scrubbing a hand over his unshaved jaw. "Grif, huh?"

"That's that drifter's name. He's feeling some better. Can sit up now and feed himself."

"Is that right. Grif what?"

"That's all the name he said. Gee, what *happened* to you?"

"Later. Put Sandy up."

Jonas limped into the house, giving Minita a bad start with his beat-up look. He collapsed on a bench at the table and did his best with a spare explanation. It soothed her consternation a little, and then he said, "Rustle me some grub, will you, Sis?"

"You are not riding out again!"

"Not right away, no. I want something to eat, then I'm going to tear off about a mile of shut-eye. We'll talk about it later, all right?"

Minita got out some leftover *frijoles* and started a fire to reheat them. Jonas rested his head in his hands, feeling a sore exhaustion in every joint. One week, Canibar had said. And he'd need a day, maybe more, just to recuperate from Dance's fists.

Glancing up, he surprised Minita watching him. Her face was troubled.

"What is it, *chica*?"

Wordlessly she went to the woodbox, lifted up some chunks of wood, and pulled out a holstered gun wrapped in its shellbelt. She carried it to the table and laid it before him. "I find this in the young gringo's things when I was putting them away," she said quietly. "I did not mean to look, but his blanket roll was very heavy. This was inside. I think I better hide it till you come back."

Jonas drew the pistol and hefted it in his hands. It was an ordinary Colt's Civilian Model Single Action .45 with black rubber grips. But the action had been worked over, smoothed and honed to a whisper; it had a beautiful balance and looked well-kept. Christ—a real old-time "thumb buster"; he hadn't seen one in years. It was unloaded.

"I never see such a *pistola*," Minita murmured. "See, it has no trigger. How can he shoot it?"

"With just the hammer, Sis. You lift back the hammer and let go. And then it shoots."

She shook her head wonderingly. "That is a strange thing, *¿no es verdad?* What kind of a man has such a gun?"

Jonas rammed the weapon back in its holster. "No kind of man you'd know. How about some coffee to go with those *frijoles?*"

When he woke that evening, he felt a sight better. Mateo Baca, worried about what might have happened to the *caporal*, had returned to Cross-B, leaving Barney to guard the recaptured mares. Tomorrow, if no word had come of Jonas's fate, Mateo had intended to go for the sheriff. While they ate supper, Jonas told of his adventure at Big Crown and his agreement with King Canibar.

"One week," Mateo grumbled. He was rheumatic and

bellicose from sleeping out and unaccustomed hours in
the saddle; even the usual stiff jolts of his potent wine
had failed to soften his mood. "From how you look, you
will not ride for a month."

"I'll ride tomorrow," Jonas said grimly. "We'll swing
back to the canyon and pick up Barney. One of you can
drive those mares to Big Crown. Two of us will go after
that stallion."

"Pa," Rainey ventured.

"Yes, son?"

"Did you see my mother?"

"Yeah. I saw her."

There was an awkward silence. Jonas turned his right
hand over, scowling at the raw knuckles. He ought to
say something more, but what the hell was there to say?
Minita rose and began to clear the table. Jonas went out
to the porch and sat down. Digging out his pipe, he
clamped it unlighted between his teeth and stared into
the cricket-keening darkness.

Seeing Welda again had kicked a few memories back
to a focus of harsh immediacy. But it was like stirring
a heap of cold ashes. Nothing left but the dregs of bitter
regret that he could consider almost impersonally, as if
all of it had happened to two other people.

Welda Delon had come from an old French-Creole
family dispossessed by the war—or so she had claimed.
Maybe it explained her hunger for more than Jonas
could ever provide. She'd looked anything but high and
mighty when he had first seen her in a Laramie dance
hall, billed as the "Silver Thrush of the Golden West."
Her voice hadn't been anything to write home about.
But Welda was beautiful. And he had wanted her with

the same stubborn intensity he brought to anything on which his heart was set.

Not to own her, though. To share with and to cherish. Welda, small and dainty and doll-lovely, had seemed made to be cherished, like a precious and delicate figurine. Maybe that had been the trouble. It was no way to feel about a woman you wanted to share your dream of a workaday cattle outfit. And that was Jonas's simple dream, a want as fierce as his desire for Welda. Two desires that could only mesh badly. Welda had dreams of her own.

None of that had seemed important in the delirium of their first attraction. They'd called it love. Whatever it had been, it had fired Jonas with a determination to hasten the day when he could bring his bride—they had wed a week after they met—to a place of their own. Before this, King Canibar, knowing Jonas's reputation for handling horseflesh, had offered him a job at extravagant wages—rejected because Jonas had hated working for anyone but himself. After the wedding, he'd accepted Canibar's offer, hoping that a few years of saving such wages, along with what he had laid by, would enable him to start his ranch.

All had gone well enough during the years at Big Crown—on the surface, anyway. Welda had loved the Canibar ranch, particularly the big house that King's late mother had tastefully furnished and appointed. Quickly recognizing Welda's own taste, Canibar had given her a job as his housekeeper—hardly a physically taxing position with so many Mexican menials to do the chores. Welda had simply given orders. And had served decoratively at lavish parties where King entertained wealthy friends and business acquaintances from the Cheyenne Club.

It must have begun early if at first unobtrusively, that fine underside of rot in the marriage. For King Canibar had found his ideal woman, Welda her ideal man. To blame either of them—Jonas could now realize, since time had salved his pride—was like blaming water for running downhill. At the time he couldn't object to Welda's contributing a substantial salary of her own to their savings—not when the work pleased her so much. Any vague disquiet he'd felt had been thrust aside as unworthy, not hard to do when the grind of breaking Big Crown's horses left him sodden with fatigue at the end of each day. (It now seemed a minor miracle that Rainey had ever been conceived.) Moreover, Jonas had no reason to believe, even in retrospect, that any infidelity had occurred. Those two simply weren't the kind. King was a stickler for the proprieties; Welda had been anything but an easy woman, even in her reduced straits.

Still, a feeling between them must have been far advanced, a torment to both, by the time Jonas had quit Big Crown and taken his wife and small son into the hills to develop his shoestring outfit.

Though she'd hated it from the first, Welda had made a valiant effort to adjust to the rough conditions. These had been damned rough at the start: living in a tent, cooking over an open fire, doing all kinds of work her frail physique wasn't up to. Jonas had done what he could to relieve her burden, while planning on building their future home to ensure every rough comfort possible.

But the erosion had begun and was irreversible. It had begun long before, he now knew, with two people who were hopelessly different. Welda was gregarious

and people-loving; she missed the fancy doings at Big
Crown where she was the cynosure of admiring male
eyes. Loneliness and isolation, long days of drudging
housework and child-tending, reduced her to weeping
spells that became more frequent. And they quarreled a
lot.

When her bitter misery had become more than either
of them could endure, Jonas had moved her to Moratown
where she'd gotten work at a dressmaker's shop. For a
while they'd kept up a mutual pretense of accomodation
to their separate lives. But a marriage in name only,
with Rainey and him paying occasional, almost formal
town calls, was worse than nothing. Then he'd learned
that King Canibar was a more frequent visitor. An
explosive final quarrel had begun the divorce proceedings to which neither of them, by now, was averse. One
month after a final decree was granted, Welda had
become Mrs. Canibar.

And now, at long last, she had remembered that she
had a son. Might even be getting it in her head that
she'd like custody of Rainey. Well, it didn't work that
way.

Jonas couldn't recall when Welda had borne motherhood with anything but ill grace. She hadn't wanted a
child in the first place, and sometimes, while they were
still together, Jonas had believed she'd hated the sight
of Rainey. In the years of her marriage to Canibar, she
hadn't once sent to inquire after the boy.

That, finally, was the one thing beyond Jonas's understanding, the thing for which he could find no forgiveness
or extenuation. Through the crucial years when a mother
would have done Rainey good, Welda had been silent and
indifferent. Now it was too late . . . 'way too late.

Jonas gave his empty pipe a hard, absent knock against the step, then stuffed it into his pocket and got up and went inside.

Rainey and Minita were at the table working their lessons; Mateo had already shuffled off to bed. Jonas went to Minita's room and looked in on the drifter who called himself Grif. He was sitting up by lamplight, laying out a solitaire game on the counterpane. He gave Jonas an oblique glance and went on slapping down cards. Jonas pulled up a chair by the bed and straddled it, crossing his arms on the back.

"How you feeling?"

"Not bad. Be out of here soon as I can sit a saddle."

The kid shuffled the cards together and laid them aside. The least of his bruises were fading from darkly livid to a yellowish green. His stitched-up face was tautly wary, the eyes chill and withdrawn, asking nothing and wanting nothing.

"Well, no rush about it," Jonas said mildly.

No reply. Only the cold half-polite attention of that dark stare.

"What's got you so knotted up, boy? You on the dodge?"

"No." Polite and quiet.

"Anyways, it's your business."

No reply.

Jonas felt a baffled irritation. There was something about this kid . . . maybe he saw in him an echo of the footloose down-and-outer he'd once been. But that worked-over Colt suggested faster company than Jonas had ever moved in. Still, Grif had relaxed that sullen guard of his with another youngster: Rainey.

Hell, Jonas thought abruptly, no odds in his trying to

play the mother hen. He hadn't feathered his own nest any too snugly, come to that. He swung off the chair, walked to the doorway, and paused. "Take your time," he counseled lamely. And went out, closing the door.

In the room he and Rainey shared, Jonas opened a commode drawer and took out the drifter's gun. He turned it in his hands, scowling at it as if trying to make up hs mind. Hearing Rainey's quick step, he shoved the gun under a pile of shirts and closed the drawer. Rainey came in, whistling between his teeth as he webbed a length of string between his fingers.

"You turning in, Pa?"

"Uh-huh. You too. Rainey—"

"Yes?"

"That Grif . . . don't get to liking him too much."

"Why not?"

"Just don't," Jonas said roughly.

Jesus, he thought, always the questions. But looking at the droop of his son's mouth, he had the feeling he'd best start dredging up some good answers. And soon.

A kind of inspiration struck him next morning. It came at breakfast while he was half-listening to Mateo grouse about his rheumatism. Pretending irritation, Jonas cut the old man off short: "All right, forget it. No need for you to go out with us again."

Mateo dropped a fork in his surprise. "Heh?"

"We'll collect that stallion without you. Three of us'll be enough."

"¿Tres? You and the Negro are two."

"Barney and me and Rainey. That's three."

Rainey almost fell out of his chair. "Oh gosh, Pa, you *mean* it?"

"Why not?" Jonas casually poured himself a third cup of coffee. "You can ride, you can rope. You got learned by *el viejo* himself, and a boy couldn't learn any better."

Mateo was on the edge of a bristling objection, but the last words mollified him a little. He subsided, muttering into his cup as he sipped coffee. Then he shuttled a sly glance at Jonas, his mustache stirring to an understanding grin. "Truly, *caporal*, and I can teach no more. The rest must come by doing. I think the boy is old enough. Not that Mateo Baca is *too* old, mind you. But I catched plenty *caballos* in my time. What is one more?"

"Nothing, to one who's caught so many." Jonas drained his cup and pushed away from the table. "Get your stuff together, son. Slicker, blankets, change of duds . . . you know what you'll need."

Rainey hurried to their bedroom. Jonas and Mateo went to the corral to ready the horses, and Jonas quietly told the old man about the drifter's gun Minita had found. "Keep an eye on him, *viejo*. He's in no shape to give any trouble even if he's a mind to . . . but watch him."

"Hah! What did I tell you? This wolfling, it has teeth."

"His teeth are pulled. For the time being, and I don't expect we'll be away long."

Mateo grunted pessimistically. "You be careful, *amigo*. *Diablo Rojo* won't be so easy to catch this time. With the boy along, you be careful."

Chapter Six

By high noon Jonas and Rainey, leading a string of spare horses, arrived at the canyon where Barney Blue had set up camp. The ride had been a steady, aching punishment for Jonas, warning him that he wasn't yet in shape to push himself too hard. He told Barney to take the three mares to Big Crown, then rejoin them. Meantime he and Rainey would do some easy reconnoitering for sign of Diablo Red. When Barney returned, they would resume the hunt in earnest.

The two Bonners picked up the stallion's trail where he had left the canyon. They spent the rest of the day following it through the brush and rock fields to which Diablo Red had cannily clung in his flight. Several times they lost the track, but Jonas worked the ground with patience, honing his old skills while he studied out the wilding's pattern of movement.

The work was so pleasantly absorbing that he forgot to be annoyed with his son's persistent questions. Abruptly, and with some surprise, he realized that he was enjoying this more than he'd enjoyed anything in years: being on a track with his son, breaking him into a familiar game.

The day was a good one and the evening was better yet. Something about the age-old rituals of setting up camp, preparing a simple meal, talking beside a cozy fire, made magic between a man and a boy. This was what Jonas had hoped for, remembering his Ohio boyhood and the father who had found time to take him on such outings. Too easy for a man settled in a day-to-day grind of living to forget these things. Things as essential to the business of living as working and eating and sleeping.

Next morning they took up the tracking again. Jonas felt a sight better by now, and an eager impatience was crowding him. This was cold trail and it was getting colder; Diablo Red would cover as much ground in a couple of hours as they could cover in a day. They made a noon camp and a fire with plenty of smoke to guide Barney to them, for he should be on his way back. And he found them at midafternoon. They took council, squatting on their heels while Jonas sketched a rough map in the dust.

"He's been moving southeast," Jonas observed. "Going on a tear at first, but last track showed he wasn't in any rush. He'll still be on a caution, after running afoul of us. So he won't be ranging after mares for a spell. He will stick to the wild places and he'll be spooky at hell."

"He moving into the badlands, looks like," said Barney.

"They some mighty mean country south o' these foot-hills. Lot o' places he can hide and no open country we can run him. One thing sure, you ain't gonna box him like we done before. That's if we even catch a sight o' him."

"We'll need a lot of luck," Jonas conceded. "And a lot of good teamwork. We got to think out our moves and his, too. Let's get to it."

They traveled steadily through the day and that night made camp on a timbered bench at the edge of the bad-lands. At first light Jonas was up and glassing the broken ranges to the south and east.

The terrain was a choppy maze of cliffs and canyons where a whole band of horses might easily lose itself. Attempting to track a single horse across it would be hopeless. Jonas planned to keep to the high benches that marched irregularly along the west slopes of the Never-summers and fell off to the badlands at their east ex-tremities. Thus they'd have a constant overview of the rough country for miles. With any luck at all, they might spot their elusive quarry. It would be somewhat like groping for one needle in a very large haystack, but it seemed their best recourse.

For two days they worked south along the benchlands. They spent hours just scrutinizing with field glasses the rollaway of land to the west. It was slow and monotonous work and didn't bear much thinking on without feeling a deep discouragement. Be too damned easy to miss one red horse in all that rugged immensity. He might be just out of sight wherever you looked. Or he might be miles away. No way of being certain, even, that he was any-where in the whole area.

On the morning of the third day Barney, who was

working a quarter mile ahead of Jonas, came riding back on the gallop. "I seen him, *caporal*," he reported gleefully. "You had him pegged just right!"

"You sure?"

"He was on the move, didn't see him for but a few seconds. But ain't no way a man could mistake that critter. He shine like fire a mile off."

Jonas whistled for his son, who was riding drag some yards behind. Boylike, Rainey had felt the boredom more acutely than his elders; now he perked up, squirming with impatience, as the two men surveyed the country below and discussed the situation.

"He's lining due east of Echo Breaks," Jonas said. "I want to turn him southwest."

"Toward the Breaks?"

"Right square into 'em."

Barney shook his head ruefully. "I dunno, *caporal*. He might go plumb wild in that place."

"That's the idea. He's onto us now, enough he could start outthinking us. Best way to get him in a corner is get him so confused he can't think at all. Then—"

"Then we'll have a sack o' hell on our hands for certain-sure. Man, he could go so loco in there he would butt hisself to death on a wall. It's happened."

"We got to take the chance. You get behind where you seen him. Tail him up, but no crowding."

From Diablo Red's position and the direction he was moving, as Barney sized it, he was working south along a chain of bisecting canyons. Now as Barney rode down off the heights to reach the stallion's backtrail, Jason and Rainey pushed hard to get ahead of him. Their horses were lathered when they achieved an open saddle between the benches. From here Jonas swept the canyon-riddled valleys to the east and north with his glasses. He caught several glimpses of the stallion and knew they had pulled a good lead on him.

And something else: a glittering snake of water that made a twisting track southward. That would be Cibola Creek, wide and shallow and boulder-strewn, and Diablo Red was following it midstream. It gave Jonas an idea.

After switching to fresh mounts, he and Rainey headed down a fairly easy incline where the saddle tapered off. Setting a quick pace, they sood reached Cibola Creek and rode down a shallow cutbank into the water, then headed south. The banks rose high and steep on both sides for perhaps a half mile before they came to a place where, Jonas thought, the stallion might be turned in the direction he wanted. The creek's east bank dwindled to a mild slope; the west bank remained steep, but not inaccessibly so.

Jonas dismounted and draped an empty flour sack over a boulder in midstream. His gamble was that Diablo Red, newly alerted to the ways of men, would try to foil their "spooks" the way he had in the old days. Logically a horse confronted by a man-scented object would leave the stream, making for the easily negotiable east bank. Diablo Red might just cannily reverse that expectation—and tackle the high west cutbank. Once out of the stream, the terrain would force him to cut briefly in a westerly direction. But Barney at his back would keep hustling him south and west. It was Jonas's job to lay the "spooks" that would prevent him from turning aside.

Leaving the creek now, they pulled off into a concealment of scrub timber. Jonas explained the ruse to Rainey. The boy's eyes shone with excitement. "You know, Pa?

Mr. Baca said you're half horse yourself. I sure can see what he meant."

"Maybe," Jonas said wryly. "I hope so, boy. But you just never know with a critter like this'n. I could be outsmarting myself."

Yet he felt with an intuitive certainty that he was right. He couldn't say how or why. Only that where this horse was concerned, some bone-deep knowledge guided him, as if Diablo Red's eyes and ears and brains were his own.

Presently the stallion came trotting into sight along the creekbed. His head was up, his tail switching; wind ruffled his mane. Rainey stifled a soft cry. Diablo Red's nostrils twitched at the strong man-smell. For a moment he halted, motionless. Then he tossed his head and lunged up the south cutbank with the ease of a goat. He breasted through a tangle of brush and was gone.

"He did it, Pa! He did it!"

"He's going where we want . . . now," Jonas muttered. "Only holding him that way will be one tricky business, boy."

The rest of this long day followed a run of touch-and-go calculations. While depending on Barney to keep Diablo Red always, steadily, on the move, Jonas depended on his own knowledge of the country and constant guesswork to lay spooks that would keep the stallion headed on one course. He and Rainey drove their animals hard to press always ahead of the blood bay, planting eack spook with the same eye to his wily contrariness.

Three more times they repeated the procedure; each time Jonas weighed the stallion's actions correctly. By sunset they had covered nearly twenty miles in this manner. About then Jonas began to sense Diablo Red's mounting nervousness. The horse couldn't anticipate just what (outside of capturing him) the men's purpose was, but the knowledge of being constantly driven and turned was flicking small warning signals in his behavior.

"I reckon he is getting onto us." Jonas said. "We're close to Junction Pass now. If we can rustle him through that, we can push him into the Breaks. But it'll be mighty touchy from here on. Reckon I will put our next spook so it'd turn an ordinary *caballo* right into that pass. You see what I'm about?"

Rainey gave a jerky nod. He was slumped in his saddle, blinking exhaustedly.

"It's going to get a sight rougher, son. We can't stop now. Got to keep pushing him along. If you ain't up to it, say so."

"Sure, Pa." Rainey straightened up. "I mean, I can make it. I'm all right."

They made a wide swing to reach the head of Junction Pass.

The broad floor of the declivity was overgrown with thick brush, but an age-old game trail was worn clear through it. If Diablo Red were leery about pushing into the pass, he might plunge sideways into the flanking brush before he reached its mouth. And now Jonas made his second big gamble: that the stallion had sensed the trick being run on him and would now try to turn it to his advantage. Deliberately Jonas laid his spook as he would have for any other horse, in order to head the animal into the pass.

The light was fading as he and Rainey concealed themselves in the brush. Dusk began to fur the landscape as they waited; Jonas had to strain to make out details. His eyes were starting to ache when Diablo Red appeared and, reacting without hesitation to the spook, headed straight into the pass.

Jonas and Rainey followed him now, and before they were halfway through the pass Barney caught up with them. He had collected the various spooks Jonas had planted along the way.

"You have done it, *caporal*," he said in a near-reverent voice. "Clean as a whistle. Now you got him this far, I'm 'bout ready to believe anything. You tol' me you could witch up a hex that'd let you walk right up t' him, I'd believe it."

"Be a little harder than that," Jonas said dryly. "I had to outguess him any more, I be like to bust a blood vessel. He's confused as hell now, and we want to keep him that way. We got to run him to a frazzle and ourselves, too."

The pass debouched on a vast gorge that Jonas knew a man couldn't see the end of, even by daylight. Towering cliffs walled it on every side and its whole expanse was cut up by ruggedly eroded spires and chimney rocks. Toward this end was a brush-rimmed seep where game watered. Full dark had rushed down by now and all they could make out were contorted shapes of stone against the sky. As they approached the seep, the stallion's angry bugle lifted out of the darkness. A splash of water, the swift brush crackle of his retreat, then a clatter of hoofs as he raced away down a rocky aisle, creating a shower of echoes.

The three dropped out of their saddles. Barney built up a roaring fire while Jonas scattered a number of spooks across the end of the pass, hoping this would be enough to keep Diablo Red from bolting back through the broad cleft come daybreak . . . or even before. They were all too bone-weary, too tense with excitement, to feel hungry.

Rainey sprawled in a tired daze by the fire as Jonas and Barney tended and watered the horses. Then Jonas spread out his son's blankets and motioned him to crawl into them.

"Get your sleep, son. You only got a few hours. Soon's it's light enough to see, we're going after him."

"Is he trapped now, Pa?" Rainey murmured drowsily as Jonas tucked the soogans around him.

"Sort of. He can't get out 'cept by this way, but will run himself ragged up a lot of blind alleys trying. I hazard by first light he'll know what sort of bind he is in. About then he'll be one spooky piece of horseflesh, for certain."

"What do we do with him when we catch him?"

"Boy don't you ever come to an end of questions?" Jonas let a grin in his voice take the edge off his words. "Well, *if* we catch him, we'll have a mighty big responsibility to him. We'll have to shut him away from what he's known all his natural days. I don't much like to think about that . . . ."

He let his voice die gently. Rainey was asleep.

Jonas and Barney split the hours of dark into two watches so each could catch a couple of hours of sleep. Jonas took the second shift, alerting his ears to the occasional stamping echoes from deep in the gorge as Diablo Red vainly sought a means of egress. The minutes dragged till he wondered if false dawn would ever show. Gradually it came, picking out in slow relief the gray world of the Breaks with its monolithic crags and weirdly fluted columns. When the sky was almost pale and the landscape faintly stressed, he shook Barney and Rainey awake. Rainey raised only a small objection when Jonas told him to remain here, laid up in a nearby cluster of rocks with his rifle, and not move from that spot on any account. If Diablo Red were to cut back this way and he was in a panic, no amount of spooks was likely to deter him. Rainey was to start firing as fast as he could in an effort to turn the horse. If he reached the pass, all their work would be for nothing.

The two men rode into the crazy quilt of towering rock, their animals' shod hooves throwing out a tinny pulsation of echoes. As the gorge floor tended steadily downward, the echoes deepened to a hollow and ominous pitch. In the colorless light of predawn, it was easy to imagine that they were descending into a monstrous pit of another world. Long ago the earth's crust had split and shifted here, webbing the scape with myriad canyons. Erosion had done the rest, sculpting the rough masses of rock between the fissures into contorted shapes.

Before he saw the stallion, Jonas heard him from somewhere ahead. His frenzied high whinney was hurled back tenfold from the craggy clefts. After hours of wandering the rocky maze and listening to tortured echoes of his own making, Diablo's nerves must be strained to a breaking point. He could tell that mounted men were coming but couldn't pick out their direction with any certainty.

Jonas's guts ached with tension. Luck had ridden on his shoulder so far. The next minutes would tell the story.

Coming around a sudden turn, they saw the red horse as the end of a stony corridor. Diablo Red saw them at the same time; he wheeled and dashed out of sight.

"Get around him if you can," Jonas told Barney. "Try to get him between us."

Barney merely nodded, his face a dark mask. But Jonas could feel his tenseness as palpably as his own.

Barney rode back around the bend; Jonas pushed

forward. He had no more idea than Diablo Red of the many twists and turns in this labyrinth. All he and Barney could do was maneuver blindly, using their man-sense against the stallion's.

Jonas turned his peg pony nimbly down one cross canyon after another, feeling the animal's panic as the waves of echoes beat at them from all sides. Now and again he heard Diablo Red's frantic, angry squeals. He could only guess at their direction and try to keep working along this side of him, trusting Barney to come up on the other flank. All he was sure of was that they were close to the south end of the gorge now.

Abruptly Jonas saw the stallion again. And now he kneed his pony straight toward him, shouting at the top of his voice. Diablo Red swerved away at right angles and vanished once more. But Barney must have spotted him, too. Barney's yells echoed Jonas's now, playing one echo of another in a crazy cacaphony. Seeing the south wall of the gorge loom in front of him then, Jonas veered hard to his right at a breakneck speed.

He pulled up swiftly.

Diablo Red was just ahead of him. Standing in the center of an elongated bowl, facing Jonas now, and trumpeting his mad fury. His ears were flattened; his coat was drenched with lather. All his marvelous cunning was gone, swallowed in a crazed confusion that only made him more dangerously unpredictable. He was, Jonas sensed, ready to turn on his would-be captors.

Jonas palmed his Winchester from its boot and fired twice over the stallion's head. Waves of shot-sound erupted through the bowl with a magnified roar that was deafening. Diablo Red whirled away from him, only to face Barney as he surged into sight, yelling.

The stallion's way was blocked at both ends of the bowl. Another time he might have charged either rider. Now, the last ravel of his poise gone, he reared high and came down running; he bolted sidelong into a slot of spur canyon that showed every promise of coming to a dead end. And it did. Hollering and firing, Jonas and Barney raced into the draw and saw it rapidly pinch away to a fissure through which no horse could pass.

Driven to bay, the stallion turned to face the men. His teeth were bared; froth dripped from his muzzle. In that unnerving moment of his hesitation, the two men unlimbered their lariats and whirled out their loops.

Diablo Red charged.

He ran straight into Jonas's noose; it settled around his neck. At the same time Barney undercut a deft loop that was no larger than a barrel rim as it snapped around the blood bay's forehoofs. Jonas had quartered sideways across the stallion's path; he felt the savage shock as Diablo Red's hurling weight piled into his animal's rump.

The peg pony staggered but kept its feet against the impact. For Barney had made a lightning-fast dally and there was hardly a foot of slack in his line. Even as Diablo Red hit Jonas's horse, his footing was yanked away, he was going down.

He crashed on his side and scrambled wildly, trying to regain his feet. Barney pegged his pony away, keeping a steady pressure on the rope. Scissored tightly together, the stallion's forelegs flailed helplessly; he fell back. Jonas dropped to the ground and whirled the slack of his rope around the thrashing hind legs. He moved in fast, jerked the line taut, and hog-tied Diablo Red where he lay, writhing helplessly.

Barney dismounted, too, and they looked at each other

over the twisting, grunting body of the downed stallion. Jonas felt no exultance. It was too soon to be sure of what he felt. But he wondered if his own face mirrored the awe he saw in Barney's.

Chapter Seven

THOUGH he was roped and hobbled, the wildling fought them every yard of the way back to Cross-B. Jonas chose a far straighter and easier route than they'd covered in pursuing him; even so, it took them three full days. They were worn to a sheer exhaustion, their clothes crusted to their bodies with dirt and sweat, when they finally turned Diablo Red into the stable at noon of the fourth day.

Jonas and Barney took turns soaking in the wooden tub in water heated as hot as they could stand. Rainey, having been spared most of the brutal work, eagerly spilled out the whole story for the Bacas. The two men paid hardly any attention, and after wolfing some food they toppled into their blankets and slept the clock around. Both were ravenous when they woke, but they were also beaten sore and lame, and it was too soon to think of anything but resting up.

Mateo had tried to tend Diablo Red. But as they sat down to a late breakfast, he admitted that so far it was a hopeless task. "*Un ladino pure*," the old man told them, shaking his white head. "He won' eat or drink. If he wasn't hobble', he kick that stable to pieces. Maybe, I'm think, he die of *acolambrao*."

"What's that?" Rainey asked.

"Is no word for it in your talk, *niño*. Sometimes the *vaqueros* say of a wild one, he die of a broken heart. *Acolambrao*."

"Just pine away," Barney said. "That's 'bout as near as you can say it, young 'un."

"You're wrong," Jonas said quietly. "He won't go that way, Mateo. Not Diablo Red."

"Hah," Mateo said sarcastically. "Maybe now you're my teacher, I'm the learner, hey?"

"He won't go that way," Jonas repeated. "He's life . . . that stallion, he's life itself."

The overpowering conviction was more than he knew how to say well. He attacked his food, scowling. After a moment Barney said gravely. "Sure hope you're right about that, *caporal*."

The drifter boy Grif was at table with them, but he made no comment on that or much of anything, except for a polite request to pass this or that dish. He was still raw enough to keep all his movements slow and careful, but seemed to be healing in good fettle; Mateo had taken out all the stitches. His guard had relaxed a little; he looked absurdly young and fresh-faced with his beard scraped away and his hair neatly combed. The clean, worn shirt and trousers Jonas had lent him were baggily over-size on his gaunt frame.

During the next couple of days, the kid hobbled around outside, testing his strength. He had little to say to the men but seemed to relax with Minita and Rainey. Several times Jonas heard Grif and Minita laughing together. Mateo made a grumbling comment or two about that, but Jonas told him there was no point stirring up a fuss about it; Grif wouldn't be staying much longer. He was the same restless and footloose sort Jonas had been at that age. Though Grif's presence made him uneasy on Rainey's account, Jonas felt a kindred sympathy with the drifter. Still—best all around that he be on his way soon.

For now, at least, Grif showed no inclination to drift. He seemed oddly content at Cross-B; he took an interest in the place and its prospects and unbent enough to ask Jonas a few questions. But always that polite remoteness clung to his manner, as if part of him were sealed away and untouchable. After some hesitation, Jonas returned the kid's pistol, though he hadn't asked about it. Except for a word of thanks, Grif made no comment at all.

By the third day, Jonas and Barney felt sufficiently rested to tackle the next piece of business: training Diablo Red to accept a rope and its restraints on him. By now, as Jonas had anticipated, thirst and hunger had decided the blood bay to abandon his food- and water-strike. He too was well rested. They wrestled him out to the corral on a tight hobble, with Jonas and Barney hanging to a rope on either side.

Even holding him securely checked, they felt the same awe of the stallion's power. He'd lost most of his fear, quickly adapting to the terms of his captivity as he saw them, which would be to seize the first opportunity for escape. He snorted wickedly and pawed the ground, his whole body bunching and rippling with a superb play of muscle. Even in the rangy condition of an animal who had always run wild, he must have weighed over a thousand pounds and would probably top twelve hundred at his full weight. The glossy flame of his hide was marred only by a pale row of scars on his neck and similar marks on one haunch, legacy of an encounter or two with cougars— probably in the defense of his *manada*.

Getting his vinegar up, he dragged the men around the corral, snorting and pawing, till Jonas could get him snubbed to a post. He and Barney stood back, flexing their hands. The ropes had burned almost through their heavy gloves.

"He something for sure," Barney said. "But damn' if we ain't got our work cut out, *caporal*. Gonna take weeks just to get him used to us."

Jonas swiped a gloved thumb across his jaw. "He will. Like I said, he's too smart to 'sull' himself to death."

"That, maybe. Getting him busted out o' that pure wildness is somp'n else. I dunno we ever make it."

"I don't either," Jonas admitted. "But we're going to give it the hell of a try. What we do now is get this fence built up. Or he'll take it in a walk, first chance."

After returning Diablo Red to the stable, they got to the job of reinforcing the corral. With Barney cutting and dragging pine timbers from the hills, Jonas and Mateo set to sinking extra posts and building the top rails higher than any horse could jump. Rainey and Grif lent a hand with the lighter work.

As they were finishing up the job next day, Tigre's wild barking signaled the approach of riders. They all knocked off work and were waiting in the yard as the visitors rode in.

Jonas felt a disagreeable surprise, and an instant tinge of worry, at sight of King Canibar, his wife, and his sister. Careful to show nothing, he stonily invited them to dismount. King swung to the ground and helped Welda out of her sidesaddle.

Jonas did the same for Meg Canibar, ignoring the faint amusement in her face. She was sidesaddle too, but now he noticed she was wearing a peculiar sort of riding costume with a divided skirt. He had seen the like on circus equestriennes, but it was the kind of rig no decent female was supposed to be caught dead in. He decided that he wasn't surprised.

"This is Rainey, eh?" King said genially. "My name's Canibar, young fellow. And I hope you know your mother."

Rainey was already goggling at Welda, who made quite a picture in her green corduroy riding habit. "Oh, gee," he whispered.

Welda had eyes only for him, too. She came quickly to him and bent down, kissing him on the forehead. "Rainey," she murmured, and Jonas was startled at the radiance of her look, a kind of joyous hunger in it.

Rainey took a step backward, blushing.

Canibar peeled off his gauntlets, glancing around at the ranch layout with this quiet arrogance of his that wasn't quite aware of itself. "First time I've seen your place, Bonner. Picked a fine location for yourself."

Jonas, in no mood to match King's ponderous effort to appear friendly, said flatly: "Thanks. Reckon I done something right to deserve this honor."

King smiled easily. "Well, naturally I wondered how

you fared with that red horse. I give you a week, and it's been near two weeks. Not that I'm here to lean on the deadline, anything like that."

"Is that right," Jonas said. "When did you start taking generosity pills?"

King eyed him for a moment, then decided to chuckle. "Call it that. Anyway, I'm willing to talk it over. You been out on the hunt, I suppose. Just how do you size your chances now? Of catching him, I mean."

"Better'n good." Jonas paused, watching him with a kind of wicked relish. "I got him."

"What? The devil!" King's jaw fell in amazement. "You serious? You *got* him?"

"Snug as a mouse in a pillow. Want to see him?"

"Hell, yes!" King said vigorously. "I—"

"King," Welda cut in with a note of sharp impatience. "Would you *mind?* Can't we get on with it?"

King gave a mild shrug. "It's your party. Bonner, my wife wants a private word with you. Meantime I'd like a pasear at that Diablo horse . . . if you got him close by."

"In the stable, Mr. Canibar," Barney Blue said. "I be pleased to show you."

"Good."

Minita was gazing wide-eyed at Meg's riding habit. "I have not seen such a thing," she murmured.

"Times change," Meg said cheerfully. "Why don't we all go look at that horse?"

Chatting girl-fashion, she and Minita moved off after King and Barney. Mateo grumbled something at Rainey, and they and Grif followed.

Welda lowered her eyes, tapping her riding quirt against one palm. "I don't know how to say this so you'll understand, Jonas. That always was a problem with us."

"Just get it said."

"Very well." Her glance came up, coldly. "I want you to consider giving me custody of Rainey. We can—"

Jonas cut in flatly. "You been out in the sun too long, I reckon," and turned on his heel, walking to the washbench. He rolled up his sleeves and ducked his head, splashing water on his face.

"Listen to me!" Welda said behind him, her voice rising with anger. "The least you can do is listen."

He straightened, reaching for the frayed towel. "All right. Talk."

"I started to say that we can do so much for the boy— King and I. We can give him so much."

Jonas toweled his face and hands and flung the cloth aside, only then turning to face her. "Nobody ever tried to keep you from him," he said in a hard, low voice. "You had your chance when we busted up. You never said a word to contest me taking him. Not a damn word. And you never paid him a lick of attention since."

"I know . . . I know." She twisted the quirt between her hands, biting her lip. "I don't deny any of it. I simply wasn't ready for motherhood."

"Now you are. Just like that, huh?"

"Yes," she said quietly. "I was too young, Jonas . . . and everything was so wrong with you and me. I blamed you for all of it. It took a long time for me to see how wrong I was, too. That you and I were simply different. Too different ever to be happy together."

"That ain't exactly news. And what's it got to do with the price of eggs anyway?"

"I'm trying to explain, will you please *listen?* I have a good life now. King and I are as right for each other as you and I weren't. I *can* be a good mother . . . and King would be a fine father to the boy. A fine stepfather," she added quickly. "I wouldn't try to turn Rainey against you or prevent you from seeing him when you choose."

"That's just fine." Jonas clamped his temper with an effort. "Only suppose we work it the other way. Let Rainey stay right smack here and you come see him whenever you want. You're a mite late getting to your proper duty that way. But, fine you can start any time."

"Jonas, I am not making myself clear." A brittle impatience edged her voice. "I can understand how you feel, but you're being unreasonable now. You're certainly aware that I can give Rainey a great many advantages that you can't. That is no reflection on you, it's simply a fact. Don't you care about your son's having the very best?"

"Somehow," he said softly, "I had the idea I'd done pretty fair by him."

"But you have, I'm sure. I'm not being ironic, I mean that. You're a clean and decent man, and I know you must be seeing to his education, after a fashion—"

"Thanks."

"But he should attend a regular school in the valley. Have the companionship of other children his age. Later we could send him away to private schools, the very best—"

"Why?"

"Because we can afford to, that's why! Why shouldn't our son have the best that's available to him? To help him realize the best that's in him? Surely you can see the value of that."

"Maybe I'm a mite confused. Just whose son you referring to? Mine and yours? Or yours and King's?"

Welda was silent a moment, her green eyes unreadable.

"I know you don't like King," she said at last. "But I'd think you might be big enough to put aside a mere personal dislike. He's every bit as good a man as you. In his own way, which happens not to be yours."

"I know. He's all right, he's just hungry."

She tossed her head; her eyes sparked. "Successful is the word, I believe. What would be the word for you, Jonas? Jealous?"

He shook his head slowly. "We had them years together, and you don't know me any better'n that?"

"Oh, I do." She gave a short bitter laugh. "I know very well how you think. To you, there's something not quite right about a man who aspires to as much as King Canibar has. But I'll concede that you genuinely feel that way. Not that you're right, merely honest. Perhaps it's me, then. It must have injured your pride when I turned to King. But that's water under the bridge, isn't it? Surely you don't care any more—not enough to want a petty revenge on me."

"If I did," he said flatly, "I'd hold you and him and his whole damn crew off with a gun before I'd let you near Rainey. I just offered to let you come see him, remember?"

"Oh yes. On your terms. Everything has to be on your terms!"

Jonas felt a hot spurt of real anger then. "Who's got more right to set 'em?" he said harshly. "A pa who's done his damnedest by a boy all these years? Who fed him and clothed him and give him a proper raising? Or a ma who never gave a whisper of a damn? Till she decided she could just waltz in, la-de-da, and have it all her way. You want a kid of your own so bad, get one. What's the matter? Can't the great man you married deliver that much?"

In his anger he wanted the words to hurt, and they did. The color ran out of her face. She said quietly, almost inaudibly, "Apparently not, if it's any satisfaction to you. Whatever the reason—we've not been able to have children."

"So you up and decided to take Rainey."

"He's my son too, Jonas! Nothing, nothing you've said, can change that! I have a great deal to make up to Rainey. All I ask is the chance!"

"You're asking a sight more'n that."

"Very well," she said coldly. "Think of my reason as selfish, if you like. What about yours? How much does Rainey's welfare really concern you, when you know full well that I can give him so much more—"

"More of what? What he needs most is a home where he belongs. You want to put it like that, put it to him. Ask Rainey what he wants."

"You know very well what he'll say. He's used to you—your way of life, your opinions, and your feelings. No doubt including your peculiar belief that horses are somewhat superior to people."

"Depends on the people. One thing, I never knew a mare that deserted her young."

She shook her head with a faint, icy smile. "You can't stop belaboring that, can you? Same old Jonas. You never change."

"You have," Jonas said gently. "You have become quite the grand lady, Welda. That's what you wanted, and I don't begrudge you a jot of it. But you ain't taking Rainey."

"As to that, you may be surprised. May I speak to him now?"

"All you want."

The others were returning from the stable now, and Welda went to meet them. She said something to Rainey, smiling, and he shyly returned the smile and nodded. The two of them walked off a little distance. King Canibar came tramping up to Jonas.

"Quite a critter, that horse. Now you got him, Bonner, what you going to do with him?"

"I'll worry about that."

"I think you will," King said agreeably. "You plan to geld him?"

Jonas shrugged.

"You won't, if I know you," King said shrewdly. He took a cigar from his pocket and clipped the end. "Too bad. No other way you'll ever bust the starch out of a crazy *ladino* like that'n." He threw a bemused glance toward Welda and Rainey. "Well, what did you tell her? What's your answer?"

"You'd never guess."

King chuckled, lighting his cigar. "Hell, I told her you'd never give him up of your own accord. Don't reckon she really thought so either, but she had to give it the big try."

Jonas didn't intend to comment, but curiosity prompted him to say: "Just how do you feel about it? Taking over another man's son?"

"I'm realistic, Bonner. We've had no luck starting a family of our own and I want one almighty bad. You've a fine boy there, and I can tell you done a fine job raising him up. Good as I could do, and I'd do my damnedest . . . if I had a son."

Jonas felt a fresh rise of irritation. "Why the hell don't you adopt one? There's orphans and orphanages."

"Look, I'm not het on taking a man's kid from him. But Welda . . . Rainey's her own blood. You understand the feeling."

"What Welda wants, Welda gets. Is that it?"

"Just so," King said in an impersonal tone. "Anything she sets her heart on, I get for her. One way or the other. No matter what it costs."

Jonas had braced himself for this, half-expecting it. "Rainey included, eh?"

"Afraid that's how it'll have to be, Bonner. Sorry."

"Just how the hell you think you'll manage it?"

"All nice and legal with ribbons on it. We'll get a court order demanding that you give custody of the child to his mother. It'll take time and a battery of lawyers and a passel of red tape and moving a lot of cold cash around. But we'll get it."

The man's matter-of-fact certainty touched Jonas with a quiet chill. "You think so, eh?"

"I don't think, I know." King flicked ash from his cigar. "We'll prove to the court that you're an unfit parent. Raising your boy wild as an Indian, 'way back in the middle of nowhere, not a lick of proper schooling, in the company of a nigger and a pair of greasers. It's going to get rough as hell. But you'll never learn just how rough till the sheriff comes here to serve that court order."

Jonas's jaw knotted with the effort of self-control. When he could trust himself to speak, he said: "You try to take my boy, Mister, you're the one's going to find what rough is."

King nodded with a kind of wry regret. "Yeah. It'll come to that, knowing you. But I got all the edge, Bonner.

I got the money and I'll have the law. And I'll have the men and the guns too, you carry it that far. You're going to lose, fella. Any way it goes, you're going to lose."

Chapter Eight

FOR the time being, all Jonas could do was wait. On regular trips to Moratown to pick up supplies, he kept his ears open and asked questions. The ordinary channels of gossip told him that King and Welda were not bluffing. They had put in motion the legal apparatus to take Rainey from him; lawyers were preparing briefs on their behalf. Jonas decided the best he could do was keep his vigilance to make certain when the time came that he got his own day in court.

He tried to submerge his freight of worry in a constant grind of work. There was plenty to occupy him on the range, and meantime the taming of Diablo Red proceeded after a fashion. He and Barney and Mateo spent several hours each day trying to condition the stallion to the rope. Repeatedly they led him around the corral roped by the neck and brought him up against the snubbing post. And he fought them unceasingly. After a week of it, they fastened a tow sack on his back and let him try to buck it off. He raced around the enclosure pitching crazily till exhaustion claimed him.

This went on for another week and then, though he had little indication the horse would accept a back burden, Jonas decided to try the saddle. That proved even less productive. At each session Diablo Red bucked himself into a lather and refused to quit till he was dead spent, blood leaking from his nostrils. Jonas had to steel himself to continue with the business; his own heart lay with the stallion's unquenchable spirit. But the breaking had to be accomplished. Keeping the horse penned indefinitely in a state of unchecked savagery was out of the question; his own lusty energies would wear him to death.

"He don' stop fighting ever," grumbled Mateo Baca. "You don' get him to take the saddle, how you think we ever top him, eh?"

"It's happened," Jonas said. "Horse can fight a rope and saddle and still break under a man. I reckon it's about time to try."

Mateo and Barney exchanged glances, and Barney said: "How many years since you rough busted a wild 'un, *caporal?*"

Jonas shrugged. "Hard onto eight."

"You too old for it, man. Thirty-five be too old. Bronc-peeler's gotta have green bones, you know that."

"I busted a few bones in the game. So did you."

"We was kids then, we heal up easy. Man's bones brittle up 'fore he turns thirty. You top him now, you get busted to flinders."

"It's got to be done," Jonas said grimly. "Ain't no one else to do it, and we can't afford to hire it done."

They ran Diablo Red into the small holding pen adjoining the corral; connecting the two enclosures was a tight chute customarily used for branding. Even with a war bridle on his muzzle and a Scotch hobble that pulled his left hind leg clean off the ground, it took them twenty minutes to wrestle the stallion into the chute. Reaching inside to whip off the hobble, Barney failed to pull back fast enough; a flying hoof knocked him sprawling.

"You need sewing up, *compadre*," old Mateo observed.

Barney swiped at the blood streaming from a two-inch gash in his cheek. "I be all right. Let's get that hull on him."

The chute's confinement threw Diablo Red into a diabolical frenzy; he tried to batter his way out but was too cramped to gain any leverage. It took another fifteen minutes to cinch the double-rigged saddle on him. By the time they had removed the war bridle and slipped on a braided hackamore, he'd worked himself to a lather. Momentarily he turned quiescent, for a jerk on the hackamore would cause its heavy knot, resting under a tender spot back of his teeth, to give his lower jaw a painful wrench.

Jonas swung to the top of the chute and stood astraddle it above Diablo Red. He looked at Rainey and Minita and Grif watching from the fence. He smelled dust warmed by the morning sun and felt a clammy sweat cool his flesh under his clothes. Sight and smell and sound washed against his senses with an unreasonable clarity. So did a sudden conviction that he was being a damned fool. Even in his green days he might have balked at taking on a *caballo* like this one. Reckless as he'd once been, he had never encountered the likes of Diablo Red.

Barney might be more than right. This could be suicidal.

Don't think about it!

He lowered himself into the saddle, feeling a convulsive quiver run through the stallion's coiled muscles. Barney was waiting to open the gate.

"Let 'er rip," Jonas said hoarsely.

The gate scraped wide. Diablo Red came high-rolling into the corral like a gargantuan jackrabbit. At once he erupted into a series of pile-driving plunges. Jonas kept his body alternately braced and slackened, rolling to the stallion's violent pitching. Though he tried to take each jolting impact limp as a dishrag, he felt his spine threaten to wrench apart from the pounding.

Coming out of the pile-drivers, the stallion switched abruptly to sunfishing. Jonas was prepared for it, shifting his weight to the left as the horse's right shoulder dipped. Diablo Red twisted high and came down, and once more Jonas was ready, throwing his weight the other way as the horse shifted leads. The stallion emitted a squeal of rage as his rider refused to be dislodged; he sunfished again and again, and each time Jonas successfully shifted his center of balance.

Suddenly Diablo Red had bucked his way to a corner of the corral. Jonas braced for the spinaround he expected. Belatedly, he realized that Diablo Red meant to smash the fence flank-on.

He jerked his right leg free of the stirrup and swung it high an instant before collision. The stallion's rump slammed against the poles with a force that shuddered the whole corral. Wheeling, he raced for the center of the enclosure, wheeled again and lunged for the fence at an opposite angle. Jonas barely got his right foot securely in the stirrup before kicking his left leg free. Again the crashing impact that would have crushed his leg had it remained between fence and horse.

Diablo Red raced around the corral now, bucking in loose circles and figure eights. Then he went on the pile-drivers again, plunging up and down stiff-legged. His hind hoofs struck ground ahead of his forehoofs, and it was like being caught on a seesaw gone out of control. Jonas's body was snapped back and forth; his spine took a savage whiplashing on each leap. Earth and sky gyrated crazily.

With an uncanny swiftness, Diablo Red, who had never felt a rider's weight before, was falling into the calculated patterns of a seasoned bucker. He started to "pioneer" now, changing direction at every plunge.

Jonas tried to anticipate his calculations, bracing and slacking his body just so. The battering shocks sent the blood surging to his head; he felt it gush from his nose. That part of it was an old story to him, but the tearing agony, as if his bones were being unseamed at the joints, was something else. With the pain came a bitter knowledge that he could no longer cut the mustard at this game.

Dimly he heard Barney yelling, "Take a dive, man! He too much for you! Take a spill."

The sudden reeling of his senses told Jonas that he was losing contact, losing that cold clarity that would enable him to head off the stallion's tactical switches. Only the salt-sharp taste of his own blood seemed to anchor him to reality; everything else was fuzzing away in a world of rocking, battering fury and the fog of choking dust.

No man alive could take this kind of punishment for long. Always a dragged-out contest between man and horse had to hinge, finally, on who could outlast the other. If there were any faint diminution of the stallion's brute, rawboned power, any sign at all that he was tiring, Jonas couldn't detect it.

"Take a dive!"

Damned if you do and dead if you don't. Was that the choice?

Jonas could feel the actual weakening of his pain-wracked muscles now. His timing was off; his dulled nerve-ends no longer mustered a rhythmic adjustment to the horse's savage plungings. On each one, his body was flung backward against the cantle, then jammed forward across the horn. At any moment Diablo Red could start sunfishing again, and that would be the end.

On the next pile-driver, Jonas let his body go wholly loose, leaning out from the saddle so that the jarring impact shook him off. He tried with his last fragment of physical will for the horse-breaker's roll and half-managed it. Hit the ground like a sack of meal and rolled twice before his body slammed against a corral post.

He lay stunned, unable to move. Then he felt a grip of hands pulling him sideways as Barney dragged him out of the corral.

Nothing was broken that he could tell, no bones any-way. Jonas was less certain that some of his innards hadn't torn loose; his whole carcass was so pain-whipped it might take a day or two to be sure. But one thing was bitterly clear already: his horse-breaking days were done with.

He spent a painful day and night in bed and didn't drag himself out of it till the next evening. A grinding misery savaged his body at every step he took very gingerly, but he could manage to get about by himself, and he guessed he could keep some food down. He sat down to supper with the others and took almost no part in their conversation; the depression that weighed on his mind went deeper than any physical hurts.

His private gloom affected the table talk, which kept awkwardly dwindling off as if everyone hesitated to touch the subject that was nettling him. Minita made an effort to perk things up by saucily twitting her grandfather: "What a skirt for riding that Miss Canibar has, *Abuelito!* Can I get one like it?"

"Blood of Christ! What indecency is this?"

"Was my mother not a *mestenera?*" Minita said demurely. "She rode with the men. Yes, even like the men. Is it not so?"

Old Mateo cleared his throat with embarassment. "It was a wild way we lived. It was not good for a woman." Quickly changing the subject, he grunted, "Well, Jonas, the thing must be said, eh? What will it now be with *Diablo Rojo?*"

Jonas shook his head glumly.

"There's still a way, *caporal,*" Barney said quietly. "You can geld him."

"Maybe," Jonas said heavily. "Maybe we'll have to do that."

But the thought turned his gorge. He shoved his plate away and stood up and limped outside. Settling himself on the porch, he stuck his pipe in his teeth and watched the sun's last flare die along the dark hills. *Gelding.* He had always hated it—the mutilation of animals that was necessary to men's work, the kinds of work he'd always done. But to castrate a critter like Diablo Red was almost more than he could stand to contemplate. Bad enough to take away his freedom . . . .

The door creaked open and Grif came out.

Plunking himself beside Jonas, the kid came straight to the point. "Mr. Bonner, I reckon it's time I moved on. You been mighty kind and all, but it ain't right I go on taking board and bed without I can pay you for it."

Sunk in his gray musing, Jonas gave an indifferent nod.

"I been thinking, though. Maybe there's a way. I am surely owing you, and could be I can pay my reckoning if you let me."

"How's that?" Jonas said absently.

"Well, I been listening to all you fellows say about horse-busting, a man needs green bones and all. You reckon I'm green enough?"

It took a moment for the words to sink home, and then Jonas peered at him sharply. "It takes a sight more'n that. You ever done the like? Ever topped anything like this horse?"

"I rode the edges off a few rough broncs."

"So's anyone, if he's worked cows. That ain't what I asked."

"No, sir."

"You seen Diablo Red in action. He ain't a critter any man'll snap his fingers at, green bones or no."

"I seen that, all right."

"Then, why?"

"I'm beholden to you. I'm a fellow always pays his debts. I am healed up right enough, now. I know some about horse-busting, I can learn more. You can learn me the ropes."

"Takes more'n picking up a few tricks," Jonas said

grimly. "More'n just climbing on a saddle. That takes cheap guts. Having the bottom to stick on him, ride him out—boy, that's something else."

"Look, Mr. Bonner," Grif said impatiently, "you need it done, don't you? It means plenty to you. It means something to me, too. I wish you'd let me try." He ducked his head, scowling. "I never had a home I can remember. Grew up with an uncle who allus drifted here and there. He never stuck long at anything, and I reckon I never did either. It ain't easy to say, but—"

"You want a job here?" Jonas broke in, reaching a decision quickly. "I'll give you one. You want to work your tail off for not much more'n your keep, you got it. And," he added, "you don't need to take on Diablo Red."

"I'll take the job. Thanks." Grif paused, then said stubbornly, "I'll ride that red horse, too. I want to."

"We'll see," Jonas said quietly.

Next day, they all assembled at the corral again.

Once more Jonas and Barney fought Diablo Red through the holding pen into the chute. His recalcitrance hadn't dimmed by a jot; if anything, his savage spirit had taken on a fresh edge. Finally they banged the gate on him, and Jonas climbed atop the chute. Barney handed up the Porter saddle, and Jonas dropped it on the pawing, grunting horse. Barney flipped the cinches through the bars under the animal's belly to Grif, who reached through the opposite side to grab them and whip the latigos through the rings. With the saddle laced up, the hackamore on and the hobble off, they were ready.

Jonas had put in some time coaching Grif. He added a cautioning word as he clambered down from the chute and Grif went up. "You mind what I told you. I give the word, you take a dive. Ain't no disgrace to it if a man's getting the worst. He can always come back and try again."

Grif gave a tight nod. Jonas knew what he was feeling: the fluttery knot in the pit of your stomach, the sharp last-minute misgiving and knowing you had to, all the same.

That was all right. What concerned him was how Grif would hang in. Jonas wanted the boy to make it: wanted it at least half as much as he wanted to see Diablo Red brought to taw. This was what came, he wryly supposed, of seeing your younger self in another man. Grif, he was sure had always followed a loose and easy path in all he did. Ordeal like this one could break just enough sap out of him one way and build his manhood just enough in another way . . . depending what the kid had in him to start with.

It might break his neck, too. But Grif had volunteered, he was going in with his eyes open. And it was a better alternative than his old life had allowed. If he returned to it (after sooner or later tiring of a placid, drudging interlude at Cross-B), he'd more than likely find an early death on a lonely trail. That worked-over gun told the story . . . .

Grif dropped into the saddle, shifted his butt around a little for a settled feel, and said tightly: "Let 'er go!"

Barney opened the gate.

Diablo Red came bucketing out with all his vinegar up. He pitched and spun and "pioneered" with a dizzying fury, and then he ran for the fence. Grif brought his leg up a second before the stallion's rump crashed against a rail, splitting it with a sound like a pistol shot.

Standing on the outside, Jonas realized—as he hadn't before—the animal's cruel intelligence, even in his frenzy, for gauging the feel of a rider: judging Grif's balance in the saddle, spinning abruptly in an effort to snap him off, even feinting runs at the fence.

Barney limped excitedly up and down, yelling advice: "Ride him high 'n' low boy! Watch out, he gonna double-shuffle you, look out for that fence, now! Don't let him sunfish on you, knock him down!"

Grif was still hanging on gamely as the stallion went into that savage pile-driver of his. But the boy was showing the strain, his body reacting sluggishly, his head snapping up and down. Blood burst from his nostrils.

"Take a jump!" Jonas roared. "You hear me, Grif? Get off him!"

But the youth hung on as Diablo Red switched again, racing around the dusty arena. Whatever he tried next would put the kid down for sure. Swearing bitterly, Jonas seized his rope and shook out a loop. At the same moment the horse sunfished for the first time, and Grif took a header over his shoulder. He crashed into the moiling dust and lay still.

Jonas ducked through the rails as Diablo Red thundered to the end of the corral and came back on the run, straight for the fallen boy. He squealed and reared up a scant six feet away from Grif.

Jonas underhanded a hooley-ann throw, a hasty cast that went true, popping up and over Diablo Red's fore-hoofs. Barney, coming in on the other side, sank his noose around the stallion's neck. Canted over by the pull of ropes from two directions, Diablo Red went down heavily on his side.

While they made him fast against the snubbing post, Mateo hauled Grif's limp form from the corral. The boy was still out cold, stretched on the ground with Mateo working over him, when Jonas and Barney came tramping over to them. Both Rainey and Manita wore looks of scared concern.

"Did he break anything, *Abuelito?*" the girl asked.

"He did not," Mateo growled. "We would not be that lucky."

"You are wicked to say that!"

The boy groaned and sat up, rubbing his head. Barney gave him a hand getting to his feet. Grif pulled away, walked unsteadily to the fence and leaned both hands on a rail, head down. Jonas followed him and grimly waited till Grif's glance pulled around toward him. The kid's face was pale, full of a wild, sullen anger.

"Want to get back on him?"

"Don't make fun of me, Mister! I don't like it!"

"I ain't making fun," Jonas said quietly. "I asked a civil question of you, boy."

"Maybe you want to see me killed, that it?" Grif snarled. "That damn devil horse of yours near—"

Jonas caught him by the shoulder and whirled him around so hard and fast that Grif's back slammed against the rails. Thrusting his face almost into the boy's, he said in a sight low voice, "Now you hear me, sonny boy, hear me good. You went in full of cocky steam and got dumped hard enough to knock some sense into you. Only it didn't. I told you to go down, and you didn't."

"I—"

"Shut your mouth, I'm talking. I gave you a choice with the horse. Now I'll give you a different one. You ducked out on a lot of things in your life, kid, ain't you? If it gets too rough, just walk out and give yourself some half-ass excuse. Or maybe you push that gun of yours under a better man's nose and figure that evens things up. In my book, it don't make you a man by half. That goddamn gun is just another easy out." He had an iron grip on Grif's arm, shaking him. "Not this time, kid. It's put up or shut up. Tomorrow you get on that horse again or you pack your warbag and clear out. Finish what you started or put your tail between your legs and run!"

White with anger, Grif jerked his arm free and walked away.

But he did not immediately pack and leave, as Jonas had expected. Nor did he say a word to anyone till next morning at breakfast: two sentences, soft and sullen.

"I'll do my best with the horse. I can't do no more."

"I judge you will," Jonas said in a neutral voice. In fact he was far from sure.

When Grif topped him this morning, Diablo Red dumped him inside of three crow hops. Grif climbed out of the dust with a bloody nose, and Jonas thought sinkingly that he'd lost his nerve altogether. But Grif said nothing at all, just grabbed a rope and helped them get the horse snubbed.

Then it was into the chute again and out of it, with Diablo Red pitching into the full range of his savage maneuvers. He was still bucking with an undiminished fury when Jonas yelled at Grif to get off. The kid took his fall, pawed his way out of the corral, and vomited for a half minute, then insisted on trying again. But he was so wobbly he could hardly stand, and Jonas called a halt for the day.

It was the start of a long and brutal week. After that first time Grif never offered a word of complaint. Each day he returned to the contest except for a couple of days when, battered and lame from head to foot, he had the sense to rest up and marshal his faculties. He was thrown countless times; each time he threw himself back into the fray with a dogged, redoubled zeal for as long as he could keep it up. Vomiting up most of his food and often unable to eat at all, he lost weight he could ill afford to spare, turning gaunt as a scarecrow. It seemed a sheer miracle that his limber young carcass, even given youth's second saving strength, could soak up all this punishment and keep coming back with nothing busted.

In all his experience, Jonas hadn't encountered such an instance of undiluted grit and guts. A dozen times he was on the verge of telling Grif to throw in the sponge —that he had proved whatever needed proving—but he didn't. Jonas sensed this was a task the youth had set himself for the deepest of reasons; nothing he could say would dent Grif's insensate determination. It was an arena of self-proving that belonged to a man's world governed by a man's code; you kept your mouth shut and let the other fellow do what he must.

For the same reason none of the men ever said a word of praise to Grif's face, but Barney said privately, laconically, "He getting his growth fast, that boy. He doing fine." And even Mateo Baca grunted a reluctant assent.

Nevertheless the daily strain told on them all to one degree or another, wearing tempers thin in this usually pleasant household. One evening Minita burst into tears and called Jonas a brute, then ran to her room crying. Passing a rougher judgment on himself, Jonas decided to allow one more day of it—then order Grif to quit.

One more day. One more fierce trial between man and horse. But it went differently. At the height of Diablo Red's routine of savage pitching, Grif disobeyed

Jonas's command to take a fall. He held on like a lean burr, blood spraying from his nose and mouth. At the same time, whether Grif had sensed it or not, something else was happening.

Without warning, suddenly and unbelievably, Diablo Red was breaking stride.

Even as his furious gyrations began to weaken, he was perceptibly staggering. And it was over almost before they knew it. The stallion came to a stop, legs braced and head down; dirty ropes of lather streamed from his flanks.

Grif wasn't even aware of it. He fell sideways and hit the dust face down. The men piled through the rails and pulled him to his feet, yelling and pounding his back.

"You done it, boy!" Barney crowed. "You done it! You whupped him!"

"What?" Grif lifted his head, his eyes staring out of focus. "Got to get back on . . . where is he?"

"You damn fool, you young *bobo!*" Mateo swore. "Where is your head? He is beat. You have beat him!"

Grif tried to straighten up, but his knees gave way. He bent against their supporting arms and was sick. Again he tried to pull himself erect and succeeded. He wiped a hand across his bloody face; his eyes found a hard focus on Jonas.

"That squares us, Mr. Bonner," he whispered.

Jonas nodded, grinning widely. "If you say so. What about it? You want to ride on, now your score's paid? Or you feel mean enough to be one of the family?"

Grif's gaze moved past all of them to Minita, and almost shyly he smiled. "I'll tell the world I do," he said.

Chapter Nine

SOMETHING had gone out of Diablo Red. Jonas felt its loss keenly and with a sense of regret, necessary as the breaking had been. They hadn't so much broken the stallion physically, he thought, as they had crowded him to some cruel acceptance of his fate.

Not a crushing of his spirit, no. But an irrevocable loss to his nature all the same. No way to make up, even partly for that deprivation except by patient and kindly treatment, and Jonas saw to it that the horse's taming continued along gentler lines. He spent all the time he could in Diablo Red's vicinity, getting him accustomed to his sight and smell, the sound of his voice. He talked to the horse as he would talk to a human comrade, making no attempt to ride him. He gave Grif the job of working him daily, training him to a rider's touch and command, under Jonas's own watchful eye.

The blood bay was the apple of Rainey's eye—and Diablo Red's first positive response to a human was his reaction to the boy, nosing up to the rail to take a hunk of sugar from his hand. Jonas encouraged his son's absorption with the animal, wanting to take Rainey's mind as much as possible away from the brewing situation with his mother that could change his whole life.

Welda's visit had wakened a pensive moodiness in the boy, making him really aware for the first time of a mother's reality. He would have liked to be with her now and then, he confided to Jonas, but he didn't want to live at Big Crown. Yet Jonas knew, with the troubled self-doubt of an introspective man, that Welda had spoken the simple truth when she'd charged him with having the advantage of familiarity. If Rainey had gone with her six years ago, no doubt his present allegiance would be to Welda.

What *was* best for Rainey? It annoyed Jonas, who liked to be damned sure of himself, that he had no certain answer. Not really.

What it boiled down to was that each of them wanted Rainey, possessively and, he supposed, jealously. He couldn't shake the unforgiving resentment he felt toward Welda's old, cold indifference—nor a conviction that it effectively canceled any "rights" she might claim. At times he wondered if he couldn't temporize with her and somehow reach an accommodation on Rainey's future that would be satisfactory to both of them and the boy too. Always his stubborn gorge rose to beat the idea down: Damned if he'd bargain for his own son as though he were a colt. Welda's cold intent to wrest Rainey away by legal chicanery was enough to shrivel any seed of compromise before it took root. And finally there was the hard admission that neither he nor Welda was the kind who'd make large concessions on anything that cut this close to the bone.

The day came for which Jonas had waited and dreaded, his day at a court hearing. And long before it was over, he knew he had lost.

The Canibar lawyers had their arguments thoroughly and skillfully marshaled, while Jonas had no recourse but to defend his own case—clumsily. It went exactly as King Canibar had predicted, every appearance of cold fact being relentlessly juggled to make him out an ignorant yokel, an irresponsible ne'er-do-well, and an unfit father. Burning with humiliation, he let his anger blaze out of control, told them all to go to hell, and stalked out of the courthouse.

By the time Jonas got back to Cross-B that afternoon, a grim fatalism had settled in him. Remembering King Canibar's matter-of-fact threat, he knew it would be worse than useless to fight. He'd lost a battle; why lose the whole damn war? If they wanted Rainey, they would have to come take him. To take him, they would have to find him . . . .

As he approached Cross-B headquarters, Jonas heard a popping of gunfire. Not knowing what to expect, he heeled Woboy into a run. Then, as the ranch buildings came into sight, he slowed to a trot, feeling a wash of relief.

Grif and Rainey were standing a little distance from the house. Having reloaded his pistol now, Grif fired as fast as he could at a litter of tin cans sixty yards off. Every shot sent a can bounding away. Jonas pulled up in surprise. It was a marvelous piece of shooting for the distance, considering the notorious inaccuracy of the ordinary Colt revolver.

Rainey was watching the exhibition with open-mouthed awe. Seeing his father now, he came running over to him as Jonas stepped out of the saddle. "Pa! Did we win?"

"No," Jonas said tersely. "I'll tell you about it later." He glanced at Grif as he came tramping up, punching the empty loads from his gun. "Getting in a little practice?"

"Mr. Bonner," Grif said soberly, "when I put this thing away last, I didn't figure ever to take it out again."

"Why did you?"

"Reckoned from how things been going, there might be a need. Seems that look on your face says it. You are going to need some help."

"Not that kind," Jonas said quietly. "You can put it away again, Grif."

"Whatever you say." Grif eyed him keenly. "What'll you do then? Won't the law be coming to fetch Rainey away?"

"They won't find him. Rainey and me are packing out of here tomorrow morning. We'll go up in the hills somewheres and make a cold camp. Will stay there till I figure something out. Might be we'll have to get clear out of the country. I don't know yet."

He told Grif and Rainey to assemble the gear and provisions that would be needed, for they would depart at first light tomorrow. Meantime, with a few hours of daylight left, Jonas headed for the corral. It had occurred to him, thinking of Diablo Red's great speed and endurance, that the stallion might be useful to have along. Once Rainey turned up missing, King Canibar would fill the hills with men to search for him: no telling what need might arise.

Jonas still hadn't essayed to mount the blood bay, and it was time for a trial run. So far, Diablo Red was used to one rider, Grif.

Jonas saddled the stallion and put a special twelve-foot rein on him, then led him out to the corral. Afterward he coiled the rein and thrust it into his belt; if Diablo Red elected to dump him, Jonas could grab the rein before he got away.

"All right, fella," he muttered. "Let's just see how you take to the *caporal*."

Seizing the cheek strap above the bit, he dragged the stallion's head around till it almost touched the saddle, leaving him unable to ruckus till Jonas was securely mounted.

Diablo Red left the ground in a flurry of rail-fence pitches that were easy to anticipate and meet. Jonas made no effort to control him, letting him exhaust his stock of ornery crow hops. Then he pulled the horse's head up, nudged him over to the gate, and reached down to open it. Bracing himself for anything, he gave the blood bay his head.

The stallion crow-hopped a little more, perhaps for a spine-jolting minute or so, then launched himself into a run. Jonas didn't try at all to check or guide him—not yet. This burst of energy was to be expected after the weeks of confinement. He felt a sudden confidence in his ability to curb the stallion once he had run his edge off.

Diablo Red lined into the open country, avoiding the pine-clad hills. All he cared about for the moment was running fast and free.

Then, as the horse settled into a steady mile-eating

stride, Jonas became aware of something incredible, something he'd never experienced. He had seen the stallion on a riderless run when he was still uncaught. It had excited him almost to envy: that effortless stretch of the horse's pace as if he were floating free, hardly touching the earth. But Jonas had never hoped or expected to learn the sensation firsthand.

Having come this far in his taming, Diablo Red could afford to ignore his burden of saddle and rider. He bore them like feathers. No, less: as if they didn't exist at all. Yet Jonas himself felt as though he were fused one-to-one with the surging roll of power under him, merging with the stallion's liberation of nerve and muscle as if it were his own.

A little recklessly now, he decided to put the blood bay to a sterner test. And test his own control at the same time. He applied the bit gently, and Diablo Red did not fight it. Good. Ahead and to their right was a stone outcrop about fence-height, and he headed the stallion directly at it. Diablo Red lifted up and over it so smoothly and effortlessly that he might have been flying. Jonas turned him gradually to the left now, putting his toward a rock slide that spilled down the flank of a steep hill.

The stallion's muscles gathered and surged, and they were climbing up, up, at an undiminished pace. There were footholds here and there on the shale slabs, and Diablo Red's hoofs sought them unerringly. God . . . what power! What a coordination of instinct and muscle! Even where there seemed no footholds at all, he advanced like an irresistable force. With a great bound he topped the slope and kept running. Jonas pulled him into a wide circle, down one slope and up another, till finally he was pointed for home.

Halfway there, Jonas pulled him from a run to a gallop, to a canter, to a trot and a walk, and finally to a halt. Diablo pulled up obediently and pawed the ground, tossing his head. Why, the old cuss, Jonas thought exultantly, he's having the time of his life. And so am I, by God.

He stepped to the ground, pulled a handful of grass, and gave the stallion's sweated coat a rubdown, working from his neck and back down to his cannons and fetlocks. Diablo Red didn't so much as shift a foot; he stood quietly, giving a restless grunt or two, as Jonas picked up his feet one by one, inspecting his hoofs for sand cracks and the frogs for stone bruises.

"Just fine," Jonas murmured, patting his arched neck. "You're my horse and I'm your man. Ain't so much owning . . . it's more like belonging. And you know it too, don't you? By God, you do know it."

Mounting again, he headed the stallion south at an easy lope, but reined in abruptly. Two riders were coming over the brow of a nearby hill, coming fast, and they were already so close that he recognized Grif and Barney Blue at once.

Trouble. Jonas knew it in his bones before they pulled their horses to a lathered stop in front of him.

"They taken him, *caporal!*" Barney said harshly. "They done taken your boy—"

"What?"

"The sheriff and a pair o' deputies. They come in waving this paper and said it was a court order authorized 'em to take Rainey with 'em. Judge done turned him over to his ma, they said . . . ."

Jonas raised his knotted fist two inches from his pommel. "And you let 'em?" he said incredulously. "You let 'em take—"

"Mr. Bonner, we took the gospel like you read it," Grif cut in softly. "No gunplay. No way we could stop 'em otherwise, was there? They was law and they had paper to show their right. I read it, and it sure looked in order."

Jonas groaned. "All right—all right." He dropped his fist to the pommel. "How long ago?"

"Right after you left," Barney said. "They rode in and took him away on a horse they brung. Didn't take 'em five minutes. Didn't even leave the boy time to collect his things. Reckon from how they was armed, shotguns and all, they 'spected a mighty ruckus from you. Counted 'emselves lucky you was away and wa'n't about to wait on you. They wa'n't letting no moss grow, that's sure. Looked like they'd pushed their hosses blamed hard."

"Can't of got far, even so—" Jonas pointed at the rifle booted under Barney's knee. "Give me that."

Wordlessly Barney pulled his Winchester from its scabbard and handed it over. Jonas quartered Diablo Red around, and Barney and Grif promptly hauled alongside him. He yanked to a halt and regarded both of them flat-eyed.

"This ain't your set-to. Stay out of it."

"Mr. Bonner, if you aim to fight now—"

"Now I got no choice. But you men ain't buying in, neither of you. I am going to draw lightning after today, and I ain't drawing it on nobody else. *Stay out of it!*"

Diablo Red lunged ahead at a touch of his heels, and Jonas didn't look back. Even if they followed, he would easily distance them, and he gave no more thought to the matter.

He set a beeline for where the bridge crossed the Washoe River on his west boundary. Better than even chance he could cut ahead of the sheriff's party at that point. If he couldn't, he should overtake them in short order.

Damn! Again he groaned aloud, hammering a fist against his thigh. He should have guessed at something like this. Knowing he wouldn't passively accept their victory, King and Welda would have anticipated that he might try to spirit Rainey away before their men came to take him. Once the decision had been declared in their favor, the proper document readied, Canibar would have urged the sheriff to move at once. And Herb Retlaw wasn't a man slow to act when urged by the powers that be.

The ground was a racing blur of green and tan under the stallion's hoofs; the wind tore at their bodies. Diablo Red's ability to cross difficult terrain was now worked to the full as Jonas guided him up and down valleys and hogbacks, holding as well as he could on a straight line for the river crossing. They slammed through tangles of brush and breasted treacherous slides. The stallion's raw power, communicated to his rider, lifted in Jonas like an angry banner.

A red, ungovernable rage flamed in his head. He wasn't thinking any more, not of what he might do, not of the consequences. Of nothing except that his son, his flesh and blood, was going out of his hands.

It don't work that way, Welda. It don't work that way at all!

Diablo Red boiled with undiminished speed onto the crown of the final hill, and Jonas brought him up hard. Swiftly he scanned the rollaway of country beyond. To his right the Washoe cascaded down its narrow cut; the bridge he and his crew had laid across it was perhaps a hundred yards downstream. Brush and trees made a dense screen between this hill and the road, but he saw at once the four riders following the rutted switchbacks toward the bridge.

Without hesitation, Jonas poured down the hill and sent the stallion in a reckless crashing run through the brush, twisting between the tree boles. He heard a thud of shod hoofs on the bridge, and then he broke free of the brush and swerved onto the road.

Sheriff Retlaw and his deputies had reached the far side of the bridge. Now they turned, facing him across it. The bull-shouldered Retlaw and one deputy, a nervous, sallow-faced youth named Jurgen, sat their horses in front of Rainey and the other deputy, a man Jonas didn't recognize. This one had a secure hold on the bridle of Rainey's mount.

Retlaw lifted a shotgun from his pommel. "Hold it there, Bonner!" he shouted above the roar of water.

Deliberately Jonas nudged Diablo Red forward onto the bridge, holding the rifle pointed upward. Seeing both Retlaw and Jurgen tensing up then, he halted. Jurgen's rifle was already bearing on him.

"Your boy's in line!" Retlaw bellowed at him. "Don't be a fool!"

The stubborn fury beat in waves against Jonas's brain, and now, slowly, he brought the Winchester down to line on Retlaw's broad chest. He'd never be sure of what he might have done next, for as his rifle ended its downward arc, Jurgen fired.

Jonas felt a clubbing blow in his right leg.

He heard the sheriff yell, "Goddam you, Jurg!" and then the world went pinwheeling out of control as Diablo Red shied and reared, pitching Jonas sideways. He felt himself leave the saddle, and now the bridge timbers seemed to rush up and slam him in the face.

He wasn't aware of rolling and falling again and hitting water. Not till the Washoe's choking rush closed over his head. The icy water shocked him to his senses, but already he was being borne away on the churning, plunging current, swept along like a cork.

Dimly he heard Rainey cry out, but that and the rake of pain in his leg were lost in a tumult of strangling water as the current bowled him over and over. Jonas struck out wildly with arms and legs, fighting to keep his head up. He was ducked many times, his strength ebbing away, before the downrush of water leveled out somewhat. Even then, the river's force carried him irresistibly onward.

No question of striking for shore. He had all he could do to keep from being drowned or battered against the great smooth-sided boulders of the riverbed. Time and again his feet scraped bottom; he seized at rocks to break his momentum, but his hands skidded off their slick surfaces. Twisted and flung helplessly this way and that, he caught a glimpse of the bridge and the men on it looking tiny and distant now. Then he was swept around a bend, and the bridge was lost to sight. The water's chill was eating to his marrow, and he could no longer feel his arms and legs; he was hardly aware of the impacts as his body slammed against rocks.

Brought hard against a protruding outcrop, Jonas grabbed at it blindly and clung to it, letting his head clear. Other rocks reared above the water between here and shore, and maybe he could pull himself that far. Putting all his will behind a desperate residue of strength, he worked from one outcrop to the next while the water raged about him shoulder-high, threatening to rip away his numbed holds.

Finally he reached the last rock, plunged into three feet of roiling shallows, and fell. He doubled his legs under him and heaved himself upright. The water surged to his hips, but he swayed into its force, floundered to the steep bank, and grabbed at some overhanging willows. Hand over hand, he hauled himself onto the bank and fell face down, legs trailing in the water.

Jonas lay that way a while, mustering his strength. Then he dragged himself higher onto the bank and crawled into the brush . . . .

Chapter Ten

BREAKFAST at Big Crown's main house was rarely what you'd call a convivial affair. None of the Canibars were at their best early in the day, and this morning was no exception. If anything, Meg thought, they were more short-spoken with one another than usual. She had always taken this state of things for granted, till she'd learned with some surprise, while living with her mother's relatives in the East, that people could actually be civil upon rising. It had given Meg a kind of outsider's perspective on her family. She now got a certain cross-grained amusement out of watching the usual breakfast byplay.

Phil and Welda, for instance. Welda despised her brother-in-law's foppish and dependent ways; Phil, on his part, was bitterly jealous of Welda's influence with King.

Most of the time they masked their mutual dislike, treating each other with an ironic politeness. At breakfast it wasn't unusual for them to show each other a veiled contempt that fell just short of open insult. Only the presence of King, himself uncongenial at this hour and not about to brook any discord at table, kept his wife and brother somewhat in check.

The rest of the family was already seated in the big dining room this morning when King entered. He muttered a good morning, took his place at the head of the table, and tucked his napkin in his belt, swinging around a glance at his wife, sister, brother, and father.

"Where's the boy? Passing up breakfast again?"

"He isn't hungry," Welda said coolly. "We can hardly force him to eat."

King grunted, reaching for the platter of ham and eggs. "All the same, he could come to table. I'm getting a mite fed up with his sulking."

"Well honestly, what do you *expect?* It's been only a week since—"

"I know, I know," King said irritably.

Old Sam Canibar, drowning his perennial hangover in black coffee, tipped a sly, bloodshot glance at his son. "You done for his pap, Lenny. That's how he sees it. Might be a spell getting over that. Iffen he ever does."

King attacked his food, ignoring the old man as usual.

There was no love lost between them—never had been that Meg could remember. Why King kept their father around at all, much less tolerated his blunt and unwelcome observations, was a mystery to her. Phil thought it was because King needed a perverse reminder of what he'd raised himself above: a childhood of rootless poverty spent in the wake of a father who was the constant shame of his family. Drifting from one place to another, never holding a job long, going on periodic drunks. Living down that disgrace had driven King all his life, Phil opined. Older than his brother and sister, King had been the one deeply affected by all of it. (In fact Meg had no such memories of her own. By the time she was born, the teen-aged Leonard had been supporting their family and, for all purposes, was the family head.)

After a moment's silence broken only by the rattle of dishware, Meg said dryly, "Well, does anyone care to comment on that little matter? Who *is* to blame for Jonas Bonner's death?"

King swung his head up, angrily. "Look, nobody wanted that. He resisted the law and got shot for it. He was armed with a Winchester and he was set to use it and the deputy shot to wound him. Then that crazy horse of his threw him in the river. That's how Retlaw told it."

"Fine," Meg said in the same dry voice. "The fact remains that if certain parties hadn't effected, by not altogether overhanded means, to take his son away, it wouldn't have happened."

King pointed his fork at her and shook it, saying ominously, "All right, now. I don't want to hear another damn word about that. If I do, I'm going to take it a certain smart-mouthed party is tired of her nice, soft berth at Big Crown and hankers for a change."

Meg smiled and inclined her head with a mocking diffidence, satisfied to have given him a small needling.

"But she's right, King," Welda said quietly. "We've neither of us been willing to say it and it's there between us; it's making both of us snappish. Meg, will you believe me when I say I'm sorry about Rainey's father? That I didn't want or expect anything like that?"

"I believe you, dear," Meg said with only a mild irony. "But it's not me you have to convince, it's your son. Anyway, I'm forbidden to discuss the matter."

"Personally," Phil put in, "I doubt that damn Indian *is* dead."

King stabbed up a forkful of ham and stowed it in his mouth. "The sheriff's men and my whole crew and Bonner's own men hunted up and down the river for him," he growled as he chewed. "We didn't find him, and there's been no word he's turned up, dead or alive."

Phil raised a finger. "Ah," he smiled. "Your key phrase, dear brother, is *he hasn't turned up*. Long as no body's found, there's a fifty-fifty chance he didn't drown at all. That he's lying low somewhere."

"Why the hell would he?"

"Well now, he might just have his reasons."

Welda kneaded her underlip between her teeth, saying nothing, and Meg guessed that the same possibility had been weighing on her mind.

"He'll turn up sooner or later," King said musingly. "Alive or dead, I don't much give a damn. Except on the boy's account. If Bonner's dead, we're going to have a long-term problem with that kid."

Old Sam gave Meg a sober wink. "Sounds like somep'n I said, don't it?"

Meg winked back. "Sorry, Pa. I'm forbidden to comment."

King brought his massive fist crashing on the table. "*Shut up*, all of you! Christ, can't a man eat his breakfast in peace?"

Meg said sweetly, "I won't upset your digestion any further," as she finished her coffee and rose from the table.

Phil gave her riding costume with its divided skirt a sardonic look. "You going for a ride, old sister, or planning to join a circus?"

"Thanks for the thought. A few women besides circus performers *are* wearing these outfits now."

Phil grinned maliciously. "Who, the chippies?"

"Thanks again, dear." She batted her eyes solemnly. "You do have a gift for the delicate phrase."

King directed a warning "harrumph" at them both, and Meg laughed and strolled outside, heading for the corral. The morning was clear and cool. She glanced at the small watch pinned to her shirtwaist and thought: Good, I should get there just about the right time.

Frank Dance was lounging by the corral picking his teeth as she came up. Meg had the fleeting uncomfortable thought that this was the third morning in a row he'd been idling in the same spot when she showed up to claim her mare.

Dance straightened up, quirked a warped grin at her, and said politely, "Right on time, eh, Missy? Be glad to saddle Blazes for you."

As usual, Meg thought, and thanked him coldly.

There was nothing untoward in the man's speech or look, but she was convinced he'd chosen this way to discomfit her: pointedly appearing each morning with his battered face from which the scars of his beating hadn't yet faded. Ostensibly she had no grounds for complaint; all he ever did was offer assistance with her horse. But she knew that Dance, with his fanatical pride in his rock-hard strength, hadn't forgotten and would never forget that she'd baited him into that fight with Jonas Bonner.

Not that she regretted it in the least. Aside from Dance's brutality to animals, the sly and cruel delight he took in his behavior had always repelled her. So, at the time, had his battle with Bonner. She'd witnessed tussles between men, but nothing at all like that one: two powerful men out for blood, smashing each other to insensibility. Yet, in retrospect, and with no small satisfaction, she could admit that she reveled in the memory of Dance's punishment.

Dance led out the mare and held her while Meg mounted. Then she swung away without a word to Dance or a glance at him, turning northeast across the roll of green-grass hills.

It was a good day for a ride, and Meg enjoyed it to the full, along with the feel of free wind on her face and Blazes' smooth canter under her. A few days ago she had taken a fresh step in female emancipation by switching to a man's stock saddle, and it was a whole new experience in riding. It must have been a man, she thought wryly, who had dreamed up those blasted sidesaddles. She laughed softly, reaching down to pat Blazes' neck and murmur foolishness in her ear. Above all she was happy to be out with her favorite horse. It had been touch and go with Blazes after Bonner and his men had recovered her and the other mares—King threatening to have all three destroyed in order to obviate any risk of Diablo Red's "crazy blood" getting into his stock. Only the vehemence of Meg's protest had forestalled him.

Meg drew rein on a hill above Twelve-Mile Pasture, where Big Crown's stallion, Alacrán, was grazing with his harem.

Always alert to any intruder on his domain, the great black horse came circling to this side of the *manada* and watched Meg and Blazes with up-pricked ears. He was familiar with both of them; there was no alarm to his posture. Alacrán tossed his head and gave a short bugling note, to which Blazes made a soft response. If King were with them, the stallion would have come straight up to them, Meg knew. Nobody but King ever rode him, which seemed fitting. Alacrán was a *criollo*, descended from pure Spanish stock, and Meg smiled at his lordly assumptions, so like his master's. An aging lord now, but still undisputed in his own realm, and Meg could understand King's feeling for the animal. At the same time she couldn't help contrasting it to Jonas Bonner's regard of Diablo Red: alike yet different. She thought Bonner's way was the better—if a man could afford such indulgences.

Pulling off the hill now, Meg pointed Blazes northeast once more. After riding for an hour, always taking her bearings by the pinnacle shape of Castle Rock directly to the north, she came up on a windswept crag where a few stunted cedars had taken root. She tied Blazes in the trees, checked the time on her watch-pin, and took the field glasses from her saddlebag. Afterward she moved onto a ledge that tipped off the crag's steep flank and stretched out on the sun-warm rock on her stomach. Putting the glasses to her eyes, she trained them on the long expanse of Deercreek Meadow to the east.

Perhaps ten minutes later, she saw a horseman taking his way south to north across the meadow. She focused the binoculars, knowing even before she identified the man that he was Barney Blue. She followed him till he was lost to sight on a timbered slope.

Meg rose to her feet, a thoughtful smile on her lips. Barney had come from the direction of Bonner's Cross-B, but he was 'way off Cross-B range. She was now certain beyond a doubt that no ordinary ranch business had brought him here.

For this was the third time he had ridden exactly this

way at the same time of morning. Meg had first spotted Barney by chance five days ago, while she was out riding this way. Since this was a favorite of hers, it had been no trouble to check again at the same time, next day. She had watched from the crag for an hour and had seen nothing. But the third day, prompted by an unbidden hunch, she had watched again and had spotted him once more. On the fourth day, yesterday, nothing. And now on the fifth day, Barney had shown up again. He'd come this way three times at two-day intervals, each time with a bulky pack lashed to his cantle.

Certainly interesting, Meg mused. But aside from having her suspicion almost surely confirmed, she didn't know exactly what she might do about it.

Perhaps nothing at all. For now.

She arrived back at Big Crown headquarters a little before noon.

As she rode toward the corral, Meg noticed Rainey Bonner by the tack shed. He was sitting on his heels, back to the shed wall, arms folded on his knees. He was the picture of listless and lonely dejection, and she felt a swift sympathy.

Meg found David Crow at the corral and turned Blazes over to him, then walked over to the tack shed. Rainey looked up at her approach, then looked away indifferently. She didn't blame him: what was she to him but another of the enemy?

" 'Lo there. Mind if I join you?"

The boy's eyes turned down; he shrugged his shoulders.

Meg dropped on her heels beside him and settled her back against the wall. She plucked a grass stem and split it with her thumbnail and blew into it, producing a squeaky whistle. Rainey glanced at her, his green eyes defiant and sullen, and she said: "Can you do that?"

He squirmed his shoulders in another shrug.

"Stand up to them, Rainey," Meg said quietly. "Don't let 'em get you down. I never do."

"You," he muttered. "Huh."

"Let me tell you something. Will you listen? I think what your mother and my brother did was wrong."

"I bet."

"I do. Dead wrong."

His eyes probed her face mercilessly, and then he burst out: "I hate them!"

"I hate what they did," she said carefully. "Taking you away from your pa. But they didn't mean to get your pa hurt. And maybe he didn't drown in that river, you know. They didn't find him. I wouldn't be surprised if he's very much alive."

"Then where is he?"

"Maybe lying low somewhere. You know? Sort of biding his time."

"You think so?"

"I wouldn't say so otherwise."

Momentarily she debated whether to tell him what she had seen: that she was almost dead sure Jonas was alive. But suppose she was wrong? The worst thing she could do would be to buoy up his hopes for a cruel letdown.

Rainey said suddenly: "Did you like my pa?"

She smiled wryly. "Well, I can't say we have the greatest friendship the sun shines on. But I think he's a man deserving of respect. And he's sure enough in the right, at least I believe so."

"Honest Injun?" he demanded.

Meg laughed and raised her right hand. "Honest. What

do I have to do, cut my arm and sign my name in blood?" At his puzzled frown, she added, "Didn't you ever play pirate or outlaw? You know, take the oath of blood brotherhood, swear on your life, and all that?"

He shook his head, still puzzled, and Meg remembered that his backwoods life couldn't have allowed any contacts with youngsters his own age. "All the boys in my neighborhood did. So did I. Told 'em I'd tell on 'em if they didn't let me take the oath too." After a pause, she said tentatively, "You might like going to school here in the Basin. You'd meet a lot of kids, make friends . . . get to know all those things."

His face began to close up, and she said quickly, "But I suppose it was mighty fine living where you were. Wasn't it? I bet you got to do a lot of things. Do you like to ride?"

"Ride" was the key word: it opened a spillgate.

Rainey was by nature an outgoing youngster, swift to give trust and confidence, and he warmed to a flood of memories, talking quickly. Of Mr. Baca and all the things he had to tell you and teach you. Of Barney Blue and Minita and Grif. And glowing-eyed of his father and how they had caught Diablo Red. How Grif had broken the stallion and Pa had trained him and there was nothing like him, no horse in the world like Diablo Red. Listening, Meg thought enviously: Lord, but those people must be a contented crew. Happy with each other and what they've got, even if it isn't much.

She saw, though, that the boy was blinking rapidly, his voice sinking. The memories were too much, they belonged to what had been and was no more, might never be again, and they hurt uncontrollably.

Cudgeling her mind now, Meg had an inspiration.

"Rainey, how would you like to have Diablo Red right here?"

"Here?"

"Yes, brought to Big Crown and kept here for you. How would that strike you?"

His eyes blinked hard, going wide and tearfully fierce. "Do you mean it?"

"Honest Injun." She added quickly, "I can't promise anything, you understand. But I will go to bat for you with my brother—I'll argue with him till I'm blue in the face."

And you will be, too, ran her wry thought.

Twenty minutes later King Canibar had heard all her arguments and was arguing back. He strode up and down the parlor floor, raking one hand through his thinning hair, a scowl on his face. Meg had adroitly enlisted Welda on her side before approaching him, and the two women sat on the sofa listening to King angrily sum up his objections.

"I don't want a crazy-wild stud like that on the place," he declared flatly. "Not unless he's gelded. His pa was dead set against it and you can bet the boy will be too."

"Probably," Meg agreed. "But Diablo Red has been tamed, Rainey says. That doesn't square very well with your 'crazy blood' notion . . . but I've heard quite a few people, you included, say that nobody could touch Jonas Bonner when it came to training horses."

"It's true," Welda put in swiftly. "King, at least give it a chance, can't you? If we do this for Rainey, perhaps he can stop hating us. Oh Lord, I want that so much!"

The intensity of her plea held King mute for a moment. Then he growled. "The horse is Bonner's and we ain't sure Bonner's not alive. We can't just waltz up to Cross-B and take him."

"We can ask, for heaven's sake!" Meg said with asperity. "Would it tax your almighty pride so much to *ask?*"

"Go easy, Sister. I am getting a bellyful of your sharp talk."

With an effort Meg swallowed her impatience. "I apologize," she said gently. "Look, all I'm asking is let *me* go to Cross-B and put the request to Bonner's men. If they understand it's for the boy's good, I'm sure they'll be agreeable."

"I don't know," King grumbled. "We'd have to keep that damn horse away from Alacrán . . . . It'd make a sight of trouble or I miss my guess."

"It's up to you, of course," Meg said calmly. "But it may be your only way to the boy. He worships Diablo Red. The *only* way, Lenny. I'd think about that."

"Dammit, I am thinking!"

"Please, King," Welda murmured.

Still frowning, hands clasped at his back, King paced a slow circle of the rug. Meg watched a slow resignation touch his heavy face, and finally he nodded.

"All right," he said abruptly. "Done. But only if Bonner's people are willing. Been enough trouble stirred up with Cross-B; I don't want any more. Understand? If they turn thumbs down, there's an end of it."

Chapter Eleven

WHEN Jonas heard the horseman approaching the cabin, he raised on one elbow and looked at Grif. The youth was dipping into the sourdough crock for biscuit fixings. Meeting Jonas's glance now, he nodded, wiped his hands clean, and picked up the pistol he kept close at hand. Then he walked to the puncheon door which stood slightly ajar, and peered out.

"Barney coming," he said laconically.

"Something must of come up," Jonas muttered. "He ain't due again till tomorrow."

He settled himself on his back again and carefully straightened a cramp out of his right leg, steeling himself against the knife of pain. The leg was coming along, all right, but it still hurt like hell at any movement. You couldn't take a 45–70 slug clean through the big muscle of your thigh without a lot of nerve and tissue damage that would be a long time healing.

Since the grip of fever had passed, each day had been an ordeal of boredom, bitter thoughts, and a quiet raging against his helplessness. It was all Jonas could do not to show the brunt of his temper to Grif, who had patiently tended to all his needs for over a week now.

He'd tried to counter the blackness of his mood by telling himself he was damned lucky at that.

After leaving the river, he had fixed a stick and bandanna tourniquet on his leg and crawled back into the brush, laying up in a vantage from where he could watch the sheriff and his deputies combing along the riverbank for any trace of him. Minutes later, Barney and Grif had arrived on the scene and joined the search. It was Barney whose tracker's eye had spotted the faint signs Jonas had left when he'd pulled himself from the water. Correctly assuming he didn't want to be found by the sheriff, Barney and Grif had waited till Retlaw and his men had given up the search and gone on to Big Crown with Rainey. By the time the two men reached his side, Jonas was nearly unconscious from the pain of his wound. Be he'd had enough left to order them, against all their arguments, not to take him back to Cross-B.

At best he'd had only a half-formed notion of how it might work for him, but he was dead sure of one thing: he wanted everyone outside of Cross-B to believe he was lost in the river. That was important, he'd insisted. They were to take him to an old trapper's cabin, long abandoned, back in the Buckhorn Hills; Barney knew where it was. So they had rigged a horse drag and tied him on it. While Grif returned to Cross-B to apprise the Bacas of what had happened and fetch some medicine and fixings for his injury, Barney began the long trek to the Buck-horns, making many stops to check Jonas's condition. Each time he'd tried to argue the *caporal* out of continuing this long and painful haul, and each time Jonas, clinging to ravels of consciousness, had overruled him. Jonas was clean out of his head by sunset when they made a halfway camp at a predetermined spot upriver, where Grif rejoined them. Next afternoon they reached the cabin. Here, before surrendering to the big onslaught of his fever, Jonas had given his men final orders: Grif was to stay with him; Barney, whose absence from the ranch would be more noticed, was to go back to Cross-B and return here every two days with such grub and medicine as might be needed, but more particularly to fetch any news.

So far there hadn't been any to speak of. Maybe . . . .

Barney dismounted and entered the cabin, said a grave hello to Grif and came over to Jonas's bunk, plunking himself on a bench beside it. "Well, *caporal*, I got a piece o'-something for you. We done had a visit this morning from Mr. Canibar's sister her own self."

"Is that right," Jonas said impatiently. "She bring any word about Rainey?"

"She tell us the boy is mighty unhappy, but I didn't count that no news. 'Peared to me she was trying to dig out anything we might know for sure 'bout you, but we-all kept purely mum."

Jonas was silent for a reflective moment, and then he said: "Canibar could be wondering how dead I am. Like as not he sent his sister to nose around. You got to be wary, Barney. You could get followed here." —

Barney shrugged. "Allus kept an eye peeled on my

backtrail, can't do no more'n that. Good tracker could pick me up, I reckon."

Jonas nodded wearily. "That's so. She tell you anything else?"

Briefly Barney told him the why—according to her—of Meg Canibar's mission to Cross-B. She wanted their consent to have Diablo Red brought to Big Crown, stressing this was for Rainey's sake. "I hazard that's so, *caporal*. Boy sets a heap o' store by that red horse."

"What did you tell her?"

"Tol' her we'd need a day to think it over. She say she'll come back tomorrow." Barney's forehead puckered worriedly. "She a sharp one, that missy. Might o' guessed we would delay to ask you the what-for, 'pending you was alive. Wonder if mebbe I was follered just now."

"Well," Jonas said grimly, "it's no great shucks if you was, except I hope to keep the Canibars in the dark that I'm still kicking. I'll do what I got to even if they know I am, but it'll be harder to manage."

"You'll do what you gotta for certain," Barney agreed soberly. "That Canibar lady comes back, what do I say about Diablo Red?"

"Tell her you decided he's Rainey's horse now. If he's fetched to Big Crown, it ought to pick the boy up some."

"Would do him a heap more good to know his pappy is alive, *caporal*."

Jonas nodded. "That's why you're going to fetch Diablo Red to Big Crown yourself. It will give you a chance for a word with Rainey . . . . "

When Meg Canibar returned to Big Crown next day, she was accompanied by Barney Blue leading Diablo Red. All the Canibars were on hand to view the reunion between Rainey and the red stallion. Diablo Red was a little skittish at this strange place and a crowd of strange people; he grunted nervously and fiddlefooted against the lead rope fastened to Barney's saddle. The afternoon sun shimmered red-gold on his coat.

Frank Dance and David Crow stood a short distance away, watching.

"Man, that's a horse," the half-breed said admiringly. "I never figured to see him this close up."

Dance said nothing. He rolled an unlighted cigarette from one corner of his thick mouth to the other, studying the stallion through half-lidded eyes. Bonner's stallion. Just the thought sent a pulse of hatred through his guts.

Barney stepped out of his saddle and replied with a broad grin to Rainey's excited greeting. "Good to see you, too, young 'un. Here's your horse for you."

As the boy started boldly toward Diablo Red, Welda said anxiously: "Be careful!"

The stallion promptly quieted as Rainey spoke to him; he extended his snout to lip a hunk of sugar from Rainey's outstretched hand.

"He got his edge took off for sure," David Crow observed. "Even you got to admit it, Frank. That Bonner had some touch with horseflesh."

"I never said the bastard didn't," Dance growled.

King Canibar gave Barney a curt nod. "Blue."

"Howdy, Mr. Canibar. Thought it best I fetch the horse here myself. He mighta ruckused some if strangers brung him in."

"Good thought. But he might's well start getting used to all of us." King glanced toward Dance and David Crow. "You fellows take him over to the breaking corral. We'll keep him there for the time being. And Frank," he added warningly, "you be easy with him, hear? He belongs to Rainey."

"*Bueno*," Dance grinned, thinking as he moved forward at his bouncy rolling stride: Sure, boss-man. Anything to get you on the little bastard's good side, huh?

Barney dropped an arm around Rainey's shoulders. "You be having plenty o' time with Diablo Red, young 'un. S'pose you 'n' me talk a little bit 'fore I head back. Want to know how things is doing at Cross-B, don't you?"

The two of them moved off at a slow walk, Barney talking quietly to the boy, as Dance laid hold of the stallion's leadrope and David Crow unhitched it from the saddle. Diablo Red's eyes rolled toward Dance; he shuffled away and laid back his ears.

Phil Canibar chuckled, tapping ash off his long nine. "Boy howdy, if he hasn't taken a pure un-fancy to you already, Frank. Sort of hate at first sight. You have to admire the critter's taste, though."

"Phil," King said flatly, "put a lid on it, will you? All right, men, move him along slow, don't get him excited."

David Crow talked quietly in the Cheyenne tongue, horse-calming words, as he took hold of the rope close to the stallion's head. Gently he pulled Diablo Red into motion. They led him across the dusty compound toward the working side of the headquarters.

Diablo Red nervously followed their lead, not balking till they reached the gate of the breaking corral. Here he planted his feet and refused to enter. Dance swore and yanked on the rope, and Diablo Red pulled back, almost jerking both men off balance.

"Son of a bitch!" Dance said savagely. "Come on, damn if I'll coddle you, get in there!"

"Quit it, Frank!" David Crow said sharply. "You get

him riled, we'll have hell's own time with him. Let me handle this."

"Injun boy," Dance said softly, "don't you rile *me* now. Come on, you red bastard, come on!"

They dragged Diablo Red halfway through the gate and then he balked solidly, twisting his head aside and back. Swearing steadily, Dance seized the rope close to his mouth. The stallion squealed and reared, striking out with his forehoofs.

One of them struck Dance a glancing blow. The world spun away; he felt himself falling and that was all.

When he came to, he was stretched on his back outside the pen. He sputtered; water was dribbling over his face.

David Crow stepped back, letting his hand with the empty dipper fall to his side. Dance crawled slowly to his feet, shaking his head; drops of blood flew from it. He clapped a hand to his head and grunted with pain. The cut angled from his scalp to his left eyebrow; it had laid his forehead open to the bone.

Dance dug out a dirt-crusted bandanna and scrubbed at the blood streaming down his face, then held the bandanna over the gash. He turned a long, slow look on Diablo Red who was inside the pen now, the gate closed and secured. Dance's thumb nudged the whip coiled on a hook at his belt.

"Don't think about it, Frank," David Crow said quietly, adding as Dance's gaze swung toward him: "You asked for what you got. I'll tell it that way if need be."

Dance drawled thickly, "Of late you have got right talky for an Injun boy."

"You be surprised just how talky I can get."

David Crow's stare was flat and uncompromising, and

Dance met it a moment longer, then gave a mild shrug. "Let's say my foot slipped and I fetched my head agin' a post, all right?"

"We'll say that."

"Sure. Now I be obliged if you do a mite o' sewing on me."

Shortly after dusk, Dance returned to the pen.

He opened the gate and closed it behind him, talking soft and easy as he approached the stallion, a hackamore in his hand. In the gray darkness Diablo Red stirred restively, gave a short whicker, and turned away, rounding the fence at a trot, keeping a measured distance away from Dance.

This was going to take time, Dance knew. That was all right. He ought to have plenty of it. The corral was located well away from the bunkhouse, and nobody would be stirring out at this hour.

He had allayed David Crow's alertness with friendly talk when they had gone together to Dance's shanty. After the half-breed had sewed up his forehead, Dance had expressed his gratefuls by producing a bottle which they passed back and forth. David Crow had been pretty unsteady when, an hour later, the cook's triangle had summoned them to supper. Full of food and booze, he would be snoring in his bunk by now.

Dance laughed softly. Wasn't an Injun alive had a head for likker. Him, he had already finished off another bottle and—in spite of a pounding headache—was riding a feeling of heady, reckless strength. By damn, he could wrassle giants right now.

Slow and easy does it, he thought, moving unhurriedly after the stallion's dark circling form. Talking always in a low encouraging voice, most of it obscenities. His tone and manner were getting to the horse; he continued to retreat, but Dance could feel the wariness going out of him.

Dance grinned in the darkness. "You going to be all right," he sing-songed mildly, "you going to be just fine." And he would be, too. If you had the touch for it, you could use a whip to comb over any critter from a man to a mouse and never leave a mark except in the heart of him.

At last the stallion stood tensely quiet. He let the man fit the hackamore on him and fasten him tight against the snubbing post.

Stepping back then, Dance took the whip from his belt and slowly uncoiled it. "Now you red son of a bitch," he murmured. "It's all between you 'n' me."

Chapter Twelve

NEXT morning after breakfast, Meg and Rainey left the house together and headed for the breaking corral. Meg had to marvel at the change in Rainey since the arrival of Diablo Red. He was like a different boy, chatting and laughing and bright-eyed, eager to see his horse. Remembering his long and earnest talk with Barney Blue, she shrewdly wondered if the stallion were the whole reason for his high spirits.

As they neared the pen, Rainey said suddenly: "Meg, how would you like to ride Diablo Red?"

"Me? Why, I'd love to . . . if you mean it, Rainey."

"Sure." He added wistfully, "I'd sure like to get on him myself, but Mother doesn't think I should. Not just yet."

Mother. He and Welda were talking together now. That was a change for certain.

"I don't want just anyone riding him," Rainey said seriously. "I thought maybe you'd want to."

"I do," Meg said, and meant it. "I've wanted to from the moment I first saw him."

But something wasn't right. She saw it even as Rainey approached the gate: Diablo Red's tense stance and the wicked roll of his eyes.

"Wait a minute, Rainey. I wouldn't go in there just yet."

Rainey halted, eying the stallion carefully. "Gosh," he said softly. "He's like he was after we caught him. What's the matter, boy? Don't you know me?"

He reached an arm through the rails and Diablo Red trotted swiftly to the fence. Rainey yanked his arm quickly back; the stallion's long neck reached; his teeth snapped.

The boy's spirits sank like a stone. He looked at Meg, his lips quivering. "What happened with him? This is a strange place and all, but he wouldn't change just like that. Would he?"

"I don't know," Meg said slowly. "The change might have spooked him a bit. Let's don't tell anyone about this. We'll stay close to him all we can, you and I, and we'll talk to him. Maybe we can get him over it. Let's try."

That was how it went for the next three days. The two of them, singly or together, were at the breaking corral every hour. Meantime some of the crew came to have their look at the horse and, after a glance, shake their heads. David Crow, too, was a frequent visitor at the pen, but he only looked thoughtful and made no comment. King Canibar, occupied with other matters, didn't come for another look at the horse till the evening of the third day. By this time Diablo Red was calm again, his wild eye placated.

Standing beside her brother as they watched Diablo Red nuzzle sugar out of Rainey's hand, Meg said abruptly: "Lenny, I'm going to ride that horse. Tomorrow, I think."

As she'd known he would, King scowled. "Why?"

"Because I want to, that's why. Besides Rainey promised me a ride. Didn't you?"

"Sure did," Rainey said promptly.

King didn't put up too much of an argument, despite a lingering distrust of the stallion's mettle. Wanting Rainey's good opinion, he was trying to oblige the boy as much as possible. However he insisted that David Crow work any kinks out of Diablo Red before Meg took that ride. At supper Welda added her own endorsement to the idea and suggested that she and Meg go for a ride together.

In the morning David Crow began working with the stallion. Rainey stood by, keeping an attentive eye on the proceedings. Within an hour the half-breed was riding Diablo Red around the corral, the stallion merely unlimbering a few playful crow hops.

"What do you think?" Meg teased. "Is David as good as your pa?"

"Nobody's good as Pa," Rainey said firmly. And noting the bronc-peeler's quick grin, he added: "But you're mighty good, Mr. Crow."

That afternoon David Crow took Diablo Red for a short ride to wear off any excess of spirit, and when he returned to the corral, Meg and Welda were ready for their outing. Welda's mount—and her favorite horse—was a clean-limbed sorrel gelding named Sarchedon, noted for his even gait and his amiable nature. He showed only the best disposition toward the red stallion, and Diablo Red, after a curious and thorough examination of the friendly gelding, appeared to be satisfied with him.

King, naturally, was on hand for the event. Rainey proudly held Diablo Red's headstall while Meg stepped into the saddle. She took a firm seat at once and said, "Let go of him, Rainey," and expertly curbed the stallion's mild fiddlefooting. She rode him in a short circle and pulled him up, pleased at his response to a rider's touch.

She patted his neck and smiled at them. "He's just fine."

King helped Welda onto her sidesaddle. She carefully adjusted the drape of her skirt, daintily tucking it here and there, and Meg felt a touch of envy. Her sister-in-law knew the proper outfit for an occasion and how to wear it, anything from a ball gown to a riding habit. Her cheeks flushed and her eyes sparkling, Welda made a stunning picture. Rather careless of attire herself, Meg decided it was just as well; emulating Welda would only lead to unwelcome comparisons.

Quite abruptly Diablo Red began a nervous side-shuffling; then he quartered roughly around, tossing his head. Occupied with getting him under control, Meg took only a fleeting notice that Frank Dance had joined the group, lounging quietly up beside David Crow. Dance was hatless, showing the grimy bandage on his forehead.

"Come on, now, boy," Meg murmured. "Whoa there! What's the matter?"

Frowning, King said, "Listen, you'd better get off him if—"

"It's all right; I can handle him."

But it took her another ten seconds to get the stallion

under control. And still she could feel a tension coursing through his muscles, his head straining against the bit. Something's wrong, Meg thought, but what? It's like three days ago—

In the same moment her gaze crossed Frank Dance's: saw the faint, sleepy grin on his lips and his hand idly lifting the coiled whip from his belt and toying with it— a sunflash wobbling on its metal tip.

That instant's impression merged with a half-dozen others. And then Meg forgot about everything else as Diablo Red unwound like a released spring. He reared high and pawed the air and came down; a bitter squeal tore from his throat as he cut sideways in a powerful leap. Springing up and out as a cat might, all four feet leaving the ground.

His full weight smashed into Sarchedon's flank. The gelding emitted a shocked whicker of hurt and surprise as he crumpled sideways under the impact. Both horses crashed to the ground in a kicking tangle.

Even as she felt Diablo Red going down, Meg instinctively kicked her right foot free of the stirrup and thrust her body away from the direction of the fall. She felt her other foot yank from its stirrup as she landed with a bruising force. That pain was lost in the blow of an outlashing hoof striking her hip.

David Crow must have gone into motion even as the incident started to happen. Suddenly the half-breed was beside Meg, grabbing her shoulders and throwing her bodily aside, away from the flailing hoofs. Then he leaped to seize Diablo Red's rein as the stallion, getting his legs under him, surged upright.

"Whoa! Hold still there!"

Sarchedon was still down on his side, legs churning

wildly, his terrified squeals mingling with Welda's anguished scream. Sidesaddled, her lower body had gone down under the gelding's weight. She was pinned, her trunk twisted at a frightening angle.

King leaped in now and caught hold of Sarchedon's headstall; he gave a mighty heave that wrenched the gelding's head up and started him to his feet.

Welda lay like a crushed moth in the voluminous spread of her skirts, her body still twisted. King hurried to her, bent and turned her on her back. Another terrifying scream escaped her. King pulled his hands back, the color draining from his face.

"Welda, *what is it?*"

"I can't . . . don't touch me. Please."

"What is it?"

"I can't . . . move. My legs, King. I can't feel them . . . can't move them."

"Just be quiet, honey," King said softly. "Just stay quiet." He straightened up and around, his face like granite. "David, you're riding to Moratown. Take our two fastest rackers. Get Doc Vestal here. *And don't spare the horses.* Ride 'em to death if you have to. Frank, fetch me your rifle."

Diablo Red stood quietly now, shuddering a little. Silently, David Crow held out his bridle to Rainey who moved slowly to take it, his face white as paper. The half-breed loped away toward the stables. King peeled off his coat and rolled it up. Dropping to his knees by Welda, he gently raised her head and pillowed it on his coat.

"Is that all right, honey?"

She moved her head in a nod.

"Good. Meg, you fetch a couple of blankets."

Meg had climbed to her feet, trying to brace her weight

away from her bruised hip. She was still dazed by the fall and the sudden turmoil of events. Now her head cleared quickly. Frank Dance had already gone to his shanty close to the corral and was coming back on the run, his rifle in his fist.

"Here y'are, Mr. Canibar—"

King grabbed the rifle from him and swung around, tramping toward Diablo Red. Shocked to muteness, Rainey didn't at once understand what was happening. But Meg did. She made a stumbling try to head off her brother, crying, "Lenny, don't!"

There was a crazed shine on King's eyes. He didn't slacken his bullish stride, just swept out a heavy arm and knocked her aside. Meg hit the ground on her injured hip and the scream that left her held as much pain as anger: "*No, Lenny!*"

King came to a stop and said thickly, "Get away from him, boy," as he brought the rifle up.

Rainey's eyes widened; comprehension rushed over him and he gave a strangled cry of outrage.

"King—" Welda's painful broken whisper. "Don't, oh please don't. *King, he's Rainey's horse!*"

The rifle hung steady on the stallion's head, but King did not put his eye to the sight. He looked slowly at Welda and just as slowly shook his head once, then let the rifle sink in his hands till it pointed groundward.

"Get that goddam devil horse out of my sight," he said in the same thick voice. "You hear? Get him away from me."

After his arrival on a lathered horse, young Dr. Vestal supervised the moving of Welda to the house. He made a thorough examination, afterward reporting to the family that there was some spinal damage, he couldn't be sure how extensive.

"It might heal or it might not," he said matter-of-factly. "It will be at least six weeks before we can be certain."

"You're saying," King Canibar said in a forced, labored tone, "that she might not walk again. Is that right?"

"It depends on the degree of damage to the spinal cord. That, Mr. Canibar, we've no way of determining. We simply wait."

"God," King muttered. "Ain't there operations for this sort of thing? There's got to be *something!*"

Dr. Vestal shook his head. "A specialist might—in some instances—recommend surgery to relieve pressure on the spine, but the cord must heal itself. My own judgment is that such an operation would be an undue risk to Mrs. Canibar's life. That you would be better advised to wait and let nature take its course. However, I can give you the name of a physician in Cheyenne who specializes . . . ."

"Do that," King said grimly. "I ain't taking the word of any one-horse, tank-town sawbones."

The doctor shrugged gently. "As you wish. But the odds are that Dr. Phelps will tell you what I've told you."

"Then I'll get another goddam sawbones. I'll see a hundred of 'em if need be." A suppressed rage shook King's voice, and then it sank to a whisper. "She can't live like this. Jesus, she can't!"

Meg took the word to Rainey. She found him in his room, face down on his bed. Sitting on the edge of the bed, she told him as gently as she could.

The boy was silent for a time. Then he said in a choked muffled voice, not lifting his head, "It's my fault. It's all my fault."

"It's not." Meg laid a hand on his shoulder. "It's nobody's fault. You might as well blame your mother for taking you from your pa or me for wanting to ride Diablo Red or . . . it's just that so many things all led to it. Don't you see that?"

"I . . . I don't know. What happened to him, Meg? Why did Diablo Red act that way?"

"I can't say, Rainey. Not for sure." She frowned, touching back on that kaleidoscopic impression of Frank Dance an instant before Diablo Red's upset. "But I don't think it was his fault either. Something went wrong that we don't understand . . . yet."

He turned a tear-stained face toward her. "What will happen to him?"

"Nothing," she said firmly. "But my brother might—well, he might still make up his mind to destroy your horse. Before that happens, Rainey, I think we'd do well to send him away."

"Where?"

"Back to Cross-B. I'll tell David Crow to take him there . . . today. Is that what you want?"

Rainey stirred his head once, up and down.

The Seth Thomas clock on the wall chimed midnight. Phil Canibar slumped in a big wing-backed chair, gently swirling the brandy glass in his palm. From time to time he took a sip of liquor, smiling a little. His thoughts were mellow and pleasant. He let his gaze touch idly across the familiar furnishings of the great parlor, the huge fieldstone fireplace that occupied the west wall, the trophy heads of grizzly and bighorn mounted above it along with a collection of weapons. Phil's eyes lingered on the Martini express rifle, imported from England, that King had acquired after a visiting Britisher had told him that hunters in Africa and India used this make of gun to bring down elephants and buffalo.

That was like King. If he owned anything, it had to be the biggest or the best or the fanciest. Phil had once felt a corrosive envy for his brother's ability to get what he wanted. Over the years, though, he had learned to relax and enjoy the fruits of King's labors.

A soft chuckle escaped Phil. Why not? He wasn't the man King was, but damned few men were. Rolling with life's punches, getting as much as you could with as little effort as possible, was the key to easy living in this vale of tears. A man was damned lucky to have a brother who generously provided for his kin and made no demands on them except a concession to his authority.

Privately, during the two weeks since Welda's accident, Phil's frame of mind had been cheerier than usual.

King had brought three different specialists to Big Crown to examine his wife and offer their bleak verdicts on the graveness of her condition. All had agreed that surgery would be too dangerous to attempt. And, pressed by King for the cruel truth, that the chances were she'd be paralyzed from the lower back down for the rest of her life. Not that King had given up: he was determined that Welda would walk again, and he was growing desperate enough to try almost anything.

There was an excellent possibility, as Phil understood it, that even if a master surgeon could be found who would consent to perform an operation, it might prove the death of Welda. A possibility that Phil found immensely brightening to his own prospects.

He and Welda had hated each other since King had brought her to Big Crown. Phil knew she despised him thoroughly, and he couldn't have cared less. He had watched with deepening resentment as her influence over King had grown till she could twist him to almost any whim of hers. Behind it lurked Phil's worry that if anything ever happened to King, Welda would fall heir to all of Big Crown; King himself had made that clear. And the day that happened—as it easily could, given King Canibar's consuming appetite for work and play that would have burned out a lesser man long ago—Welda would give her brother-in-law the boot.

Momentarily a brooding frown creased Phil's face. If there were only some way, a *safe* way, to wipe that little bitch out of all their lives . . . !

Hearing King's heavy tread in the hallway, Phil composed his expression to blandness. King had come from Welda's room, and, entering the parlor now, he tramped over to the walnut sideboard and picked up the nearly empty decanter and a large tumbler. He gave the decanter a shake, scowled, and glanced at Phil.

"Sorry," Phil said mildly. "There's a full bottle under the sideboard."

Without a word King broke out the fresh bottle, yanked the cork, and filled his tumbler to the brim. He drank it straight down and refilled the glass. Then he began to prowl the room restlessly, combing a hand through his thin, rumpled mane.

"You really been packing that stuff away of late," Phil observed tranquilly.

King halted and looked at him. Phil raised a placating hand. "Just an observation," he said.

King emptied his glass again, paused for another refill, and continued to prowl. Suddenly he gave a savage curse and flung the tumbler at the fireplace. The crash of glass made Phil's eyes, half-lidded and drowsy, jerk wide open. King stood bear-big in the middle of the room, his feet apart and his hands clenched. An inner anguish was tearing him apart, Phil knew. An indomitable man used to having his way in all things, he was confronted at last with something against which all his overbearing strength was useless.

Light and mellow in his own thoughts, Phil felt a good-natured nudge of sympathy. He rose to his feet and walked over to his brother, laying a hand on his arm. "Buck up, Leonard. There's still a chance that spinal lesion may heal. And there are plenty of physicians to be consulted yet . . . . "

His voice trailed off as King turned an iron look on him. King's eyes were red with fatigue; the brandy he'd taken must have hit his empty stomach like a hot stone.

"What the hell do you care?" His speech was slow and slurred.

"Of course I care," Phil said warily. "I'm worried about you. You haven't eaten a thing in two days. You'd better . . . . "

"Like so much shit, you care," King cut in so softly that his labored words were almost inaudible. "You'd like to see her die is what you'd like."

Phil dropped his hand and took a step backward. "You don't know what you're saying, Leonard. You—"

"Shut your goddamn mouth!" King roared suddenly. His arm shot out and seized a fistful of Phil's shirt. "You think I ain't got eyes to see with? Ain't nothing would pleasure you like having Welda hurt—crippled—dead! Yes, by God, dead!"

Red lights kindled in King's eyes; all the explosive tensions in him were loosened by liquor and boiling to the surface. A chill of fear clutched Phil.

"No," he said in a reedy whisper.

"Shut up! Why did it happen, Phil?" King shook him like a dog shaking a rat. "Why did that goddam horse go crazy all a-sudden that way? He was all right enough—and then—*why?*"

"I d-don't know, Leonard—God, l-listen to me—"

"Liar!" King bawled. A bloat of rage swelled his face. His massive arm swung back and forward; his open hand smashed Phil like a club. "*Liar!*" Phil gave a bleat of pain and terror that was crushed on his lips by another sledging cuff. "*Liar liar liar—*" White lights popped in Phil's eyes; he was aware of another blow and another. Then King flung him with a crash against the wall.

Phil hung there with his palms flat to the wall, not daring to move. The freeze of fear around his brain was as sharp as the taste of his blood. Just once before in his life he had seen his brother in a blind drunk rage: that time King had wrecked a barroom and had broken two men's jaws.

Slowly the crazed frenzy ebbed from King's face. His eyes squeezed nearly shut; tears streaked his cheeks. "*Why*, Phil?" he whispered.

A noise in the doorway. Phil inched his head around just enough to see Meg, aroused from the bed and blinking at them uncomprehendingly. The shock in her face slowly faded, altering to a quiet sorrow.

"Lenny," she said gently. "Oh, Lenny."

King turned and tramped heavily past her. The door of his room slammed.

Phil spat a gout of blood and pushed away from the

wall, nearly falling. As he swayed for balance, Meg came
toward him. "Phil, let me—"

"No," Phil said carefully. "Keep away." He tongued his
broken lips and fumbled out his handkerchief, mopping
at his mouth and chin. "He said I crippled Welda. *Me.*
Did you hear him?"

"He didn't know what he was saying. I was on Diablo
Red . . . not you, not Welda. Phil, please—"

"The hell with you. Get away from me."

Meg bit her underlip; she pulled her gray wrapper
tighter around her and folded her arms over her bosom,
shivering. "What is it?" she murmured. "What's happening
to all of us?" Her eyes looked beyond him as she spoke,
and then she bowed her head and turned, walking slowly
from the room.

Phil crossed to the sideboard and scooped up the
brandy bottle. His hands shook, chattering the bottleneck
against his teeth, as he took a long drink. Afterward he
walked unsteadily to the window, one hand grasping the
bottle, the other wiping gently at his mouth. He stared
blindly out at the darkness and took another slug of
brandy. The shaking and the fear washed out of him; his
brain throbbed with a hot and savage clarity.

Briefly and very softly, he chuckled.

You're going to pay for that, brother mine, Phil
thought. Jesus, how you are going to pay.

Chapter Thirteen

LIKE most men who had worked cattle in the West's heyday, Jonas had always owned a handgun and even packed it a good share of the time. It came in handy now and then for knocking down a ringy steer or shooting at a rattlesnake. Given enough time to aim and a little luck, you could usually hit the steer. He had no faith in the ordinary Colt's virtues as extolled by Ned Buntline's yellowback thrillers, but he knew that some few men, anyway, could achieve pretty lethal results with the weapon. So he had Grif give him shooting lessons.

They practiced every morning back of the old cabin, setting up all kinds of targets—bottles, cans, pieces of wood—at different distances. By the end of a week, Jonas was able to group his shots in a six-inch circle at fifty yards, and Grif assured him that this was doing passably well.

On the morning he managed the feat, Grif told him: "Just one thing, Mr. Bonner. You plan on making anything stick with that old gun, you could just be shooting at the stars. In the time we been working out, your mainspring has busted, your pawl has busted, and your cylinder stop spring has busted."

"You done a good job replacing all of 'em, Grif. It's working fine now."

"Sure, but you get using that thing in a tight place and a hammer notch goes on you or the cylinder stop bolt goes on you, where'll you be? Look, take my gun, why don't you? You can have the damn thing. I wouldn't promise nothing with a thumb-buster like mine, but leastways it ain't likely to let you down at the wrong time."

Jonas shook his head. "I'm used to this old piece. Only kind of Colt I'm any good at breaking in has four legs and a tail."

Privately he felt repelled by the killer's weapon Grif toted—used to tote. Jonas didn't like the look of it, much less the touch. And he had no intention of using any gun at all unless he was pushed to it. But, sizing the odds he might face in the light of what he planned to do, it might unavoidably come to that. He didn't intend to be caught flat-footed if it did. Getting in solid practice with his own gun, a familiar easy-feeling thing in his hand, was a kind of stubborn talisman for him.

Grif racked up another row of targets. After burning a good deal more powder, Jonas repeated his accomplishment twice.

"That ought to do it for today, Mr. Bonner. No use

putting too much strain on that old smokepole."

Jonas's leg was starting to ache. It had healed cleanly and well, but there was no point putting a strain on it either. "Set 'em up once more," he said. "Then we'll. . . ."

He broke off. A couple of riders were coming through the notch at the west end of this thinly wooded valley. That was the way Barney always came, but he'd always come alone.

When they got near enough, he recognized Barney at once. At first Jonas didn't want to believe it, but the rider with him was Meg Canibar on a man's saddle. Evidently she hadn't come willingly, for Barney had a grasp on her rein, and Jonas thought wearily: Oh Jesus.

As they pulled up in the yard, Barney said meagerly, "Look who been follering me."

Meg swung to the ground, giving them a tranquil smile. "Hello."

Jonas glared at her.

"My, you look chipper for a drowned man," Meg told him. "Mean, too. Don't blame Mr. Blue. I did follow him, and he very adroitly spotted me and waited for me in some trees."

"We was already close to here," Barney said glumly. "Figured she knowed what's up anyways, so I brung her along. Let her tell you what she's up to. Me, I ain't hearing a thing."

He dismounted, tied his and Meg's horses to a tree, unslung a sack of supplies from his pommel, and tramped into the cabin. Grif glanced from Jonas to Meg and back again, then shrugged and followed Barney inside.

Jonas said thinly, "I don't reckon this was just an accident."

Meg explained that she had suspected for some time

Barney's reason for riding this way at regular intervals and had decided to verify her suspicions. Today she had followed him to within a half mile of this valley, and then he had picked her up.

"So now you know," Jonas growled. "What are you going to do with it?"

"Why, nothing. Goodness, it's no crime for a man to pretend he's dead. Is it?"

"I mean," he said with a thinning patience, "who you fixing to tell about it?"

The amusement in her face gave way to a searching gravity, and slowly she shook her head. "Nobody," she said quietly. "If you say not to."

Jonas eyed her with a baffled uncertainty, and she said swiftly, "Listen, Jonas, I'm on your side. Your son believes that. I hope I can make you believe it."

"That could take some doing. Why the hell would you be?"

"I'm beginning to wonder. I'd guess Mr. Blue has already told Rainey that you're alive."

"What if he didn't?"

"Well, I'd think Rainey would like to know, wouldn't you? I hoped I'd be able to tell him that. But if you don't—"

"He knows," Jonas said flatly. "If that's all you come for. . . ."

"Not exactly. I hoped I could help some way."

"Help how?"

Meg shook her head with a kind of weary patience. "All right, if I have to say it all. You plan on getting him back, don't you?"

"Go on."

"Well, it's pretty obvious, isn't it? What would I do

if I were your kind of man in your position? I'd make believe I was dead, hoping it would relax everyone's guard. Then I'd find a way to spirit my son away from Big Crown, and then I'd clear out of the country with him. What your plans might be after that, I've no idea. I suspect you'd lie low for a spell, but then? You might go somewhere a few hundred miles away and change your name. Or you might go clean to Canada. Or to the North Pole, for all I know. That's no concern of mine. The thing is, I might be able to help you *here*—in getting Rainey away from them."

"You might at that. But why would you?"

"That, at least, is a reasonable question," Meg said dryly. "I just don't like what Lenny and Welda did. I do like Rainey. And I don't like what's happening at Big Crown . . . to him or any of us. You know about Welda, of course."

Jonas nodded soberly. "That wrangler of yours, Crow, told Barney and the Bacas when he brought Diablo Red back to Cross-B. Wasn't sure then how bad it was with her."

"It's bad. Very."

Meg repeated what the doctors had told them about Welda's prospects. And she added her suspicion that Frank Dance had played a part in the panicking of Diablo Red. All she could base that feeling on was the slyly casual way that Dance had been fondling his whip when the stallion had gone out of control. Yet she wasn't sure why Dance's presence or the whip would have had that effect.

"Unless he used it on him," she said slowly. "He had the chance. And he might have done it because he got a bad clip on the head when he and David Crow were putting the horse up that first day. Dance and David both claimed he fell against a post. I doubted it then. And after what happened with Welda . . . but I just couldn't be certain."

Jonas gazed thoughtfully across the valley, nodding gently. "Reckon it's as sure as need be, if you know Dance. The son of a bitch was looking to get you hurt, not Welda." He glanced at her then. "Sorry."

Meg smiled. "I don't mind a man swearing. Around Lenny, it's never done much good to mind. One thing Welda's not been able to curb is his language."

"She never cared for rough talk," he agreed dryly. "But then that wasn't exactly our problem."

"I know. I think I know you a little, and I do know Welda." Meg gave him an oblique, veiled look. "She and I get along quite well, by the way. Does that surprise you?"

Jonas shrugged. "Never thought about it one way or the other."

"No, you wouldn't." Meg's smiling glance held on his face, and she added: "She's made King a fine marriage, and she's pleasant company. Of course, she likes having her own way too well, but a Canibar can hardly complain about that."

"Pot calling the kettle."

"Look who's talking." She grinned and held up a hand. "Let's not, all right? We've nothing to quarrel about. I do want to help. Honestly."

Jonas gave a grudging twitch of a smile. He felt automatically on his guard with this woman, and he wasn't sure why. He was nonplussed by her forthright ways, and she was a Canibar; maybe that was reason enough.

Why should he trust her? She could be attempting to

mislead him—or this could be the mere whim of a bored
and spoiled girl. In fact she looked rather like an overgrown kid: facing him hipshot, dangling her hat from
one hand by its chinstrap; her other hand poked idly
at the blonde fall of her hair, full of tawny glints in the
sun. Her attire was indifferent, well-worn and dusty, and
she carried herself with a tough, wiry grace. Unusually
tall, full-breasted yet almost too slender for her height,
she must have been gawky and self-conscious in her teens.
Jonas had been the same, and he remembered how he
had covered the feeling with a free and easy, almost
brash manner. Now, though, Meg Canibar was plainly
a person not in the least preoccupied with herself—and
the realization startled and pleased Jonas.

She'd gone out of her way to be kind to Rainey—the
boy had told Barney and the Bacas that Meg had inter-
vened with her brother to save Diablo Red. Unsuccess-
fully, for Welda's word had swayed King's temper. But
she had tried. Jonas made his decision swiftly now.

"All right," he said. "Here's what you can do."

As she rode back toward Big Crown, Meg had plenty
of food for thought.

She wasn't sure why she had offered the Bonners her
aid so unreservedly. Maybe she hadn't really expected
that Jonas would unbend enough to accept it; in that case
it had been a cheap gesture. But no—she had meant it
sincerely, had felt a distinct pleasure at the trust that
his acceptance implied, and did not experience any mis-
givings now.

Meg's part would be simple enough: tomorrow afternoon she would offer to take Rainey for a ride. King
and Welda would have no reason to suspect anything

awry; they knew she'd been trying to cheer the boy up, and an outing on horseback might be just the medicine for his melancholy. She and Rainey would rendezvous with Jonas at the foot of Castle Rock, and Jonas and Rainey would be on their way to a place of hiding. (Jonas hadn't divulged his specific plans thereafter, and she hadn't asked.) Then she would return to Big Crown to brave King's wrath, which wasn't likely to be damped by her story that Jonas had come on them by surprise and had taken Rainey away. Naturally, she'd been helpless to prevent it.

Would King believe her? Probably he would in the end—after mulling over a wide range of natural suspicions. He'd have no reason, finally, not to believe her—nothing to verify otherwise. Jonas, after all, might have been spying on the ranch for days, waiting an opportunity of this sort. Still, she was about to betray blatantly the interests of a brother who had done immeasurably well by her all her life—and she couldn't pretend any happiness on that score.

Yet, because she was convinced that King and Welda were in the wrong, Meg felt no genuine regret, either. Whether he believed her story or not, King would rant and rave—and Welda would be unforgiving. But I'm going to do it, she thought calmly: no use dwelling on what might or might not come of it. . . .

The sun was high and hot in her face; the day was sticky and windless. Halfway back to Big Crown, Meg thought of Arrowhead Spring in a wooded glen a little distance to the southwest. She hadn't been there in a long time, and thinking now of the clear, cold water and deep shade trees, she turned Blazes in that direction. It was a slight detour to this favorite place of her girlhood, where she had dreamed away many a summer afternoon with a favorite book.

It was exactly as she remembered it: a small glade set in a motte of old ironwood trees, the spring bubbling up over mossy rocks and cascading into a wide, deep pool. After she had let the mare drink and then tied her to a tree, Meg knelt on a stone ledge by the pool and cupped water in her hands, drinking and bathing her face. Her teeth ached from the chill, but the water was welcome all the same.

Meg unbuttoned her blouse and slipped it off, her camisole too, and bent to the pool again. She spilled handfuls of water over her head, shivering as the icy runnels coursed down her shoulders and back and arms, bracing the large firm cones of her breasts and tightening their pink nipples to smooth, hard nubs. She sat on the warm stone, head thrown back, and luxuriated in the quick warmth of sun on her naked upper body till her skin was dry. Then she slipped on the camisole and the blouse, standing up to button them.

A horse's whicker came from somewhere in the trees. Meg's hands froze in place; she looked swiftly around.

Frank Dance was standing on a far side of the glade, watching her with a glazed, slack-jawed look. He must have come noiselessly out of the trees behind him. But how long had he been standing there? And how long had he watched her from the trees?

Mechanically, Meg finished buttoning her blouse, and then, fighting down the queasy and polluted feeling in her stomach, she said evenly: "Whatever else you are, Frank, I never thought you were a plain-out fool."

"Oh," Dance drawled gently, "you are some beauty to look at, Sister." He waggled his head in a slow semicircle. "You are for certain sure."

A brightness lay on his glazed eyes; he swayed a little from side to side. He's drunk, Meg thought. Not with any surprise, but feeling a strong thread of fear now.

Don't say anything, she warned herself. Just get away from here. She turned and walked toward her tethered mount, trying not to hurry.

"You want to get that nag killed," Dance said in a slurred, pleasant voice, "jist keep on walking."

She halted and looked back. He was holding his rifle in one hand, pointed slackly down, and now he raised it till the muzzle was leveled on Blazes.

"Frank." She fought to keep her voice steady and reasonable. "You know what will happen, don't you, when my brother hears about this."

"Oh, he ain't gonna. You know why."

His stare gained a sheen of hard focus; Meg realized he wasn't as drunk as she'd thought. The panic tightened in her throat.

"Because I follered you today, sister. Been wondering what-for you been riding out this way alla time. All I done was, I kept a goodly ways behind you. Follered you straight to that cabin where Bonner is. Kept back in the trees and watched. The King, he wouldn't be overjoyed to know you been keeping company with Bonner right along. Now would he?"

Meg shook her head quickly. "You're wrong, I—" She saw the futility of the words even as she spoke. "What do you want, Frank?"

"Well, for a start, like. . . ." Dance moved now, skirting around the pool at a shambling trot. "I seen half o' what you got. Would purely admire to see the rest—"

Meg whirled and ran for the mare.

She tore the reins loose and got one foot in the stirrup just as Dance's hand closed like a vise on her arm. The swift, powerful clamp of his fingers sent blue pain squirting along the muscle strands. Meg bit back a scream and did not resist as he pulled her away from the horse, then swung her to face him.

"You goddamn high-'n'-toney bitch—" A drunken fever reddened his face. "You won't look cross-eyed at a man 'cep'n' when you look down your long Canibar nose at him. 'Cep'n for that goddamn shoestring bum Bonner. You been a woman to him, you can be a woman to Dance. Won't cost you nothing you ain't give—"

His face had gone slack with a wildness of lust; his hand was shaking her, rocking her slowly back and forth. At the same time his grip had unconsciously relaxed a little. In a pure terror now, Meg yanked free and wheeled to run. Dance was on her in an instant, his hand closing on her shoulder, and he wrenched her around, dropping his rifle as his weight carried them both to the ground.

Meg fought with all her strength, thrashing her head from side to side in an effort to avoid his slobbering mouth. Suddenly she raked her nails down the side of his face. Dance cursed and gave her a savage cuff that half-stunned her.

Dimly she was aware that his hands were tearing at her clothes; she felt them rip and pull away from her flesh. Then the roughness of Dance's hands. She was sick and limp-muscled under the fierceness of his attack, his wet mouth and whiskey-stink, yet she continued feebly to resist. Her outflung hand tore despairingly at the ground. And closed over something: the sharp edge of a fist-sized stone. It was loose in the soil.

With a blind surge of strength she brought the fragment up and around, crashing it against Dance's bullet head.

She heard his grunt of shock and pain. And she struck again. Dance's body sagged across her. A desperation of panic fed her muscles as she heaved against his weight and rolled him sideways. She scrambled to her feet and ran to the mare. In a blaze of fury now she snatched the quirt dangling from her saddle horn.

Dance groaned and crawled to his hands and knees. Meg stood over him and lashed at his head, her mind empty of everything but the need to hurt and punish. She got in three hard strokes; then Dance gave a howl and grabbed at the quirt, tearing it from her hand.

It shocked Meg back to a cold sensibility. She backed off from him, then moved swiftly to Blazes, seized up the reins, and flung herself into the saddle. The mare snorted and capered; Meg fought her to a standstill. She sidled the animal away from Dance, watching pitilessly as he climbed laboriously to his feet. He swayed like a stocky oak, pawing befuddledly at the blood pouring from his scalp.

Meg spoke then, her words icy and measured. "You won't say anything about this, Frank. Not about any of it. Because King will kill you if you do. And if you ever come near me again, I'll kill you."

She turned Blazes on a quick rein and rode away from the glade, not looking back.

Chapter Fourteen

KING Canibar stood by the breaking corral with his brother, watching David Crow in his patient careful way at breaking a skittish colt to saddle. But King wasn't really paying attention, and presently he muttered softly, musingly, "Damn. I wish I knew."

Phil shuttled a glance at him. "What?"

"What she's lying about."

"You're really sure she is, eh?"

"Damn sure," King said grimly.

She had to be, he thought. A half hour ago he had surprised Meg sneaking into the house by the kitchen entrance. Sneaking had to be the word for it. Always her habit had been to enter or leave the house by the front way. Why had she turned furtive all at once? Somehow her excuse that she was embarrassed to be seen in her disheveled condition, with her clothing shredded and her face bruised, had seemed a piece of awkward dissembling. King had concluded long ago that his sister was beyond embarrassment if not shame. Also her explanation that Blazes had shied from a rattler and pitched her off in some chaparral had failed to ring all wool and a yard wide.

. King didn't like household secrets. What the hell, when you'd raised a kid sister by hand, indulged most of her wishes all her life, given her more than any five girls should need or want, you expected a little loyalty in return. They were all the same damned way, he thought darkly, the whole pack of satellites that moved in his orbit. All except Welda. With her alone there was a total giving, a total sharing. But the rest of them . . . !

Phil, for example. King gave his brother a narrow-eyed glance. Since the night he had struck Phil in an unreasoning fury of drink and worry, Phil had been quietly unforgiving. Not in any way you could lay a hand on; outwardly Phil had accepted King's gruff apology for the incident gracefully enough. But King was as keen as a wolf on deer-scent when it came to probing the moods of those around him. Something was still amiss with Phil, and now Meg, he thought with a steady rising anger, was holding out on him for one reason or another.

Phil tipped his head toward the trampled lane between the tack shed and the blacksmith shop. "That looks like Dance coming."

"About time, too," King growled.

The blackness of his temper took a sharper turn yet as he watched the bronc-peeler, slouched in his saddle, start this way and then veer aside in the direction of his shanty.

"Hey you, Dance!" King roared. "Get your ass over here. Now!"

Slowly, as if reluctant, Dance turned his mount toward the corral. Before he was a dozen yards away, King's brows pulled together in a scowl. Dance's face was criss-crossed with several red weals; he had a drawn and pasty look, and he seemed to have trouble focusing his eyes.

"What the hell happened to you?" King demanded.

"Ah, nothin'," Dance said sluggishly. "Rattler skeered my horse and he piled me."

Phil glanced at King, tilting his brows with a mildly quizzical irony. "A regular epidemic, it seems, of rattlers and skittery broncs," he murmured.

King could see, since Dance's hat was angled carefully away from the injury, that his temple bore a swollen lump wider than a silver dollar; the side of his face was blood-crusted. "You got fetched a good one, eh?"

Dance gave a sallow grin, touching his temple. "Yeh. Come down square on a rock. Then I got switched chasing the son of a bitch through the brush."

"That's too damn bad." Sarcasm roughened King's voice. "Listen, you shorthorn. You had a day's work cut out for you, remember? You're supposed to be working ornery horseflesh, and we got plenty on hand right now. I ain't paying you to go tomcatting off to Sanchez's or wherever the hell you been. You been gone half the goddam day!"

Dance waggled his head humbly. "Yeh, well, I know, boss. Reckon I got paid for it in right hard coin. My head is ringing like a church bell."

"When the hell you ever hear one?" King said scathingly. "All right. You hear *this*, now. Mostly I've give you a free hand and damn few orders in your work. I see that's been my mistake. From here on you keep regular hours like everyone else. I catch you sojering around just once, I'll boot your ass off Big Crown! I'll boot it so hard you'll wear out rolling. You got that?"

"Yessir."

King swept him with another disgusted look. "You sorry bucko. You ain't in no shape to walk, much less work. You might's well take the rest of the day off. It's going to be your last for a month. *You got that?*"

"Yessir."

King wheeled and stamped away toward the main house, pulling violently on his cigar. In his still-flowering anger he shredded it between his thick fingers, then threw it aside with a furious "Ah-h-h!"

Halfway to the house he slowed, frowning over his two sources of irritation. Phil was right. Both Meg and Dance being unhorsed the same way was stretching the long arm of coincidence. Not that it couldn't have happened to either or both; but both the same day—it was just too damned obvious an excuse. King's frown deepened. What had Frank said about getting switched chasing through brush?

Yes, that could happen, too. But he thought of those three bloody stripes crossing Dance's face: as clean and even and alike as if they had been painted on. A whip might lay welts on a man's flesh that evenly . . . but a random chase through the brush?

King swore softly; his thoughts reeled with the sudden force of suspicion and just as suddenly hardened with conviction.

He tramped onto the veranda and into the house, flinging the door wide and not bothering to close it as he stalked up the stairs and down a hallway that branched into bedchambers. Coming to his sister's room, he didn't pause, just wrenched the door open, and strode in.

Meg whirled from her pier table, coming to her feet. She had changed to a clean frock and had touched up her disordered hair. But a wide, swollen bruise marked her jaw like an angry testimonial, and the sight of it tightened King's voice with an ominous fury.

"Where's your quirt?"

"What? Lenny, what is—"

"That braided Mex quirt I gave you last Christmas," he said harshly. "I want a look at it."

After a space of three heartbeats she said quietly, "I don't have it."

"What do you mean, you don't have it? Take it along every damn time you go for a ride, don't you?" His eyes narrowed. "Come to think, though . . . you didn't have it when I caught you sneaking in awhile back. Where is it, Meg?"

Her gaze moved uneasily across his face; she moistened her lips. "I . . . I'm not sure."

"Goddamn it—" He took a long step; his hand closed on her shoulder. "You had it on a thong around your wrist, didn't you? If you took it off, you got to know where and when." He gave her a violent shake. "*Where is that quirt?*"

"Lenny, you're hurt—don't!" Grimacing with pain, she tried to pull his hand away; it was like a vise on her flesh and now tightening relentlessly. "Arrowhead! Arrowhead Spring . . . I left it there! Lenny, *let go!*"

Slowly he released her, saying tonelessly then, "What happened there, Meg? What were you and Dance doing there?"

It was a shot in the dark, but King knew from her look that it had struck home. An unreasoning rage poured through him, and now his hand seized her arm. "Damn you, *what happened?* What did he—"

"Nothing! He did nothing!"

"Nothing, for Christ's sake, clothes all tore, face banged up, you call that *nothing?* Meg, what in hell is it?" His voice began to shake. "Why didn't you tell me directly you come in? Why cover up . . . ?"

She shook her head woodenly.

King flung her lifted arm down as if it were contaminated. "Jesus," he said in a wry and unbelieving tone, shaking his head slowly back and forth. "I have thought now and again there might be a fine bitch in you just waiting to cut loose. But nothing like that. Nothing like that."

"That's not—you don't understand. . . ."

"Shut up."

He let the words fall cold and flat, cutting her speech like a knife. "Something's got to be done for you," he said tiredly. "What, I don't know. Right now I don't much give a damn. But you stay away from me for a spell, all right? Just don't let me have to look at you."

He turned and tramped heavily out of the room and down the stairs, ignoring—for once—Welda's voice faintly calling from her room, "King, what is it, what's the matter?"

He left the house and moved across the headquarters area at a solid, implacable gait, heading for the breaking corral. A numbness clung to his brain so that he was hardly conscious of feeling anything at all. As he passed the corral, he heard Phil call a question at him and he ignored that too, tramping on toward Dance's shanty.

The door stood partly open and King gave it a kick that slammed it against the inside wall, and walked straight in.

Sitting at a crude table in the center of the single room, Dance had a bottle of whiskey open before him; he had just poured himself a drink. His hand raising the glass froze halfway to his mouth; his jaw dropped. He had no time to say anything, for an instant later King's huge fist crashed into his face.

The sheer power of the blow sent Dance kiting over backward, the chair falling with him, and then he somersaulted out of it and fell against the wall. While he was still in a dazed sprawl, his legs pulled up against his chest, King seized the table in both hands and flung it out of the way, then bent and caught a handful of Dance's shirt and dragged him to his feet. A second sledging blow smacked Dance backward with such force that his shirt tore away in King's grasp. The bunk bed caught Dance behind the knees and dropped him across it with an impact that split the bunk's support rail. Then his head met the wall with a savage rap.

King reached down, took hold of Dance's belt and hauled him up again. Dance was glassy-eyed, his head lolling between his shoulders, as King slapped him with a meaty palm. Once, twice, three times, till the smarting cuffs jarred Dance back to a semblance of alertness.

"Huh? Wha—?"

King let go of him, and Dance swayed backward, then caught his balance. He stood blinking and befuddled, rivulets of blood running down to his hairy chest from his mashed nose and lips.

"Frank," King said thickly, "right this minute you're awfully close to getting dead. So don't lie to me, don't even think of lying, or that could tear it. All right?"

"Jesus," Dance muttered, "I didn't do noth—"

He tried to flinch away as King's fist came up, but the solid clout caught him on the ear and sent him crashing to the floor. Again King dragged him to his feet and this time dropped him into a chair, then leaned over him, hands on hips.

"Frank, next time I could bust your head. Once more, now. I want the truth out of you, all right?"

"Wha' you wanna know?" Dance's words left his pulped lips as a sodden mumble.

"Were you with my sister at Arrowhead Springs today?"

King's right fist stirred off his hip as he spoke, and Dance said quickly, "Yessir."

"Were you having a . . . rendezvous? Were you supposed to meet her there?"

A naked fear crawled on Dance's broken face; he swallowed and shook his head.

"You met by accident, did you?"

"Nossir. I, uh, followed her."

"Why did you follow her, Frank?" King's voice was deceptively gentle.

"Well, she been taking these rides same time every day, see, and I got curious where she went. She, uh. . . ."

"Speak up."

"She been seeing Bonner, looks like. Follered her to this ole cabin back in the Buckhorns, and I see her there with him. . . ."

"Hold it. Back up," King said softly. "Jonas Bonner . . . you saw him? *Alive?*"

"Yessir, he's sure 'nough alive. Seen him plain as day with my glasses."

"What went on between them?"

"Nothing I could tell cep'n they talked. Then she got back on her horse and rode away."

"To Arrowhead Springs?"

"Eh, yessir."

"And you followed her there?"

"Yessir, and I dunno what happened then, I seen her by the spring and I dunno what happened to me, I just went all sort of, uh, crazy or somep'n'. . . ."

"That will do it, Frank," King cut him off mildly. For a long moment he studied Dance's battered face, but oddly the anger had drained out of him; he felt emptily calm. "You get your warbag packed and see Phil. Tell him I said to give you your time. Then start walking. I don't care which way you go. Just be off my land by tomorrow. Don't ever set foot on it again. Don't ever come near me or mine again. You do, and I'll kill you on sight. Got that?"

It was more than a warning; it was a raw pledge. Dance blinked and nodded. King turned on his heel and walked out, heading back for the house.

He walked slowly, taking out a cigar and clipping it, then lighting up. The strange calm held in him as he pondered what Dance had told him. Bonner was alive and Meg had been seeing him. But only to talk to him, apparently. King considered this with a kind of irritable relief; the truth fell far short of his worst fear. Nevertheless Meg had known Bonner was alive and had said nothing. More: she'd been determined not to tell him, which was why she'd kept mum about Dance. She'd feared that if King's anger focused on Frank, the truth would come out, as it had.

Mulling over the implications of all this, King paused

by the veranda to smoke his cigar awhile. Then he dropped it and ground it underfoot, and tramped into the house and up the stairs. This time he passed the closed door of Meg's room without a glance. He entered the master bedroom and closed the door behind him. Welda lay in the vast bed propped up by pillows. Her face, pale in the black tumble of her hair, turned quickly toward him.

"King, what happened? I heard you and Meg. . . ." Her glance tipped to his right hand as he settled heavily into a chair by the bed. "Your hand is all skinned. Oh King—!"

"Meg ain't hurt," he said tonelessly. "I combed Frank Dance over with that hand is all."

"Dance? But why?"

King told her what he had learned, carefully marshaling the facts as he saw them. The important thing in all of this was that Jonas was alive, and a man needn't look far to see his reason for playing dead. The wan pallor of Welda's face did not change, but King had the feeling that any color in it would have vanished with the effect of his words. Her eyes turned large and frantic; she clutched at his arm.

"King. You know what he's about, don't you? He wants us to think he's dead so we won't look for him to. . . ."

"Take Rainey away? He won't," King promised grimly.

"You can't let him, King! You can't!"

"Easy, honey. I said he won't get Rainey. Now we're ready for him, he'll never get the chance."

"Oh, God, but he'll try! Jonas will bide his time, and then he'll dare any odds; there's no telling what he'd do if he took it in his head! King, you don't *know* him!"

"Maybe I do," King said thoughtfully. "That ornery varmint. He might at that. We'd have to kill the bastard, then. But he could get some of us, too."

"Then go to the sheriff! Have him—"

"What?" King said in a quietly savage tone. "Tell him Bonner's been playing dead? No law says a man can't play dead if he's a mind to. So far that's all he's done. And you can't arrest a man for what he might do."

"He tried to take Rainey away from the sheriff—"

"Hell, he didn't have time to try anything then, except get shot by that gun-happy deputy. That's no grounds for diddle-de-damn. Except *he* could likely bring charges against that deputy, was he minded."

"Then what do we do?" Welda whispered. "What can we do?"

King rose and paced a short circle, one hand rubbing the back of his neck. "I could bring in a 'warrior,' " he said slowly. "A hired gun. I could have Bonner ambushed and shot. Nobody could ever prove a thing."

Welda's eyes widened with shock. "Oh, God, you can't be serious. King!"

"No," he said wryly. "That's never been my style. I'm just thinking out loud. We got to figure what we won't do before we settle for sure what we will. What it boils down to as I see it, we can't move Bonner no way. But we can move the boy."

"What do you mean?"

King came back to the chair and sat, taking both her hands in his before he answered. "This. We can send Rainey a couple of thousand miles away. Way back East, to a good private school. Honey, I know it ain't easy to think about, you and the boy just starting to get close and all. But it's the only way I know of. If Bonner comes after the kid as you're sure he will, there'll be gunplay for certain. If Bonner gets killed then, it'll be all up with you and the boy. It won't be no accident this time, and he will know it, and he'll hate you the rest of his life."

Welda's head stirred to a slow, bitter, resigned nod. "I know. I couldn't bear that. But King, even that won't stop Jonas if he learns where we send Rainey. . . ."

"No reason he ever should. We'll do it this way. Tomorrow I'll give the crew a day off. We'll all ride to town with the boy and put him on the night train east. Send along two of our crew to guard him as far as Omaha. Meantime I'll wire ahead to the Parkinson Detective Agency there. They'll have a couple of their operatives waiting for Rainey when he switches trains at Omaha, and our men'll deliver him into their hands. The Parkinson men will see him all the way to Maryland where relatives of my ma's will be waiting for him. They'll take care of him till we've settled on what school he's to attend."

King spread his big hands. "Now, you tell me where there's a flaw in that idea. There's no way Bonner can tell what's up till it's way too late, but even if he does, we got all bases covered. What can he do afterward? Nothing, less'n he can find out where we sent Rainey. And nobody on this end will know that outside of you, me, and the Parkinson folks. And Meg," he added judiciously.

"Meg? But you say she's been friendly with Jonas. . . ."

"Yeh," King said musingly. "I dunno just how friendly. She's took a liking to the boy and him to her, so could be her sympathy just naturally follows his. Maybe that's all there is to it—her passing messages between Rainey and his pa. Or maybe she is fixing to help Bonner get the boy back."

"Would she do that?"

"Wouldn't surprise me none, headstrong as she is. No use putting it to her; she'd only deny it till hell freezes. But it don't matter. Whatever the case, she's got too damn pert and uppity for my taste. Still she's my sister, and I got a duty to her. What she requires is to be took down a peg or two. Best way to do that is send her back to Maryland for a spell. Right along with Rainey."

Welda nodded slowly. "That would be good. All I'd object to in your plan would be sending Rainey to live with strangers. It would be so much better if Meg were with him. But King, suppose she tries to get in touch with Jonas? She could always write him."

King chuckled. "The postmaster at Moratown, old Bill Condo, is a good friend of mine. Any letters get posted there for Jonas Bonner will have to pass through Bill's hands. They'll pass straight along to us."

Welda was silent for a long time. Then she curled her fingers around King's, squeezing them tight. "Can I tell you something, Mr. Canibar? How very grateful I am for all you've given me . . . all you've done for me? And that I love you very much?"

"All I done," King muttered. He felt the heavy mask of his face starting to crack; he had to blink against a sudden wetness. "I can't begin to say what you give me," he said huskily. "My God, we've had a good life."

"The best," she murmured. "Only the very best. I made up my mind after I left Jonas never to settle for anything less than the best. And I never have. That includes you, my darling."

"You're going to walk again." King's voice shook a little. "That's another promise."

"Don't try to hand me the stars, dear," she said gently. "You've given me more than I ever asked, and I've never asked for the impossible. We have to face it. There is no sign of improvement and very probably won't be. Every doctor we've consulted has agreed—"

"Then we'll keep looking," King said fiercely. "You're going to walk again. I swear to God you are!"

Chapter Fifteen

JONAS had waited all afternoon at the base of Castle Rock. Long before sunset, when Meg and Rainey still failed to appear, he was certain something had gone wrong. Yet, hoping against hope, he continued to wait till the last streaks of twilight had melted into dusk. Wholly and bitterly convinced by then, he lost no time making his next move, for he had settled on it hours ago. He pointed Diablo Red southwest toward Big Crown headquarters, leading a well-laden packhorse and a spare mount he'd brought for Rainey. The night was clear; a frosting of starlight plainly picked out his way so long as he clung to open hills and flats.

He rode slowly, wanting to reach the place at a late hour. The darkness would cover his approach, making it easier to steal into the heart of Big Crown than on the occasion when he had sneaked in by daylight. Apparently there was no ranch dog, for none had picked him up then. All to the good, but then Jonas had considerably more at stake this time. Yet, having no idea what difficulties he might encounter, he had no plan in mind any more concrete than just getting Rainey away. He'd simply have to move one step at a time and be as prudent as possible. Taken by itself, this venture was an exercise in pure recklessness, but the savage determination in him would brook no delay.

What had gone awry with Meg and Rainey? King's and Welda's suspicions might have been somehow aroused, or Meg's offer of help might have been an impulse she'd later regretted. Not knowing the truth, Jonas had no recourse but to move now. If there was a danger the Canibars might be expecting him to do just that, there was a greater danger that to wait for another time, another night, might enable them to put Rainey beyond his reach.

The very possibility, once it had occurred to him, gnawed steadily in Jonas. It lent a sharpening sense of urgency to his purpose. No waiting, then. Unless his reconnaissance of the place showed beyond any doubt that it would be hopeless to try taking Rainey away tonight, he was going through with it.

When the black outlines of rolling hills gave way to the long grassy flat where Big Crown headquarters was situated, it was close to midnight. Every building was dark except for a few lighted windows in the big house: exactly what you'd expect at this hour, whether everyone had actually retired or whether a trap was waiting to be sprung.

As he had before, Jonas came up on the timbered

flank of the headquarters. He groped his way into the same motte of trees where he had previously tied a horse. Leaving Diablo Red and the other animals there, he went ahead on foot through the random clumps of shrubbery till he reached the carriage house. He slipped cautiously along a side wall, pistol in hand, to a front corner of the building. From here he had a clear view of the main house, its two-storey hulk boxlike and black against the cobalt sky, except for those yellow squares of windowlight.

With a cold dismay, Jonas saw that all the light emanated from front and side windows of the lower floor where the parlor was, an indication that the household hadn't yet retired. It would have been easier to surprise them in their beds. Yet with a moment's reflection, he wondered if it wouldn't be better to catch the Canibars together in the parlor, if possible. After all he had no idea which room was Rainey's, and once the family did retire, they might lock the house up securely for the night. If he could slip inside quickly and get the drop on all of them, he could make them bind and gag one another, giving Rainey and him a respite in which to get well away before the alarm was raised. Once that happened, Canibar would have the whole Big Crown crew on their trail. The entire business was fraught with risk anyhow he looked at it, so why hesitate? Might as well go boldly in and take his chances.

Bending low, Jonas crossed the gravel drive at a run and moved noiselessly onto the veranda. He eased over to the front door and turned its knob with infinite care, knowing if it were locked he might be stymied at the outset. But it turned easily and silently. He inched the door open a slim crack, enough to peer into the great vaulted parlor.

It was empty.

He stood motionless, listening. The house might have been deserted, it was so quiet. Yet low-turned lamps burned in each corner of the big room, as though lighted against the occupants' return.

His muscles tight with anticipation, Jonas slipped inside and softly closed the door. His glance raked across the room and stopped on the stairwell that led to the second floor. He knew the house's interior somewhat from eight years ago, and he knew that the sleeping area opened off the head of those stairs. Had the whole household retired? The parlor lights argued that they were only gone for the evening, but if so, wouldn't they have returned by this hour?

The gunbutt felt clammy against Jonas's palm; an uneasy tingle ghosted along his spine. Steeling himself, he fought the feeling down. Despite a distinctly wrong feel to this whole situation, he wasn't retreating now.

Moving swiftly, he catfooted across to the foot of the stairs and loped up the rises two at a time. He halted at the top, peering into the dark bedroom corridor. A pencil of light showed under one door. He tiptoed over to it and, holding his gun ready, palmed the knob and opened the door suddenly.

This was obviously the master bedroom: every object it contained, from commode to bedstead, was ornate and somewhat oversize. A single lamp burned on the bedside table. Welda lay alone in the great bed, and she was asleep, the bedclothes pulled to her chin.

After a moment's hesitation, Jonas took a step back and began to close the door. But Welda woke then, her eyes coming open and alert on the instant.

"Jonas. . . ." A quiet smile shaped her mouth. "We should have expected you, shouldn't we? But of course. Well, you've invaded the house this far . . . why don't you step in? Please."

He entered the room and closed the door, then said stonily: "Where is he?"

Pushing the covers partly back, Welda hitched her upper body against a backprop of pillows and folded her hands under the ruffled bosom of her demure white gown. In the lamplight, with her face framed by the loose fall of her hair, she looked almost childlike. Except for the malice in her smile.

"Guess," she murmured.

"Is he in the house?"

She gave the faintest of shrugs. "You're welcome to look if you like."

Stung to a baffled anger, Jonas started to reply. Then he tilted his head, listening sharply. The noise came again: a creak of door hinges. He wrenched open the door and stepped abruptly into the dim hallway, his gun swinging to cover a door that was slowly opening.

Old Sam Canibar came out on wobbly legs, grabbing at the wall. He was barely able to stand; his eyes were rheumy and unfocused. A bottle dangled from his fist. Jonas took a couple steps toward him and caught the heavy reek of liquor.

"Sam. You hear me?"

"Sure," old Sam mumbled, his head down. "I ain' drunk."

"You know me? Jonas Bonner?"

"Course I know you f' chrissake." He shouldered past Jonas, stumbling, and paused in the doorway of the master bedroom, swaying back and forth as if to an unheard melody. "Hey Welda. You wanna drink? Wanna drink with ole Dad?"

He staggered into the room, swayed backward, and sat down abruptly on the floor. Jonas stepped back inside now, and old Sam peered at him and held out the bottle. "You too, Bonnie, f' chrissake. Have a drink."

"Maybe later, Sam." Aware that Welda was looking on tensely now, he hunkered down by the old man and grabbed him by the shoulder, gently shaking him. "Sam, you hear me? I'm looking for my boy. You know my boy, Rainey?"

"Heeza good kid. Don' wanna hear no different."

"Sure. He's a fine kid. You know where he is, old-timer? Can you show me?"

"Sam!" Welda said sharply. "Don't tell him anything! You understand? Nothing!"

Old Sam turned his head, eying her blearily. "Why'n hell, uh, why'n hell not?"

"He's not to be told a thing! Not about Rainey, not about anything! You hear me?"

Sam took a pull of whiskey and seemed to consider for a long careful moment. "Why'n hell not? Iss his boy ain' it? Bonnie, he's one goddamn good man." He flipped a friendly hand at Jonas's arm. "Goddamn good man, I tell you."

Fighting down his impatience, Jonas said gently: "What about him, Sam? What about Rainey?"

"Shit, yeah, Rainey, he be plumb gone, boy." Sam waggled his head slowly. "King 'n' Phil 'n' the whole goddamn crew—"

"Sam!" Welda shrilled. "Don't tell him!"

"Why not, f' chrissake? They all took him to Moratown, him 'n' my girl Meg. Put 'em on train."

"What train?"

Sam's head slumped forward, and Jonas gave him a savage shake. "Sam, what train?"

"East train, goddammit. Midnight train goin' east. Ain' no other this time a night. . . ."

Old Sam's voice dwindled, and Jonas let him sag to the floor, then came swiftly to his feet. Welda gave a low harsh laugh; her green eyes catlike.

"You're too late, Jonas! That train leaves at midnight and it's nearly that now. It would take you three hours just to reach Moratown and then you'd have to fight Big Crown's whole crew—"

He was already out the door and running for the staircase. As he plunged recklessly down it, the thin mockery of her laughter followed him like a sound of splintering glass.

Idling along the starlit road, Phil Canibar was in no particular hurry as he rode back to Big Crown. His thoughts were an agreeable slush that was brightly tinged from frequent pulls at the bottle in his left fist. His right hand had a loose hold on the reins, but his horse needed no guidance this close to headquarters. The animal stepped along at a mild gait that suited Phil to a T.

He'd been feeling considerably less mellow when he had left Moratown. After seeing Meg and Rainey and their two guards safely on the train and watching its departure, the whole crew, including King, had repaired to a saloon for a night of carousing. King had soon gotten loud and ebullient, and Phil had understood his brother's need to be shed of his worries and responsibilities temporarily by going on a roaring spree in the company of a rough crowd. It was an anodyne that had never appealed to the fastidious Phil, who preferred good brandy to rotgut and a genteel parlor to a saloon. Also he had an angry memory of how King had turned on him during his last drunk; Phil had no intention of being the target of another such rampage. So, he had soon quit the party and, after purchasing a bottle of good liquor, had headed back for the ranch alone.

The buildings of Big Crown lay dark and silent as Phil rode in. That was to be expected at this hour, even if King hadn't declared a three-day holiday for the whole outfit, including the Mexican house servants who had all left to visit friends or relatives in Mextown. Only a few windows in the big house held a blaze of light as he swung past it, riding toward the corral.

Phil had reached the horse stable when the front door of the house was flung open, yanking his glance that way. A man came piling out the door. Momentarily he was silhouetted against the inside light, but Phil had no time to identify him. In a flash the fellow was off the veranda and cutting away from the house at a run; he was quickly lost in the dark.

Cautiously Phil remained where he was, sitting his horse in the shadow of the stable, straining his ears. Presently he caught the faint sound of a horse being ridden off at a fast gait.

Gigging his mount around now, Phil cantered back to the house. He stepped from the saddle and wrapped his reins around a hitching post. As he moved onto the veranda, he shoved his right hand into his coat pocket, where he kept a Henry D. He closed his fist around the small pistol and went through the open door, throwing a quick glance around the parlor as he crossed it.

Nobody else here. Who the hell was that fellow anyway?

The likely answer was already forming in his mind when he heard Welda call weakly from upstairs: "Who's down there? I hear you. Who is it?"

Phil bounded up the stairway and headed for the master bedroom, whose door hung open. He pulled up in his surprise, seeing his father unconscious on the floor and Welda beside him. She must have dragged herself from the bed, using only her arms, to reach him. Now she was pounding on his chest with a small fist, saying frantically, "Wake up! King has got to be told. Wake up, Sam—"

She broke off, lifting her angry gaze to Phil. "You? Where is King? *Where is he?*"

"Still in Moratown, I expect. I rode back by myself. What's going on?"

"Help me back to bed . . . please." Her eyes glittered with tears of angry frustration, but her voice was steely calm now. "There's something you'll have to do, Phil. There is no time to lose."

Phil said, "Oh? What might that be," as he stooped and lifted her slight weight, then carried her to the big bed.

Welda lay back against the pillow, momentarily shutting her eyes. "Jonas was here . . . he just left. You must have seen him."

"I reckon I did. He was riding mighty fast when he went."

Her eyes flew open. "Which way did he go? If he was going for town, he must have passed you on the road."

Phil shrugged. "I was already by the stable when he

came out of the house. He didn't see me, and I had only a glimpse of him. He had a horse hidden somewhere in the trees and I heard him ride away. That's all."

"He wanted Rainey," Welda said bitterly. "Sam— that drunken old fool!—told him Meg and the boy took the midnight train east."

"So? It'll be long gone by the time he gets to town."

"But suppose he doesn't! Suppose he gets *ahead* of the train somehow? Phil, it *could* be done!"

Phil nodded, rubbing his chin. "Reckon it could, at that—"

She clutched at his arm. "Phil, I want you to ride back to Moratown. Now. Tell King what's happened. If Jonas can get ahead of the train, maybe so can King and the men. They can stop Jonas!"

"Well . . . . "

"Please—*do* it!" The shrill edge on her voice betrayed her agitation. "Phil, you won't regret it, I promise! I know we've had our differences, but we can work them out. Anything! Just so *he* doesn't get Rainey—anything—"

"Easy, there," Phil counseled mildly. "I'll get to King, sure."

"Right away!"

"Fast as I can. We'll talk this out later, all right? What you want to do now is calm down and get some sleep. Doc said no excitement, remember?"

As he spoke in a patient and soothing voice, Phil reached for the bottle of laudanum and measuring glass on the bedside table. Welda's eyes, cloudy with the pain she had fought down, followed his movements as he decanted a stiff dose of the drug into the glass and handed it to her. She swallowed it quickly and settled back, her gaze wide and imploring.

"Please," she whispered.

"Be on my way soon as I've put the old man in his bed."

The fog of drink had cleared from Phil's brain; it was working coldly and clearly now, each turn of thought meshing as precisely as the gears of a clock. And suddenly he knew exactly what he would do and how he would do it. The decision came to him that calmly and easily since, in a way, it was really a decision he had made days ago.

Moving over to his father now, he reached down and grabbed the old man's wrists, then tugged his slack weight up till he could heave it across his shoulders. Tramping heavily under his burden, Phil crossed to the door and paused there, glancing back at Welda. Her eyes were already glazing to the laudanum's soporific effect; a draught that size would soon have her in a deep sleep, and then it would take the crack of doom to awaken her.

Phil gave a silent chuckle and pulled the door shut as he left the room. Instead of carrying old Sam to his room, he toted his father's dead weight down the stairway, across the parlor, and out of the house. He was sweating with the unaccustomed exertion as he finally laid the old man down under a tree some distance from the building. "You'll be all right here, Pa," he muttered. "Might take a little damp in your bones, but you've lived through a sight worse."

Afterward Phil headed swiftly for the tack shed. He moved furtively, clinging to the shadows, though he knew the ranch headquarters was deserted tonight except for Welda and the old man. The enormity of what he intended to do crowded his whole consciousness now, trying the edge of his nerve. He must do it quickly, Phil thought, do the thing as fast as he could and not give it one jot of thought more than he had to . . . .

In the dark tack shed he groped for and found four five-gallon tins of coal oil. He carried two of them up to the house, then ran back to fetch the remaining pair. He splashed the contents of the tins throughout every room on the ground floor, saturating carpets and upholstery. In fifteen minutes or less, it was done. Then he picked up one of the lighted parlor lamps and heaved it against the wall.

It broke, spattering flames across the wall and floor. Phil waited just long enough to watch the curtain of fire start to race across the parlor carpet. Then he turned and ran from the house.

With a panicky haste he seized up his reins, flung himself into the saddle, and kicked his horse into a run toward the road. He would ride back to Moratown on the double, but not so fast as to tire his horse noticeably.

Perhaps a quarter mile away, Phil pulled to a halt and looked back at the house. The whole interior of the ground floor was already a seething furnace, flames leaping from every window. He put his horse down the road once more and did not look back again.

The night lay cold against his sweating body. It would work all right, he told himself; no reason it shouldn't. When he'd left Moratown earlier, it had been dark enough that nobody had even noticed his departure, nor had Phil announced to a soul his intention of returning to the ranch. He'd make equally certain that nobody saw him slip back into town. So far as anyone would know, he'd never left; he'd simply spent the evening drifting from one saloon to another. Nobody would trouble to backtrack all his movements; they'd have no cause to.

No suspicion of firing the house would fall on him. Not when his own father had seen Jonas Bonner at Big Crown tonight and would tell it that way. All suspicion would focus at once on one man: Jonas. Of course King still remained in the picture. But maybe not for long. King's reaction would be predictable as sunrise; it might just offer a prime chance to finish the job.

And then, with both King and Welda out of the way, Big Crown would be Phil's.

No doubt King's estate would be thrown into probate, but Phil was confident that in the end he would have everything. Besides himself, his sister and their father would be the nearest surviving kin, and neither would contest Phil's claim. Old Sam Canibar was incompetent—Meg too generous and easygoing.

The idea that Phil had only idly toyed with for a long time had hotly crystallized on that night King had given him a brutal pummeling, shaking loose a buried ambition, one he had never quite dared admit to himself. It had forced him to the galling self-admission of just how sick he was of living in his brother's shadow. For days he had boiled with plans for removing the two obstacles in his path, King and Welda, only to discard each one in turn. Unless the murders of both could be made to appear either convincingly accidental or the work of someone other than Phil, inevitable suspicion would focus on him: the one who stood to gain the most by their deaths.

Now, though, blame for Welda's death would fall on Jonas Bonner. Just maybe, so would the blame for King's.

Phil turned the scheme over carefully in his mind,

mentally trimming the rough edges, and finally he chuckled aloud. It contained elements of risk, but God, the stakes were worth it; they surely were. And King himself would unwittingly set the situation up for him. While Phil's own part would be covered by an unshakable alibi.

For, after tonight, once he had set the wheels in motion, Phil shouldn't have to do a thing. Frank Dance would do it for him.

Chapter Sixteen

CLIMBING east into the Great Divide, Rocky Bench rose in a long grade that grew sharply steeper just before it leveled out. The railroad had laid its track across that bench, and Jonas remembered, on a trip he had made to Omaha some years ago, how the cars had gradually slowed as they neared the top of the grade. This was the place, if any, that he might hope to head off the eastbound train bearing his son.

To reach it before the train did, he would have to short-cut by night across miles of rugged country, with only a faint starshine and his knowledge of the district to guide him. Luckily the terrain between Big Crown and the bench also contained great stretches of open grassland, and here he could put Diablo Red to an all-out pace.

It was a supreme test of the stallion's might and endurance, and it was a ride Jonas would never forget. Even in his driving anxiety, he felt a lift of wild exhilaration in the surging power that bore him south and east across the silvered plains. In the rushing darkness as the miles fell behind, the blood bay's steady tirelessness communicated an iron confidence to his rider, causing the clutch of urgency to ebb. So long as Diablo Red could maintain this pace, running hard on flats and climbing the rough spots with that incredibly surefooted ease, they had to succeed; it seemed impossible that they could fail.

Climbing into the south ramparts of the Neversummers, the land grew progressively rougher. The terrain forced them to a slower pace, but at the same time the sky began to lighten, making it easier for Jonas to pick his way. Taking his bearings by familiar landmarks, he felt a steady rise of confidence.

He was close to the western ascent of Rocky Bench, and he was almost dead certain he was ahead of the train. Throughout this mountainous region the tracks negotiated hairpin turns and increasing grades. So the train would move slowly, too, and meantime he would gain on it. A horse like Diablo Red could shave away miles and minutes by short-cutting at many places where the cars must swing in wide loops along a carefully graded roadbed.

In less than an hour Jonas angled onto the track at the place where it began its long climb to the summit of Rocky Bench. He followed the rails upward till he reached the last steep pitch before the slope leveled off. Here he dismounted and gave Diablo Red a look-over. The big horse showed few signs of his grueling journey; his sides heaved rhythmically and his sleek coat was wet. He tossed his head and grunted, as if questioning.

"That's all for awhile," Jonas told him.

After ground-hitching the stallion in a secluded pocket between some gigantic boulders, he set to work. The flinty slope was strewn with rubble and larger rocks, many of them loose in the soil. Jonas wrestled with the biggest ones he could lift, heaving them into position across the track. His muscles cracked with the strain as he hoisted and carried and sweated, building a massive cairn of boulders the height of a man.

As he finished his task, pearly streaks were breaking along the rim of the land; the residue of night was fading in a slow washback across the sky. But true dawn was still hours away. Shaking with fatigue, Jonas sat on a rock, took off his hat, and sleeved muddy sweat from his face, and peered off toward the squashed cone of a small peak to the west. The railroad tracks curved gradually into sight around its granite-gray escarpment, and it was this spot that Jonas watched.

A slow worry began to gnaw at him. Had he misjudged, after all? Could the train have beaten him here?

Jonas heard it before he saw it: the approaching roar of the engine beyond the curve. His pulse picked up to a swift excitement. Before the locomotive came into view, he got to his feet and tramped to the pocket where he had left Diablo Red. From here, crouching almost out of sight of the track, he could watch the train's approach.

The gray light was just starting to pale; distant objects that weren't skylined were still largely indistinct. Jonas was gambling that the old engineer on this routine night run wouldn't be sufficiently alert to spot the barricade of rock till he was almost onto it. At the same time he should have little difficulty braking the locomotive on this uphill grade. If he spotted the obstruction when he was halfway up, he should be able to stop well short of it. Jonas hoped so, for he'd positioned himself where he could swiftly reach the cars once they came to a standstill.

The train began to labor into its long climb, perceptibly slowing now. Jonas sized its makeup in a glance: locomotive and tender, two freight cars, the passenger and baggage-express cars, a pair of cattle cars, and a caboose. He fixed a brief hungry look on the passenger coach where Rainey would be, then directed his attention toward the locomotive.

When the train was about halfway upslope, Jonas had a bad moment, wondering if old Woodrow Bates was asleep at his throttle. By now the engineer should be aware of the obstruction just ahead. If he failed to apply the brakes in time, the train might be derailed even at this stepped-down speed.

The dragging shriek of brakes came; the train began to slow more abruptly. Jonas tensed himself. The locomotive finally groaned to a stop ten yards from the barricade; a deafening crash of couplings raced down the cars. Jonas was already on his feet, running to the cab as the white-haired engineer leaned out the window, swearing.

"Hello, Woody—"

The engineer's head swiveled; he peered down at Jonas and his drawn gun, waited till a racket of gushing steam subsided, then spat and said, "Howdy, Bonnie. You getting a powerful resemblance to Jesse James."

Jonas stirred his head in negation. "No holdup. You got my boy aboard, Woody."

"Yeh, I know."

The fireman's sooty face thrust past old Woody's now, and he said testily, "What the hell?"

"Don't get your butt in an uproar," Woody told him dryly, saying to Jonas then: "You aim to fetch him off?"

"That's it. Meantime you stay set, all right?"

"Hell, take him off. But you best watch yourself, Bonnie. They's a couple Canibar men in that car with him."

Jonas had a half second to digest that information before he heard their voices. Voices of at least two men. They were exiting from the passenger car on its other side; he heard their boots hit the gravel of the roadbed. Stooping down below car level, he saw their legs and feet, and they were coming toward the cab on the run. Jonas straightened up, glanced at Woody and the fireman, and tapped a finger against his lips. Then he loped quietly down the train past the tender to the first freight car.

Hearing the two guards reach the cab and shout a rough question at the trainmen, Jonas dropped low and rolled noiselessly over the rail and under the car. In one unbroken movement he rolled across the ties, over the opposite rail, and out the other side, then came to his feet, gun in hand.

The two men, their rifles up and ready, were standing with their backs to him, listening to Woody blandly declare that someone had piled rocks on the track and he was damned if he knew who.

"Whoever done it has got to be close about," drawled one of the guards. "You men get out and get that track cleared off while we have a look around."

"Look back of you first," Jonas said gently. "Do it slow."

Both guards were seasoned and steady hands, and not about to make a foolish move. They tipped their heads around till they could see him, and the younger man swore tonelessly.

"Shuck your guns."

"There's three more of us on this train, Bonner," said the older guard.

"I don't think so. Shuck your guns."

The two exchanged baffled glances, then dropped their rifles. Both had six-guns holstered at their sides, and at Jonas's order they discarded these too, pulling them with their left hands and tossing them away. Jonas stepped to one side and motioned downtrack.

"Get walking," he said quietly.

The older man promptly obeyed; the younger fellow swore again, hesitating, and then tramped after him. Jonas followed them as far as the passenger car, where he halted, saying flatly, "Keep going," and watched them move on.

"Pa!"

Rainey came piling out of the car's vestibule, practically ramming him off balance. Jonas grabbed the boy up for a moment, then looked over his shoulder at Meg as she descended from the vestibule. She gave a tentative and uncertain smile.

"I might have known you'd manage," she said. "Somehow."

Jonas eyed her stonily, then set Rainey down. "Let's be going, boy. Diablo Red will have to carry double."

"Wait," Meg said hesitantly. "I—listen, I want to go with you. Will you let me?"

"Why?" he said bluntly. "So you can lay trail for your brother? I don't reckon."

"Oh. I see . . . you think I gave you away. Is that it?"

"Can't think of no better reason you didn't show up with Rainey. Or why you and him got put on this train so damn prompt."

"Pa, Meg couldn't help it!" Rainey put in spiritedly. "She told me why that happened. . . ."

Quickly the boy told of the cross-up in their plans as Meg had told it to him during the journey. It had to be the truth, Jonas thought; it had the ring of truth, and he felt a thin wash of relief. He hadn't given any involved thought to the possibility that things had gone awry because Meg had betrayed him, perhaps because he hadn't wanted to believe it.

He said with a sober curiosity, "You mean what you said? You want to come with us."

"Yes. I meant it. There's nothing for me at Big Crown any more. Nor back East," she added flatly. "Wherever you're going, you and Rainey, take me along. I can keep up well enough and I sha'n't be a burden to you. I have money of my own. When you get where you're going, I'll say goodbye. Is that agreeable?"

Jonas rubbed his beard, scowling. He owed this girl a measure of gratitude for her good intentions; he felt a degree of responsibility for her present position. But he shook his head abruptly. "Sorry. You can't go afoot, and we only got the one horse. . . ."

A smile flickered on her lips. "My mare Blazes is in one of the stock cars. I wouldn't leave her behind. You might say it's the price I exacted from King for going away without a fuss. Just give me a little time to get a few things from my luggage and change my clothes."

"We've got a long, mean trail in front of us," Jonas said grimly. "Could be some gunplay before it's done. I just don't know."

"I do," Meg said calmly. "I can always follow you, can't I? I can do that whether you agree or not, Jonas. So you may as well be agreeable."

Phil Canibar was keeping a diplomatic distance from his brother and saying nothing, as if respecting King's grief. But he kept a wary eye on him, too.

King stood with hands clenched at his sides, silent tears streaming down his cheeks, and stared at the charred wreckage that had been his home. In the murky light of pre-dawn the crewmen resembled sooty specters as they moved quietly about at small tasks, talked in hushed undertones, or merely stood about awaiting the orders that they knew must come soon, putting them in motion once more.

It had been long after midnight, but still dark, when the men of Big Crown had returned from Moratown. They were yet a good distance from the place when they'd first made out a bright leap of fire. By the time they had reached the scene, the roaring mass of flames had all but consumed the house; the blaze was sinking. Now, despite hours of dousing the fire with water passed along a bucket line from the well, the tangle of blackened timbers continued to spark and smoke; now and then one collapsed in a mushrooming cloud of ashes. Only the two stone wings and the bare columns of the field-stone chimneys remained standing.

King's first grief had been a tearing and terrible thing to see. For a while it had touched Phil with a cold fear, an irrational fear that somehow, though his part in this was impeccably covered, his brother might unearth the truth and direct a savage retribution against the right man.

God, if King ever suspected!

The ruin was still too hot to begin a search for the bodies. Everyone assumed that old Sam, as well as Welda, had been caught in the inferno. No doubt, Phil thought, the old man was still in a drunken sleep under the tree where he had left him. Phil hadn't gone near there himself, shrewdly preferring to let someone else stumble on his father. And nobody had even begun as yet to speculate on how the fire had started. But soon enough they would. And then King's bereavement would find a fresh and fierce direction.

Phil lighted up a long nine, pleased to note there wasn't a shadow of tremor in his fingers. Hell, it would work out all right. Everything had gone exactly right so far.

His return to Moratown had been as undetected as his departure. He'd gone directly to the Mexican quarter and Sanchez's whorehouse, where he knew there'd be an excellent chance of finding Frank Dance. The bronc-peeler had been hanging out in town since King had fired him. At Sanchez's place Phil had found Dance partly drunk; enlisting his attention hadn't been easy. Once the proposal had been laid out for him, however, Dance had been predictably intrigued by the prospect of putting a slug in King Canibar and making it appear that Jonas Bonner was to blame. Phil's offer of five thousand dollars, to be paid to Dance as soon as the

Canibar estate was settled in Phil's favor, had cinched Dance's agreement.

The proposition had been made, the bargain struck, just that simply. Dance was instructed in full on what he must do and how he must handle it. The whole business had taken less than a half hour. And then Phil had returned to the saloon festivities, his long absence from them going unnoticed.

Nothing to do now but wait and let events shape their own course.

"Mr. Canibar!" It was a crewman's excited yell. "Hey, over here! I done found your pappy!"

A smile touched the corners of Phil's mouth as he and others hurried after King, who was heading on the run for the tree a hundred yards away. The crewman was bending over old Sam who was snoring peacefully on his side, and now he glanced up and said: "He's sure enough alive, sir. But I can't roust him."

King dropped on one knee, saying between his teeth, "Drunk," as he caught his father by the shoulder and shook him fiercely. "Wake up, you old bastard! Come out of it!"

Old Sam's head lolled like a rag doll's, flopping back and forth. His eyes slid groggily open. "Heh? What's 'at? Jesus, where am I?"

"You're still alive," King said ominously. And gave him another vicious shake. "What about Welda? Was she in the house? Goddamn you, answer me!"

"The house. . . ." Old Sam sat up laboriously, turning his eyes toward the smoking ruin. He blinked several times. "My Christ," he said softly. "Who done that?"

King grabbed his chin in one hand and swiveled it back front. "Maybe you," he said savagely. "Maybe you was drunk enough to knock over a lamp. Or drop a lighted stogie somewhere. Eh?"

"Naw," Sam husked. "You can't believe that, son. Why, hell, I. . . ." His brows puckered; a kind of fearful glaze touched his staring eyes. "Welda?" he said with a timorous care. "You say Welda . . . ?"

"You tell me!" King roared. "What about her? *Was she in that house?*"

"Yeh . . . yeh." Sam waggled his head slowly. "I mean she sure's hell was when I . . . Bonner." His slurry sentence trailed into the name. "He was there, too, I recall. . . ."

"Bonner—what about Bonner? Goddammit, old man, *what happened?*"

"Tryna 'member," Sam muttered. "Don' crowd me, all right? Lessee. I was sleeping in my room 'n' heard talk. Bonner was there. Him 'n' Welda was talking. Ast me where his boy was—"

"You told him?"

"Well, shit yeh, no harm in that, was there? Don' rec'lect no more after that. Don't 'member comin' outside. . . ."

King got slowly to his feet.

"Bonner," he said in a tone so hushed the word was almost inaudible.

David Crow was standing by, and now, unusual for him, he spoke up abruptly: "Does that make sense, Mr. Canibar?"

King's eyes, as he turned them toward the half breed, glistened with a strangely intense, almost dazed sheen. "Eh? What's that?"

"Jonas Bonner . . . is he a man to do a thing like this? Does that make sense to you?"

But King was beyond sense, beyond hearing or reason: the look in his face was the same it had worn at other times when Phil had seen him stupefied with liquor and rage. Tonight he had been drinking for hours, and now a numbness of stunned grief was wearing away to a fury that his great driving nature couldn't contain for long, that must find a swift and expedient outlet. A fire that only direct action could damp.

With the mention of Bonner's name, it had all the fuel it needed.

Chapter Seventeen

IT was close to midmorning when Jonas and Rainey and Meg arrived at Cross-B. The three of them were bone-tired as they dismounted in the yard, for Jonas had set a hard pace. The woman and boy had caught a few uncomfortable hours of sleep on the train; Jonas had driven himself brutally for hours without a wink of rest. Out of shape from weeks of recuperation, he was tottering with fatigue as he walked toward the house.

But there could be no delay for rest or sleep at Cross-B. Once word reached the Canibars—by way of the two guards Jonas had set afoot—a posse of Big Crown men would be swarming on their trail. One of the first places they might look would be the Bonner ranch. Not knowing how much time he might have, Jonas was taking no chances. He and Meg and Rainey would linger at

Cross-B just long enough to wolf a meal, stock up on provisions, and get a change of horses, then be on their way.

The Bacas and Barney Blue and Grif were on hand to greet them. The four had been sitting tight at the place, waiting for any sort of news, and Jonas answered their questions as they all filed into the house. Afterward, while he and Meg and his son sat down to a meal of cold steaks and biscuits, Mateo and Barney and Grif readied fresh horses and Minita put up a pack of camp supplies.

As he ate, Jonas looked around the big common room and its homely comforts, wondering if he would ever see it again. Whether, in fact, this was the last time the close group of people he'd come to think of as "family" would be together. Sunk in a weary preoccupation, brooding over his coffee, he hardly noticed that Barney and Grif were standing in front of him, waiting.

Grif cleared his throat, self-consciously. "Mr. Bonner, we got something to say."

Jonas glanced from one sober face to the other, noting that Mateo and Minita were standing a little apart, listening. "Reckon you better say it."

"It ain't much," Grif said quietly. "Just that Barney and me aim to side you. Where you go, we're going. We got our minds set on't, so won't do you a wink of good to talk us down. Not this time."

Jonas leaned back, giving a slow dry nod. "You decided that, have you?"

"Boy put it clear and plain," Barney said just as dryly. "I don't reckon you can stop us."

"No good telling you what you could be going up against. You damn well know."

"I reckon we do, *caporal*."

Jonas put a hard stare on Grif, saying pointedly: "You got a sight more to lose than Barney, boy. You got a good way of things going for you right here. A whole lot of living ahead of you. Too much to take a chance on losing. It only takes one bullet."

Grif's glance shuttled to Minita. She smiled and nodded gently, and Grif looked back at Jonas. "I allow you are right on all accounts, sir," he said mildly. "But I don't allow I can do no different. Don't reckon nobody else does, either."

No amount of argument would sway either man, Jonas saw. "Better get your warbags loaded fast, then. I ain't waiting on you."

"They're loaded," said Barney. "Got our hosses ready, too. We made up our minds last night."

A worried impatience was fretting Jonas, and foremost in his thoughts was the need to get moving. North would be their direction, toward the Montana border. To get away from where King Canibar wielded influence as far and fast as possible was Jonas's first objective, and anything he decided after that was in the hands of fate. They would stick to backwoods country that he knew, avoiding settlements, and they would rest only as necessity dictated. Jonas had some emergency money salted away, four hundred dollars in gold double eagles buried in a rawhide sack under a floorboard in the common room. In plain sight of all, he pried up the board and lifted out the sack, then announced it was time to be going.

Their animals were ready and waiting at the corral: five mounts freshly saddled and five spare horses, in-

cluding Diablo Red and Meg's Blazes, and also two
well-laden packhorses.

Mateo Baca grasped Jonas's hand, his seamed old
face working a little. "Blood of Christ, *amigo*, but I wish
I might take this trail with you. If my old bones would
bear me half so far."

"Soon's we're well away from here, out of danger and
all, I'll send Grif and Barney back," Jonas said. "Meantime someone's got to hold down the place. Remember,
you and Minita got a home here for as long as you
want it."

"Ah," Mateo said philosophically. "What will be will
be. But when will the *caporal* return?"

To that Jonas had no answer.

Sitting with his back to a boulder that was still warm
with the day's heat, Frank Dance chewed up a sandwich
and swallowed it in a couple of gulps. Cold grub for a
cold camp. But Dance didn't mind too much. He had
followed longer and harder trails than this one. And
was willing to undergo a sight more discomfort than
this for five thousand dollars. Not to mention a nice
helping of personal satisfaction.

In the valley below the high promontory where Dance
crouched, a half-dozen supper fires made orange beacons
in the dusk. The men of Big Crown had kept going till
well after dark before making their camp.

Dance had kept up with them since early this morning, hanging on like a leech to their trail. Sometimes
close, other times at a distance. Sometimes behind them,
other times parallel to their line of march. But always
at a point where he could take the best vantage of them
and still keep out of sight.

At Dance's side lay two canteens; he took a swig of whiskey from one and chased it with a drink of water from the other, wiping the back of a hairy fist across his mouth. He gave a dry, quiet chuckle.

So far it had been a cinch.

Everything had gone as Phil Canibar had said it would. Dance had followed the men from their drunken carousing in Moratown back to Big Crown where they had found the house in flames. It was still predawn when Canibar and his crew had started the long ride to Rockaway Bench where (Phil had predicted) Jonas Bonner would attempt to stop the train, as King himself had easily deduced: it was simply the likeliest place for such. On the way they had met two men trudging on foot, and from their long conference with the King, Dance had guessed these were the two sent along to guard the boy and Canibar's sister. From this he'd concluded that Bonner had been successful.

At Rocky Bench, King Canibar had put David Crow to work picking up Bonner's trail from where he had halted the train. The breed was one hell of a tracker, as Dance knew, and by noon he had led Canibar and his crew to Bonner's Cross-B. But nobody was there except the old Mex and his granddaughter, and after a hasty search of the place, Canibar had put David Crow on the trail again.

Through the rest of this long day, the breed had led them almost straight north.

Unrolling his soogans beside the rock, Dance stretched out and pillowed his head on his saddle, taking another swallow of whiskey. Idly he wondered if the Big Crown men would overtake Bonner. Good chance they might, if King Canibar kept pushing as hard as he had today.

Bonner, after all, would believe Canibar would pursue him merely to reclaim the kid. He wouldn't dream that the King was driven by a fury to avenge his murdered wife.

Phil Canibar had been coldly and incisively thorough about telling Dance exactly what he had done and why he'd done it. He'd wanted Dance to understand fully what was at stake; at the same time Dance couldn't prove a syllable of any of it. Phil was, Dance reflected, a cold-blooded bastard capable of just about anything to gain his way, including a double cross if he could work one. Only he wouldn't, Dance thought placidly, because he'd be alert for anything of the sort. And would tear the bastard's heart out if he tried it. He had assured Phil as much.

Dance yawned and pulled the blanket over him. Better catch some shuteye while he could. It had been a hell of a long night and day, and tomorrow should be rougher yet. But he could take it as long as any man alive could. The risky part was still ahead. But five thousand in the kitty and a chance to dust King Canibar and frame it onto Bonner . . . all that was worth damn near any risk.

He smiled at the stars and closed his eyes.

Jonas and his companions rode north through a long day, made night camp at the far end of the Buckhorns, and were up at first light to resume their journey. Another day in the saddle brought them into more irregular country. Tonight, in concession to the terrific weariness they all felt—both Meg and Rainey were in a quiet daze of exhaustion—Jonas made an early camp on the summit of a small, timbered plateau.

He judged that by now they had pulled a sufficient lead on any pursuit to warrant a long night's rest. Nevertheless he warned the others not to build a fire till after dark, and to keep it carefully sheltered.

Afterward, while the light held, Jonas tramped off through the trees till he came to the edge of the timber, where the plateau's south flank fell away in crumbling terraces to a flashing stream that wended north and south. They had followed the stream for a long way today, and so would any pursuers when they came.

A soft footfall at his back brought him around. Meg was there, and moving up beside him now, she said dryly: "You act as jumpy as I feel."

"You can always go back," he said gruffly.

"No. Not ever." She patted a yawn, stretched her arms, and gazed thoughtfully across the hills. "Things change. People change. A time comes when you can't go back any more. It's hard to explain . . . something you feel in your bones is all."

"It's your life. But you have put a mighty deal behind you."

"Such as money? Belongings?"

"Do without 'em a spell and you may feel different. Ain't no sport to being poor."

Meg blinked tiredly, managing a smile. "Really? I had a long taste of it when I was a kid, you know. But you can live with poverty. Living the Canibar way with money . . . it's a great way if you can live with yourself. Have the temper for being a parasite, that is. I guess I don't any more." She grimaced. "I'll admit I might be tempted back right now, for about the price of a hot bath."

Jonas nodded toward the river below. "You can have a cold one any time."

"No thanks. Even if I had enough left to climb down there, I'd never get back up." She added seriously, "Actually, you know, I've packed along most of what was any value to me. A few clothes and some keepsakes, my mother's jewelry, some money I've saved. What about *you?* You're leaving a whole ranch, a whole life's work."

"I'll come back to it in time," Jonas said grimly. "Or someday I'll arrange to have it sold off for whatever I can get. But I'll come back to it with my boy or not at all."

They were silent for a moment, a cool brush of pine-scented wind fingering around them, and then Meg said quietly: "If King should catch up with us, you have a bargaining card, Jonas. Don't forget it."

"What bargaining card?"

"Me."

Slowly he shook his head. "I thought of it. Be a liar if I said I hadn't. You for Rainey. But damned if I'll play it that way."

"I don't want to go back. But I would, if it would head off any shooting." She smiled wryly. "And if King would go for the idea—chances are he wouldn't—and if it would keep you and Rainey together. *That* would be worth bargaining for, Jonas."

"No. I owe you better. There'll be no trade-off like that. Forget it."

"All right," she said gently. "But I won't forget you refused to do it. I'll always remember it, Jonas. Is that all right?"

She half-turned as she spoke, her body arcing around

and toward him and very close then, so close that he reached out almost unthinkingly and pulled her hard against him. He took the solid feel of her thighs and pelvis and two firm breasts against him, the supple cling of arms and the taste of her hot, eager mouth.

She pulled back in his arms, a tenderness in her face that he hadn't seen, and she murmured: "I wanted you to do that. I wanted it for a long time."

"Why?"

"To find what it's like when a man has a beard. What else? Do it again."

Chapter Eighteen

THE country to the north was uneven, but undu-lating rather than rugged, full of deep valleys and rounded heights. Giant pine that had never felt the logger's ax soared along the spines of rolling hills; mule deer and smaller game scattered from the travelers' path. Baking in the summer heat, it was a land of quietly spectacular beauty, a rich and teeming wilderness that had rarely known the sound of a white man's gun.

On the afternoon of this third day, leading his little party up the open side of a long hill, Jonas thought a good deal about the passion he and Meg Canibar had brushed against last evening, the promise of a fire that could blaze out of control. Or lead to something deeper and better. It was too soon to tell. And Jonas reflected with a bitter resentment that there seemed only a dim chance they might be allowed the time to find out.

The years since he and Welda had gone their separate ways had been lonely ones. Just how lonely had been a question he had more or less exorcised, or at least stoutly evaded, by throwing himself into a grind of work that usually left him too tired to brood on the matter. Some men, loners like himself, could occasionally satisfy the pure need for a woman and let it go at that. For Jonas that need was only part of the total having and giving and sharing he wanted with a woman. But after he'd sought and failed to find it with Welda, he had grimly conceded that perhaps this kind of fulfillment wasn't for him.

Now, he wasn't so sure. He and Meg Canibar were different as hell, but could be it was mostly surface difference. They might be a good deal alike in those ways that counted most. All of which would mean little without the fire of a real attraction. And it seemed they had found that, too. But how could any of it find the time for real fruition under the circumstances?

Time. Always there was the tyranny of time. No man alive, nothing under the sun, was excepted from it.

"Mr. Bonner—"

Grif spoke sharply as he kneed his mount up beside Jonas's.

"What is it?"

Grif hipped around in his saddle and pointed. "I reckon they are onto us," he said quietly. "Leastways someone is. I seen sun hit on metal off in them trees ... there."

Jonas tugged out his field glasses and surveyed their backtrail, moving the lenses across the flank of a distant and thinly wooded slope. He saw a line of riders moving down it like a file of ants. There must have been a dozen or more of them.

He felt a sinking in his guts. So Canibar wouldn't let it alone. And Jonas thought then: Did you really expect him to? Since Welda would never let the matter rest, neither would King, whose doggedness was legend. Once he took up the trail, he would hang to it fiercely. Maybe it had been foolish to hope a reckoning could be avoided, Jonas thought bleakly; it would have had to come sooner or later.

Here and now, perhaps, was as good a time as any. It was just possible, after all, that gunfire could be averted; King would want to minimize any risk of injury to Meg or Rainey. All the same, this open hillside was no place to be caught.

Studying the boulder-rimmed summit as they climbed toward it, Jonas thought: Why not up there? Those rocks formed a natural breastworks. You could watch Canibar's bunch coming for a goodly ways. And they couldn't come up this slope without getting shot to pieces.

If King had sense enough to see that, maybe it would buy time for a parley. Or something. Anything that would avoid bloodshed.

David Crow said, "I reckon they see us too."

King Canibar gave a faint grunt, his field glasses trained on the far hillside where the half-breed's keen eyes had picked out the party of five people. When King lowered the glasses, he said nothing at all. But then he'd scarcely said a word in three days. He nudged his horse into motion, resuming the descent of the slope, and the Big Crown men fell in behind him.

Coming to a brook in the narrow valley below, he

gave everyone a considerable surprise by calling a halt. After three days of forcing a brutal dogged pace that had worn them all fine as froghair, you'd think he'd be hell-fire to overhaul the fugitives now he was this close to them. Instead, King dismounted from his horse and ordered his men to do likewise. Afterwards, he handed his reins to David Crow and told him to water the animals, then seated himself on a rock apart from the crew and lighted up a cigar.

Phil Canibar, his nerves keyed with the strain of anticipation, felt a rise of angry frustration. What the hell was King up to?

Catching Phil's eye now, King motioned to him. Feeling as wary as a man walking on eggshells, Phil went over to his brother. King's tired and unshaved face gave no clue to his thoughts; it was the same unfeeling mask it had been through these three days.

"I had time to do some thinking." His voice was quiet and musing. "Went off all half-cocked thinking Bonner set fire to the house. Thinking it *had* to be him."

This was bad news, Phil thought. He'd known that sooner or later it would happen, but why the hell did it have to happen now?

King was a man of intense feelings, a man of action. The blind intensity of grief had fueled his first urge to strike out at something, anything; once that rage had fixed on Jonas Bonner, it had been enough to drive him relentlessly through three exhausting days and two nights. Now, raw emotion was losing its edge, freeing his brain of obsession, freeing it to assess and weigh and enlarge.

King wasn't stupid. Once he started thinking, he'd lose all taste for continuing a blind pursuit of Bonner. He would ask sensible questions and draw judicious conclusions. And now it was happening, throwing Phil's plan into jeopardy.

"Bonner was there," Phil observed mildly. "Pa said so."

"Don't signify he did it. Fire could of started by accident after he left. Drunk as he was, Pa might o' done it himself and not recall it. Hell—" Impatiently King dropped his cigar and ground a heel on it. "Bonner had a feeling for Welda once. Would he of done that to her?"

"Well—" Phil shrugged "—you never know about a man. He must have been Christ-awful mad when he found you and her sent Rainey away."

"No." King shook his head gently. "David said it back then. Mad or not, Bonner's not that kind of a man. He wouldn't burn a man's house and sure as hell not with a helpless woman inside it. He wouldn't, that's all." He paused heavily, rasping a hand over his whiskered jaw. "I been pretty near out of my head . . . ain't been thinking noway clear. I lay any odds Bonner never set that fire. But if he was there, he might know something."

"What?"

"Hell, I don't know. Anything. Something that'd point to the truth."

"How do you aim to find out?" Phil said dryly. "Ask him?"

"Just that," King said flatly.

Getting up now, he walked to his horse, and Phil followed him. King took the reins from David Crow and looked at Phil. "We're that close to Bonner, I can overtake him in an hour. You hold the men here till I get back. Be no need for 'em."

Phil's mind was working swiftly now. "Look, you better not go alone. Bonner won't know what you've got in mind. He spots you coming, he'll like as not put a bullet in you."

A hard smile touched King's lips; he shook his head. "Wrong again. For the same reason. He ain't that kind of man. If he sees me alone, he'll damn sure hold his fire. We know he's got his kid and Meg and a couple others with him. He'll be mindful of them, too. He won't shoot, he'll talk."

King stepped into the saddle, quartered his mount around, and rode away without a backward glance.

As the trees swallowed him, the men exchanged glances and a run of uncertain mutters. Phil raised his voice briefly, telling them what King intended to do, and then he walked away from them. Kneeling by the brook, Phil cupped his hands and drank from it, his thoughts racing furiously.

What would Dance do? That was what concerned him most.

Dance's instructions had been to follow them till they overtook Bonner's party. When the shooting started, Dance was to work in as close as he could, keeping out of sight, and wait his chance to shoot King from ambush, then clear out as fast as he could. Phil hoped it would appear that an enemy bullet had found King, while his own presence among the other Big Crown men would give him an ironclad alibi. For Phil the very looseness of the scheme was its chief merit. Sure, it could go awry any number of ways—but given Dance's considerable woodcraft, his chances of success had seemed good. Dance, with all his boastful confidence, had thought so, too.

There remained a possibility that Dance, whether he succeeded or failed, would get caught in the attempt.

But suppose he did? If Dance killed King and then was slain himself, nothing would suit Phil better; nobody would second-guess Dance's reason for killing the man who had humiliated and fired him. Of course if he were taken alive, he would reveal Phil's part, but it would merely be his word against Phil's; Dance couldn't offer a shred of proof.

He couldn't lose, Phil had reasoned. All the risk taken would be Dance's, not his.

But if there were no shootout between King and Bonner, things could get a sight trickier. Dance had no instructions in that case. If he did nothing at all, a golden opportunity would be lost.

The solution flooded Phil's mind so suddenly that he almost smiled. The enormity of it should have taken him aback, but it didn't. Instead, in his excitement, he felt a rush of wolfish eagerness. Turning the thing over swiftly in his mind, he thought: I can do it. By God I can. Easy as pulling a trigger. . . .

Getting casually to his feet, he walked over to Bernie Haslan, the Big Crown *segundo*.

"Bernie, I've been thinking," he said abruptly. "It was foolish to let King go on alone. We've no damn way of telling what Bonner might do if he gets him in gun range."

Haslan shrugged. "Maybe, but we have got our orders. He said wait."

"Fine," Phil nodded. "You do that. But he can't blame me for being a worried brother. And right now, Bernie, I'm worried. I'm going to join King. You hold the men here—as he said."

Without waiting for a reply, Phil strode to his horse.

Mounting quickly, he headed away through the trees in the direction King had gone.

"That's funny," Jonas muttered, lowering his binoculars.

Barney was watching through his glasses, too, and now he slid Jonas a baffled glance. "Sure is. But he doing it, *caporal*, he coming on by hisself. What you make of it?"

Jonas wasn't quite sure. He and Rainey, Meg, Barney, and Grif, had taken a position behind the hilltop boulders where they intended to wait for the Big Crown riders. After the latter had disappeared in the dense timber at the base of the slope where Grif had spotted them, Jonas and his companions had seen no more of them. Presently, though, Jonas had discerned a lone rider coming from that way across the undulating folds of land. He appeared now and then where the timber was broken by sunlit patches of open ground. And finally he was close enough to identify.

It was King Canibar himself.

Maybe it did make sense at that. King had pushed hard with his whole damn crew, it looked like, to overtake them. But having spotted them about the same time Grif saw his outfit, he had decided to come on alone and see if he could dicker a bargain without gunplay that might endanger Meg or Rainey.

Jonas spoke his thought aloud.

"Well, that's something," said Meg. "Apparently he's willing to talk, at least."

"It ain't likely to change anything," Jonas said quietly. Anyway this flat summit with its cordon of boulders was easily defensible from any side by men with rifles. The three of them, Barney and Grif and him, could stand off the entire Big Crown crew if they had to. Canibar's men were working hands, not gunmen, and they wouldn't be anxious to charge up a bare-sided hill into the teeth of gunfire. Even if they did, Meg and Rainey and all the mounts and pack animals would be back safely out of the line of fire.

Let 'em come, Jonas thought coldly.

Again he put the glasses to his eyes, intently watching King's progress between the belts of timber. And then he saw something else. A sudden flash as if sunlight had struck glass or metal, off behind King and a little to his right. Jonas rubbed his eyes and focused again, now on the place where he had seen the sunflash.

It came again. And it was followed by a flicker of movement. Only a brief sun-dappled glimpse of movement among the trees. But enough to tell Jonas that a man armed with a rifle was moving on foot through the timber to King's rear, stealthily yet swiftly in order to keep up with the man on horseback.

Also, unlikely as it seemed, the man appeared to be stalking King Canibar.

Jonas caught another fleeting sight of the man's dark form as he darted between trees. This time there could be no room for doubt: he was damned surely on the stalk for Canibar.

Jonas liked to make up his mind slowly, but when there wasn't time for it, thought and action were usually simultaneous with him. Murder was about to be done on that tree-covered hillside, and he was only a few hundred yards from the scene.

Coming swiftly to his feet, Jonas started for Diablo Red at a run, his rifle in hand. Barney yelled something at him and Rainey cried "Pa!" But there was no time for explanations. He flung himself into the saddle and heeled the big stallion forward, going over the lip of the incline and down it; loose rock rattled away from his descent.

The slope tapered off to a grassy flat, and Jonas crossed it at a full gallop. He swerved into the heavy pine growth at its far end and cut through it at break-neck speed.

Then he heard the gunshot.

Too late, he thought. But he didn't slacken pace as Diablo Red reached the base of the high, wooded slope where Jonas had last seen Canibar and the man trailing him. As the stallion's great muscles surged into the climb, Jonas heard up ahead of them a drumming of hoofs as of a horse bolting. But not coming this way. The sound indicated the animal was charging off to one side.

Two more shots were fired.

Jonas broke into a wide clearing halfway up the hill just as King Canibar, slumped across his saddle horn, reached its west edge, and vanished into the trees. At the same time a man came running into the clearing from its opposite side, levering his rifle with a frantic haste. He fired after King, but the rancher was gone. Swearing bitterly, the man let the rifle tip down in his hands.

With a cold shock that held him unmoving for an instant, Jonas recognized Frank Dance.

Seeing him in the same moment, Dance swung the rifle up quickly and fired. The shot was too hasty, but it seared Diablo Red. He gave a piercing squeal and erupted under his rider. Before Jonas could even begin to catch himself, he was spilling sidelong out of the saddle. He hit the ground hard and lay half-stunned.

With a desperate energy he rolled onto his back, still gripping his Winchester, and fumbled to bring it into play. And in that instant he saw Diablo Red charge full into Dance. The blood bay's shoulder slammed Dance with a force that knocked him backward to the ground, the rifle spinning from his hand.

Trumpeting his fury, the stallion reared up, towering above the fallen man with pawing forehoofs. Then he came solidly down. Dance screamed.

Jonas staggered to his feet, yelling at the horse as Diablo Red reared again and plunged down. Floundering against the stallion, Jonas seized blindly at his headstall and got a hold on it and threw his weight back, wrenching the horse's head aside. For just an instant, hanging close to those bared wicked teeth, Jonas feared Diablo Red would turn on him.

But he didn't. He quieted, still trembling in every muscle, and permitted Jonas to lead him to a tree and tie him. Dance's bullet had creased the stallion's sleek rump but hadn't even drawn blood.

Dance was screaming with a steady wordless rhythm. Tramping back to him, Jonas bent down and forced himself to make a close examination. At first, from the pulpy look of Dance's chest, Jonas had thought his ribcage was crushed. It might not be quite that bad, he concluded, but a number of ribs were broken, and there was no telling what internal damage had been done.

Dance's screams had died to faint trailing moans as Jonas said quietly, bleakly, "Well, you could just live a while yet, Frank. Damned if I know why. But you may have more wrinkles than a hard-boiled shirt before you see the day you can spit without leaning against a post."

Chapter Nineteen

Phil Canibar had reached the summit of the timbered hill when he heard the shots downslope and ahead of him. He reined in, hesitating. A moment later he heard the sound of a horse running, and then he saw it cut across a break in the timber on the hillflank down to his left. The rider was bowed over the animal's neck, as if barely hanging on. Phil recognized King's horse and King's gray shirt, a great stain darkening across its back.

Dance, Phil thought at once.

Frank must have been closely following King and perhaps had made the shrewd guess that any possibility of assassinating King during a pitched battle had dimmed. Being this close to King, with a ripe opportunity to take the revenge for which he hungered, had decided Dance to make his try anyway.

But he had failed. King was alive and running away, his horse heading off the slope now into a narrow valley.

Phil waited where he was, straining his eyes and ears. Surely Dance would pursue the wounded man and finish the job. Then Phil heard another shot from the timber below. He straightened in his saddle, listening, his heart pounding. Listening for another shot.

None came. But suddenly he heard a man's voice rising in an agonized scream.

Christ, what had happened down there? Phil couldn't tell a thing for the heavy tree cover, but it was clear something had gone awry with Dance. Otherwise he'd be following up King, who was getting away badly wounded.

How badly? That was the big question. Phil couldn't take a chance on the answer.

When he had left the Big Crown men and gone on alone after his brother, it had been with the express intent of killing King himself if Dance failed to do the job. Then he'd return to the Big Crown crew and tell them that King had been shot by Jonas Bonner, that he had witnessed the murder himself and had barely escaped.

Frank had done the job after all. But only halfway, Phil thought with a cold viciousness.

Yanking his horse's head around now, Phil put him down the steep west flank of the hill at a reckless run. King was cut off from his view now, but it should be easy to head him off in that tight slot of a valley.

In a few minutes Phil emerged onto the open flats of the valley. It was bisected by a twisting creek which ran wide and shallow over a rock-studded bed. The valley floor was covered by clots of brush big enough to conceal a man and horse. So Phil pushed ahead slowly now, alert and wary.

Then he reined in abruptly, seeing King. He lay face down on a finger of sandbar that projected into the stream, his legs trailing in the water. His horse stood nearby; it turned its head, whickering gently, as Phil kneed his own animal forward, splashing through the shallows.

Phil halted a few yards away and pulled his rifle from its boot, then stepped to the ground and cautiously approached the motionless body of his brother. Was he already dead? With any luck at all. . . . Then Phil saw King's broad back heave slightly; his outflung right arm twitched.

Son of a bitch. A thick cry of rage swelled in Phil's throat, and he stifled it and let the suppressed violence of it have its way with him, edging him to the final move. Abruptly he levered his rifle, the sound crisp and loud in the stillness.

To his amazement he saw King instantly move, rolling onto his side, and his left arm, the arm that had been folded under him, coming up with sunlight winking on bright steel in his hand.

Phil Canibar had time for a second's space of wrenching disbelief before the pistol roared in King's fist. And for one terrible flicker of regret before the explosion in his head ended the world for him.

Following the sound of King's shot, Jonas found the Canibar brothers sprawled at the stream's edge. He swung down off Diablo Red and walked over to them.

Phil Canibar was face down in the shallow water, and

Jonas didn't have to touch him to see that he was as dead as a man could be. King lay on his back on a sandbar, his gun in the mud beside him and one hand clamped over his belly. Dully conscious, he eyed Jonas with a kind of glazed indifference. From the look of things, though it made no sense at all, Phil Canibar had died by his brother's hand.

Jonas grabbed King under the arms and dragged him over to the grassy bank. Easing off King's shirt, he ripped it up and made a couple cloth plugs to stanch the flow of blood from the holes at the front and back of King's left side where Dance's bullet had gone clean through. Afterward he wrapped the strips of shirt around King's massive trunk for a crude bandage, and through all of it King Canibar never made a sound.

Settling back on his heels, Jonas said quietly: "There's a lot going on I don't understand."

"*You* don't," came King's sardonic whisper. "You think I got any edge on you? There's some cigars in my saddlebag. Bring me one, will you?"

Jonas tramped over to King's horse, found a cigar, and lighted it for him. King smoked with a labored care for a half minute, then said in a voice husky with pain: "You was at Big Crown three nights ago, Bonner."

Jonas nodded. "Looking for my boy."

"Who did you see there?"

"Welda and your pa. Who else did you think?"

"I dunno for sure," King murmured, his glance touching Phil's body. "Hard to be sure of anything. Welda's dead, Bonner. The house got burned up that night and her with it."

Held mute by the flat and toneless revelation, Jonas let the first shock spend itself along his nerves while he listened unbelievingly as King talked on. King's tone was soft and puzzled and half-questioning, as if he were speaking solely to wrest whatever sense he could from his own words.

When he had finished, Jonas said gently, "That's why you come after me so hard."

"Yeah," King said heavily. "I thought you done it. Then I cooled off enough to see that wasn't likely. I set out to talk to you alone. That's when Phil followed me and put this slug in me."

"You didn't catch a sight of him doing it, I reckon."

"No. How did you know that?"

"It wasn't Phil shot you. It was Frank Dance."

"*Dance?*" King whispered incredulously. "I didn't even know for Christ's sake Dance was anywhere around. How the hell you know it was him?"

After Jonas had explained, King shook his head wearily. "I dunno. I had got thinking maybe it was Phil set that fire. Don't know how he'd of managed it . . . but he'd of had a reason of sorts for getting rid of Welda and me both. But maybe Dance done that. Maybe. . . ."

From the timbered hill came a gunshot.

Jonas's thoughts jerked back to Meg and Rainey, Barney and Grif; they would have come looking for him, and by now they must have found the injured Dance. Canibar's men, too, would have been attracted by the shots. Had they clashed with his party? No—just one shot fired off had to mean that the two sides had met on the hill and were trying to raise King and Phil and himself, wherever they were.

But King seemed not to notice. He talked on slowly and doggedly in the way of a man assailed by an overwhelming doubt and unable to cope with any other thought.

After Dance had shot him and his panicked horse had bolted, he said, he had managed to hold his saddle as far as this creek, where he had fallen off. Barely hanging onto consciousness, he had gotten his gun in hand and held it under his body and waited for whoever had shot him to come finish it. When he'd heard the man dismount and approach, and then the noise of a rifle being swiftly levered to cock, he hadn't hesitated. As he'd rolled to face his assailant, the sun in his eyes had blinded him to all but the man's dark silhouette, and he had fired on the instant. Too late he had realized it was Phil. . . .

"But he was fixing to shoot," King said as if arguing with himself. "He aimed to finish me off. That had to be it. Didn't it?"

"I don't know," Jonas said tiredly. "Listen. I want to know one thing. Does all that's happened . . . does it mean you're done wanting Rainey? Will you let me and mine alone, now?"

It was as though King hadn't heard. He was silent now, his eyes oddly blank and musing. His face had a gray pallor and he looked old, far older than his years.

Jonas rose off his haunches, saying, "I'll fetch your men here," and moved toward Diablo Red. All that had happened in the weeks and days and hours now past washed together in his mind, jumbling tiredly and incoherently, so that only one clear thought emerged: We can go home now. Home for good.

Behind him King spoke at last, his voice dull and uncomprehending, almost inaudible. "Yeah . . . . it's over, right enough. It's all done. Everything's finished now."

The Legends of the Old West
Live On in Fawcett Westerns

LITTLE BIG MAN by Thomas Berger	23854	$2.50
HONDO by Louis L'Amour	14255	$1.75
HE RODE ALONE by Steve Frazee	14103	$1.75
NOW HE IS LEGEND by Gordon D. Shirreffs	14233	$1.50
A TOWN TO TAME by Joseph Chadwick	14234	$1.50
THE TALL STRANGER by Louis L'Amour	14218	$1.95
THE RAWHIDER by Charles N. Heckelmann	04340	$1.75
CROSSFIRE TRAIL by Louis L'Amour	14276	$1.75

Buy them at your local bookstore or use this handy coupon for ordering.

This offer expires 1 May 81

8400

Great Adventures in Reading

HONOR BOUND 14340 $2.50
by Theresa Conway

Honor O'Brien fought for freedom in the savage wilderness of the Old West—fleeing her Indian captors, fighting against the white men who would save her.

WINGED PRIESTESS 14329 $2.50
by Joyce Verrette

The slave: Ilbaya, of noble birth, in love with his master's concubine. He risks death with each encounter. The Queen: beautiful Nefrytatanen. To keep the love of her husband she must undergo the dangerous ritual that will make her the "winged" priestess—or destroy her! An epic of ancient Egypt.

KINGSLEY'S EMPIRE 14324 $2.50
by Michael Jahn

Here is the story of a great shipping dynasty built on the ashes of a shore pirate's wiles and with the fire of an heiress's beauty.

FAWCETT GOLD MEDAL BOOKS